INFAMOUS LOVE

A MOUNTAIN HAVEN NOVEL

LEA COLL

Infamous Love

A Mountain Haven Novel

By Lea Coll

CHAPTER 1

Elle

*C*rew, a yellow lab mix puppy—with feet larger than his body—sniffed the sidewalk, grass, and the potted plant by the door of the vet's office.

The vet's office was located on the outskirts of the historic town in a valley surrounded by mountains.

Glancing around quickly to see if cameras were following me, I opened the door. Crew preceded me inside. No one would follow me here. No one even knew who I was.

Crew's feet scrambled for purchase on the tile as he whined, pulling against the leash to get into every corner to explore. The room was vast—a reception counter positioned directly in front of the door with shelves to the right, and an open space in front of large windows with spectacular views of the Rocky Mountains.

"That's where we hold training classes if the weather doesn't cooperate," said the young woman seated at the counter.

I smiled, stepping closer. So far, people seemed friendlier, more welcoming here.

"I'm Anne. Is this Crew?" Wearing scrubs, with her hair in a perky ponytail, she stood and came around the counter to pet him.

He sat, his fluffy tail wagging as she peppered him with love.

"He's adorable. Where did you get him?"

"Second Chance Animal Rescue."

"I love getting to meet all the puppies." Her smile widened as she sat back down at her desk, placing a file in front of her, inputting information into the computer.

I couldn't imagine being happy where I worked, but I'd never worked a traditional job. Not for long, anyway. The show, the cameras, made it impossible.

"Ready to go back?" She gestured to the exam rooms.

"Sure." I followed her into a square, white room—the exam table the focal point, a counter with supplies against the wall. I took a seat in one of the chairs.

"Dr. Stanton will be in soon." Anne closed the door softly, leaving us alone.

I dropped the leash, allowing Crew to explore, sniffing under the doors, probably searching for crumbs.

I startled when the other door opened, grabbing the slack leash just as Crew lunged at the man, and his assistant, who entered. Crew was only twenty-five pounds but strong, pulling me with him.

When the vet crouched in front of him, Crew sat, sniffing his hand as if he'd met a new friend. The doctor wore a long white coat and khakis with boots, his dark hair falling over his forehead in a messy disarray. The desire to touch his hair, to push it back from his face and see if it was as soft as it looked, struck me hard in the gut.

I hadn't felt an attraction to anyone in a long time. While the show was filming, I'd been surrounded by kids—boys I went to high school with.

The vet stood; his name, Dr. Gray Stanton, was printed in blue script above the pocket on his jacket. He was tall, towering over me. The jacket stretched taut over his shoulders. His face was chiseled, the kind of face you'd see on an actor or a model, not in a small town in Colorado. His face was familiar.

A sense of déjà vu shot through me. This was the man I'd run into at the bar when I was in town to renovate the shop. His hands had steadied me, not moving as his eyes darkened, his head lowered. Thinking he was going to kiss me, I'd slipped out of his grip, apologizing, then stepped to the side to escape. Everything about him—his scent, the intensity of his gaze—drew me in.

When I moved here, I promised myself I'd focus on the business. I hadn't had the best track record with the guys in my past. With one touch, this man had my body tingling.

I held out my hand to shake his.

"You got a puppy." It was a statement, his tone lightly tinged with irritation, bringing me back to the present.

Confused at his reaction, I glanced at his assistant who smiled in apology. Was he judging me for getting a puppy? The idea he thought I was impulsive, and clearly didn't remember me, struck at my most vulnerable parts.

"Yeah. I got him from a rescue." Just as I was going to lower my hand, Dr. Stanton's fingers, firm and calloused, like he was used to working hard all day, engulfed mine.

He let go of my hand, turning to open the file on the counter. "That's something, at least. You know anything about dogs?"

"No. I've never owned one before. I always wanted one." I sounded young and naive, exactly how I felt. I was new at making decisions in my life, but I'd researched, thinking I was prepared for the responsibility.

He grunted as he nodded toward his assistant, whose name tag said Sheila, to put Crew on the table that doubled as a scale. Dr. Stanton pushed the button to raise the table to hip height.

I was grateful to have something between us besides his animosity.

Dr. Stanton kept his gaze on the rising table. "I operated on a dog this morning who was given as a gift. She darted out of the house and was hit by a car. She needed surgery and the owners can't, or won't, pay for it. They asked me to put her down, but I refused."

My heart squeezed at the thought of a dog being struck by a car. I covered my chest with a hand. "I'm so sorry. That's awful."

"I wish people would think twice before getting a dog. They aren't toys you can return when they no longer suit your lifestyle."

Dr. Stanton's words rang with a hint of warning for me. The difference was, I'd wanted a dog for as long as I could remember, someone to cuddle with when the house was empty, someone to love. I chewed my lip. "A dog getting loose sounds like something that could happen to anyone."

I stepped closer to Crew, scratching under his chin, determined it wouldn't happen to him if I could help it.

"Does Crew have any issues with eating?"

Dr. Stanton's question jarred me from thoughts. "He has a big appetite."

"You're feeding him puppy food, no more than two cups a day?" His tone softened, less gruff than when he came in.

"Yeah. I read up on dogs before I got one." I was eager to disavow Dr. Stanton of his low opinion of me. The desire to prove myself ran deep.

"That's good." From his tone, I couldn't tell if it was. Was there something about me specifically he didn't like, or was I merely the unlucky person who walked in after he performed surgery on a dog whose owners abandoned her?

Did he somehow remember who I was? I curled one lock of hair around my finger, wondering if it was a bad idea to think I could move to a new town to start over without anyone recognizing me. I let the strand go, the curl popping back into place, and exhaled slowly.

There was no way this man watched reality TV. While my every teenage move was followed by cameras and producers, he was studying to be a veterinarian.

I blinked away the memories, the ever-present pit from those days, burning in my gut as Dr. Stanton probed Crew's stomach. He opened his mouth, checking his teeth, before looking at his eyes and ears.

"You're new in town." It wasn't a question.

I nodded eagerly, hoping for common ground. I wanted to get along with people here. "I just opened the new barbershop, Smoke & Mirrors."

Dr. Stanton stilled, one hand stroking Crew's head. "You opened it?"

"Yeah."

"It's a barbershop."

"It's a dream of mine." I smiled, proud of my idea and filled with hope that I'd make it on my own so I wouldn't have to resort to signing on to yet another reality show spin-off. The producers loved my idea to open a traditional barbershop complete with wood floors, traditional old-time seats, mirrors, and man-cave signs. They wanted to offer me a show of my own, but only if I opened it in Los Angeles. I wanted nothing to do with that city, or that life, anymore.

"I never thought about a woman running a barber-shop. Don't you prefer salons or spas?"

I bristled slightly. "I'd be catering to men. They prefer barbershops."

Sheila's phone buzzed. "I'll just be a minute. They can't find gloves in room two."

Dr. Stanton nodded without breaking eye contact with me.

He seemed interested in my response. Maybe he wanted to understand me. I couldn't remember anyone ever scrutinizing my reasoning for anything. I was usually the one following directions, not making decisions.

I licked my lips, stepping closer to the table under the guise of comforting Crew when I was the one thrown off balance.

The small space between us crackled with tension. His gaze paused on my mouth before he looked away.

My plan to open a barbershop catering to men was

purposeful. It was unlikely men watched the show or entertainment news. If they did, hopefully they wouldn't care.

Gray turned, writing something in a folder. "Make sure you get Crew into obedience classes. I'll have Sheila give you a list of training programs in the area. We offer one here, outside when the weather's nice, inside when it's not."

It was a relief he wasn't focused on me. At the same time, I felt strangely let down.

"I do need to get him into training." He pulled when I walked, ate everything in sight—including furniture and shoes—but he was so cute. He was exactly what I needed. I just hoped this town was what I needed too.

"Where are you from?"

I'd vowed to be vague about my history. I'd grown up in an affluent beach town on the coast, then moved to LA for the show. It detailed our high school years until we became young twenty-somethings, trying to find our way—with too much money and no purpose or guidance. I settled for, "California."

He nodded as if my answer told him all he needed to know. "Sheila will administer his vaccines. Make sure you get him on heartworm, flea, and tick medications as soon as possible. We have those here if you want them, or I can print a prescription."

"Oh, whatever you have here is fine."

"It was good to meet you, Ms. Carmichael." His tone was brisk, professional.

"It's Elle." My voice was soft. It was still weird to go by my sister's nickname for me, and not the name I'd gone by my entire life, Giselle. Giselle was a part I played on TV. She didn't exist anymore. I could reinvent myself in this town. I could be someone else, someone people counted on, someone to be proud of.

Dr. Stanton gathered his paperwork. "Why Telluride? We may be a tourist town, but the locals are loyal to each other. We don't get many outsiders."

I stiffened. For once in my life, I wanted to belong. I wanted the locals to accept me. "I used to vacation here with my family when I was a child."

I'd always loved it here, the cold and snow versus the heat and beach.

His face softened before he said, "The locals can sniff out someone who's not genuine a mile away. So, if you're not here for the right reasons, don't even bother."

I wanted to ask him what the right reasons were, why I'd bother to open a business only to pack up and leave, but I didn't. When I turned down the offer to star in a spin-off reality show, the producers said I was impulsive, immature. I thought I could come to a town where I didn't know anyone, open a business, and make it a success. I hoped I was right.

Dr. Stanton turned to leave.

The thought of this man thinking I was less than, hurt when it shouldn't. He didn't know me.

"You don't like outsiders?" I asked before I could rethink my question or the vulnerability evident in my tone.

He paused his hand on the door. "I'm an outsider myself."

He left before I could ask any follow-up questions. Was that why he'd warned me? Did he still not fit in? Had he moved here for an escape too?

After Sheila returned to administer the vaccinations, she gathered the medications into a plastic bag and gave me a list of suggested food brands as well as obedience training classes.

I went to the front desk to check out, scanning the list of classes. I didn't know the area, so it made sense to sign up for the ones offered here.

I handed my credit card to Anne at the desk to pay the bill. "Can I sign up for obedience classes?"

"It starts next Sunday, the only day we're officially closed."

"That's perfect." The barbershop was closed too.

I signed up for the class, refraining from asking who the instructor was. If it was Gray, I might not sign up, and Crew needed training. There was no way Dr. Stanton taught obedience training in his spare time. I chewed the inside of my cheek, thinking it would be an opportunity to see him. I was intrigued by him, our encounter in the bar, and now, his instant dislike of me.

I wasn't sure who I was without producers prodding me to do or say something. Before, I was judged when my actions had never really been mine. Now, I was being judged for my choices. It was unsettling.

Leaving the vet clinic, I walked Crew outside so he'd do his business, then picked him up to place him in the Range Rover my parents gifted me—with a large red bow while cameras rolled—on my sixteenth birthday. It should have been a special moment. Instead, it felt staged.

As I drove towards Smoke & Mirrors, I marveled that this quaint, ski resort town, located at the base of a mountain, was now my home. I parked behind the barbershop, pride filling my chest as I walked around to the front. The shop represented a fresh start, a chance to be a good person, someone worthy.

The shop was in a corner brick building with two large windows—I couldn't wait to decorate for the holidays—facing the street. A wrought-iron sign hung over the door with my business name, Smoke & Mirrors, written inside the silhouette of a bearded man.

I unlocked the glass door, the bell signaling my arrival as I stepped inside, the smell of new leather combined with shaving cream greeting me. I'd carefully chosen higher quality items that were professional and inviting. I wanted the barbershop to be a unique experience, whether that was from a comfortable leather chair, a scent that brought back memories of a father's shaving cream, or the experience of a boy's first haircut.

I unhooked Crew from his leash so he could explore, knowing I'd need to keep an eye on him. Chew toys were strewn across the floor, but he preferred to gnaw on whatever he could find.

Everything was ready to go for the grand opening on Saturday except for employees. I needed to hire Piper, who was coming in today for an interview, or someone else soon. Hiring a native to the town might help me connect with other locals. I could ask her advice on attracting tourists too. The list of things I needed to accomplish before the grand opening filtered through my head, overwhelming my confidence.

The words of my producer replayed in my head, *"No one will care about your barbershop if cameras aren't following you."* Everyone thought I was going to fail. The prospect scared me, but I was determined to prove them wrong.

Today, I was supposed to be interviewing the one person who applied, Piper Rigby. I'd met her when I was setting up the shop. She'd stopped by to inquire about whether I was hiring. I was impressed with her tenacity, making me want to become friends with her.

I hoped hiring a local would help. I was nervous; this endeavor felt like the first adult thing I'd ever done. Working on a reality show, or as a stylist in a swanky salon in Los Angeles, was child's play compared to being a boss.

I'd put all my savings into this building, and the

business. If it didn't succeed, I'd have to move back home. I didn't want to be in a position where I'd have to take the contract for the spin-off reality show.

The door opened, the bell sounding again.

"Sorry I'm early. I was so excited to see everything finished."

I turned to find Piper, a petite woman with blonde hair, standing just inside the door, looking around in amazement. "It looks spectacular."

In Los Angeles, I wouldn't have trusted a statement like that. I would assume a jealous, snide comment was coming next. Everything about this woman's expression, from her wide eyes to her parted lips, was genuine. It was refreshing.

"I'm so glad you could come."

"Oh my gosh. Look at this cutie." She knelt on the floor as Crew licked her face.

"Sorry. I was going to put him upstairs before our interview." Having a dog in the shop for the interview was probably unprofessional, though she didn't seem to mind.

She stood, brushing his yellow fur off her black pants. "Like I said, I'm early. He's adorable."

Piper was so easygoing, the tension I'd held in my shoulders eased. "Do you want to head over to the coffee shop for the interview?"

"Do we need to? We can talk here." She sat in one of the maroon leather chairs meant for clients, spinning until she faced me.

"That's fine." I leaned a hip against the counter, appreciating her confidence. "Are you still working at Bliss and Bang?"

"I've been working there for five years. I'm ready for something new, something different."

The sign for the shop had scissors in place of the *and*. Curious, I'd stopped inside Bliss and Bang when I first scouted locations for the barbershop. It had a spa-like atmosphere with wood floors, paneling, fresh paint, and modern decor. The salon wasn't competition. Its clientele was different. I was confident there were enough customers for both businesses.

I wanted to be sure she understood we wouldn't have any female clientele. "Do you have experience with men's cuts? That's all you'll be doing here. If highlights are your thing—"

Her eyes held a gleam of excitement as she stroked the soft leather of the chair. "I do have experience with men's cuts. I like what you're doing here. I think this barbershop is unique. I want to be part of something new and exciting."

My gut feeling was Piper would be good for the shop, and good for me. I cleared my throat, hoping she was right. "Do you have your list of references?"

"Right here." She stood, pulling a piece of paper out of her bag, smoothing it out before placing it on the countertop.

She listed her cosmetology school, her licenses,

then her job at the salon. I hoped the salon owner didn't get upset that I was taking one of their stylists.

"The owners of the salon won't mind you leaving to work here?" I tilted my head, considering her. She was confident, had the experience, and would be personable with the clientele.

Her smile was easy. "No. The owners know I've been looking for a change."

"Do you have any questions for me?"

"I remember you saying you're from LA. Do you plan to run the shop, or will you hire a manager down the road?"

The thought of going back to LA made my stomach uneasy. "No. I plan to manage it. If you're sure about working here, I'd like to offer the position to you."

Piper covered her chest with her hand. "Are you serious?"

"Yeah, I think you'll fit in here just fine. I'm hoping you can help me with the locals."

Piper seemed surprised I'd offered her the job on the spot. Maybe she wasn't used to people taking chances on her. I had a feeling we could be good friends, and that she'd be a great employee. I didn't get many opportunities to test my instincts. I wanted to take that leap with her.

She clasped her hands together. "Thank you so much! You've made me so happy."

"Are you ready for that coffee now? We can discuss the details."

She smiled, her expression friendly.

A warmth spread through me. Piper was someone who wanted to get a coffee, chat, and possibly be a friend. It was something I hadn't had since before the show was filmed. Producers advised us only to hang out with the other kids on the show. My friends in school, then later my castmates on the show, were merely acquaintances paid to spend time with me.

"Sure. I'd like that. Let me put Crew upstairs." Calling Crew, he followed me up the steps to my apartment above the shop. I grabbed his favorite bacon-flavored treats to entice him into his crate. Locking up, I headed back down to the shop where Piper was admiring the photographs of the renovations on one of the walls. I'd taken the before and after pictures in black and white, giving it a cool feel.

"I love what you've done with the place. It's classy." She preceded me out the door.

"Thank you. I'm happy with it too." Her easy compliment eased my earlier doubts.

I'd been worried people wouldn't accept me here. Even though it was a tourist town, with the ski resort, I'd be living here year-round. I needed to fit in as a local to bring in business during the off-season. Like Dr. Stanton said, I needed them to trust I was here for the long haul, or they wouldn't invest in my business. I didn't want to sell my soul to be on TV again.

CHAPTER 2

Gray

My chest felt tight ever since I left my newest client in the exam room. I didn't know why I took my bad morning out on her. I was raw from performing surgery on a dog who shouldn't have gotten out of the house, who shouldn't need surgery or to be looking for another home so early in her young life. By now, I should be used to people's callous disregard for animals. Whether they could afford vet care or not, I wished they'd ask for help before asking me to put the dog down. It was the one aspect of the job that almost held me back from attending vet school. This morning I offered to pay for the surgery and to find the dog a new home. The owners were pleased with that option.

When I walked into the exam room, seeing the beautiful young woman with a puppy, a sense of instant familiarity shot through me. When she'd run into me months ago at the bar, I'd been attracted to her dark hair, pale skin, and the shadows under her eyes. She'd looked haunted. I wanted to give in to the desire to pull her closer, to feel the fullness of her lips under mine. Except, she'd been the one to pull away. Assuming she was a tourist, I never thought I'd see her again.

My heart pounded in my chest as irritation crept down my spine. Annoyed that the first woman I'd been attracted to in a long time was standing in my exam room, all I could see was one more person who thought it would be fun to get a dog until it wasn't cute anymore or it chewed on her favorite shoes. It was an unfair assumption to make about a woman I didn't know.

I hadn't expected her to be a business owner. The town was buzzing about the new barbershop. The window coverings had come down a week ago. I'd heard it was all exposed brick walls, plush leather chairs, and masculine colors. No one mentioned the owner was a woman—an attractive, young woman.

When she'd insinuated the appeal was a men's sanctuary, my heart skipped a beat. We were only a few inches apart, close enough to smell the citrus scent of her shampoo, to count the freckles on her nose. Her hair was in a messy bun, strands curling around her face. My fingers itched to move them back, to test the softness of her skin, to kiss the sensitive spot I knew I'd find on her neck where her sweater hung off her shoulder. Wearing an oversized sweater and leggings encased in practical boots, nothing about her said California or high maintenance.

She seemed like the quintessential girl next door, sweet and down to earth. Unfortunately, I learned the hard way, people weren't always who they appeared to be.

I grabbed the file for my next client, pushing open the exam room door at the same time I pushed out thoughts of Elle Carmichael. I had no need for high-priced barbershops when my friend, Henry's sister, Piper, cut my hair at home.

AT THE END of the day, I shut down my computer. Ed Bester—the owner of the clinic—walked in wearing his white coat, his pepper hair messy.

He still saw patients, the stalwarts who'd been going to him for decades. I took on new clients, hoping that when he decided to retire, his clients would transfer to me, not move to the new vet one town over. Telluride was my college friend, Henry's, hometown. I'd come home with him on the holidays, enjoying his family's camaraderie and the town's charm. When I graduated from vet school, he'd told me about the opening at Telluride Animal Clinic. I didn't have a home to return to, or any clear direction, so it seemed like a good idea at the time.

The town, and its people, had become a part of me. I wanted to stay, but I was prepared to leave if my past threatened to catch up to me.

"Can we talk for a minute?" Ed sat in the chair across from me.

"Sure." I tensed, worried I'd done something wrong.

"I'm thinking about retiring." The tightness in my chest eased, hearing the words I'd been anticipating.

His pensive face stymied my excitement.

He held up his finger. "I want to make sure the practice is in good hands. I don't want it to be sold to someone else who doesn't share my vision, who's not a local." This is what I'd tried to warn Elle Carmichael about this morning. It took a lot for townspeople to accept outsiders.

After living here for four years, I still wasn't considered a local. Would not being from Telluride ruin my chances?

"I don't have any plans to change anything." Not drastically anyway. I had visions of expanding, maybe offering space for rescues, a free clinic for vaccines, and annual exams for clients who couldn't afford to care for their animals. I worried about how Ed would react to those suggestions. He was generally resistant to any changes around the office, including updating the computer or filing systems.

"You went to college in Colorado, but you're from somewhere on the East Coast, and currently living in an apartment. You haven't exactly planted roots here. You see my concern?"

Panic crawled up my throat making it difficult to swallow. I was from Maine. No one besides Henry knew that. Having Ed describe my life in two sentences was unsettling. Was that really all I had to show for the past twelve years since I graduated from high school, leaving with no intentions to return?

"I'm saving all of my money to buy the practice. I don't think it makes sense to buy a home when it's just me, and I don't have a hometown to return to." I stopped short of saying I didn't have family, because technically, I did. "This is my home. The Rigbys are my family, and I have no intention of leaving."

I forced a steady breath, trying to calm my pulse. I was afraid of saying anything that might reveal my family's history. At the same time, I didn't want to sway him to sell to someone else.

Ed's eyebrows drew together. "That may be, but I have to be sure. I want the practice to continue as it is. I want my clients happy after I leave. I don't want calls in retirement begging me to come back." He laughed at his last statement, but I knew he was serious.

When I first started working here, his long-standing clients didn't want their animals to be seen by a younger vet or someone not from here. They didn't think I was capable of caring for large animals. "I understand your concern. I'll do whatever it takes to convince you I'm the right person to run the clinic."

Ed nodded in approval. "I look forward to that. The second thing is, are you able to buy the practice?"

"I am." Pride filled me at that thought. I had some money my father left for me in a trust the government couldn't touch, and I'd saved carefully over the years, living frugally. I knew better than anyone, material things mean nothing.

He held up his hands. "I haven't officially decided, but I'll have the business valued, so you can go to the bank to show you're able to purchase it. Then we'll see where we are."

I wanted to ask, what then? What if I had everything ready, but he still didn't want to sell to me? If he sold to someone else, I didn't know what I'd do. I had no connections here besides Henry's family. I wanted to own a vet practice, not work for someone else.

Ed shifted in his chair, wincing slightly. "There's one other thing I wanted to talk to you about. You're a great vet. It's just that some of the customers feel you're a little cold. Being a small-town vet means being friendly with the customers, asking about their family, knowing what's going on in their lives."

I rubbed the back of my neck. I hadn't been nice to Elle Carmichael today. I was standoffish, bordering on rude. "I'll work on that."

The words felt like sandpaper in my mouth. I wasn't friendly. I hadn't been an easy-going guy since my senior year when the proverbial carpet was ripped out from under me. I'd lost everything. My father, my home, the family business, my girlfriend. I was guilty by association. My reputation ruined at eighteen.

"See that you do." Ed stood, leaving me alone in my office.

My limbs felt heavy. I was so close to reaching my dream, yet so many things still stood in my way.

The only thing I had to show for myself was the framed degrees on the walls. I'd switched colleges from Maine to Colorado, getting as far away as I could from the headlines and the shame. I could be anyone I wanted to be, as long as my past didn't catch up to me.

Telluride's climate provided opportunities for cold-weather sports, reminding me of my hometown in Maine, yet it was far enough away, hopefully, no one would make the connection to who I was. If someone did, I'd have no choice but to start over somewhere else.

CHAPTER 3

Elle

*P*iper helped me decorate the shop windows with fall decorations, adding streamers above the mirrors to celebrate the opening. The smell of coffee from The Coffee Cowboy and pastries from Baked in Telluride, permeated the small space, competing with the new leather smell.

We'd been open all week, waiting for Saturday to hold the official open house. So far, we'd only had a few moms with boys come in during the week. I was discouraged, yet hopeful because it wasn't a customer base I'd thought too much about. It could be a nice, steady income if kids came in frequently.

Piper stared out the shop window. "We should do

something for the kids when they come in. Give them a toy, or a treat, or something."

I tilted my head to the side. "What? Like a toy car or something?"

She pointed at me, her eyes lighting up. "That would be perfect."

"You get the moms in town on board, then their husbands will come in."

"You think?" I wanted to avoid women, hoping they wouldn't recognize me from the show. No one said I looked familiar.

"I know so."

"Okay." I moved to the computer at the desk, searching for toy cars that could be delivered quickly so they'd be here by Monday or Tuesday.

"Customers will trickle in because they're curious, then you'll get more people from word of mouth."

"I hope so." I had so much riding on this, my savings from the show, my self-worth. For the first time in my life, I was doing something I wanted to be proud of. I couldn't afford to fail, financially or otherwise.

As soon as I ordered the toys, a few customers came in all at once. We were busy, intermittently, the rest of the day, which lifted my spirits. Even though the clients seemed like they were just curious about a new person in town, I kept my responses vague. I was from California; I vacationed here as a child, falling in love with the town. I mentioned loving winter sports. They seemed satisfied with that information, not asking more questions.

I'd worried it would be hard to keep my old life a secret in a place where it was assumed your stylist would talk about their life. Fortunately, they were all surface-level questions so far. A few well-placed questions kept the focus on the client's lives.

As the day went on, I began to breathe easier when no one seemed to recognize me. The producers liked me to look a certain way: blonde hair, blue eyes, and expensive clothes—the skimpier, the better. I looked different with my naturally dark hair, minimal make-up, and casual clothing.

The hype surrounding the show had died down since we went off the air last year. As long as my fellow castmates stayed out of the news, it was unlikely my face would be back on a screen. When I worked at the LA salon, people confronted me about my on-screen, bad girl persona. There's no way the townspeople would accept me if they knew.

Piper finished sweeping the floor and cleaning the tools before returning everything to its place. "I think that's everything. I'll see you on Tuesday."

"Thank you so much for your help." I didn't know what I would have done without her assistance, her knowledge of the town, or her words of encouragement. I hadn't been around anyone who lifted me up over the years. Sometimes it felt like the producers' job was to tear me down, only to build me up into whoever they wanted me to be.

"You're welcome. I need this to work as much as you do." Her expression was sad.

I refrained from asking her why that was. I respected other people's desires to keep their problems to themselves, hoping they'd return the favor.

* * *

IT WAS SUNDAY, the first day of obedience training for Crew. I was excited to get him into class. I'd taken him for a walk to wear him out like the instructor's email suggested, relieved and at the same time disappointed to see Dr. Stanton wasn't the instructor.

Walking Crew was a nice excuse to explore the town and its coffee shop, bakery, bed and breakfasts, and restaurants. You could take the gondola lifts for a scenic route to the village on top of the mountain, skiing back to town.

Checking the locks on the barbershop one last time, I loaded Crew into my Range Rover for the drive. Even though Anne said the clinic was closed on Sundays, I hoped I'd run into him. Would he look as good as I remembered? I'd thought back to our encounter several times, wondering why he'd reacted so negatively to me.

I pulled into the parking lot where three other vehicles were already parked, excited to get started. At the same time, I was worried I wouldn't be able to train Crew.

I followed the instructions, walking around the side of the clinic with Crew pulling on the lead, seeing a few people milling about with their dogs.

I approached the man who was there by himself, presumably the instructor. He was tall, wearing a thick sweater against the cold, and dark wash jeans with boots. He turned to me, my heart rate picking up at the sight of his familiar dark, messy hair and chiseled jaw. "Dr. Stanton?"

"It's Gray. The instructor called in sick." His expression was tight, his words tinged with annoyance.

He looked like a Gray: serious, uptight, and grumpy. I bet his apartment was all black, modern lines with no personal effects. I'd gotten pretty good at reading people in LA. I could spot a fake or hanger-on easily now. Gray was the opposite. It seemed like what you saw was what you got. "So, you're going to be the instructor?"

The thought made me feel energized as if I'd drank several cups of coffee. The cold wind lifted my hair, whipping over my shoulders.

"Just for today." His lips were set into a straight line like he wasn't happy. I wasn't sure if he didn't want to teach, didn't want to be around me, or a combination of both.

My heart beat rapidly in my chest as he crouched

next to Crew, his face softening, the lines around his mouth smoothing out as he spoke to him.

I stilled, not wanting to move a muscle or say anything that would lower the perpetual shadow over his face. He looked younger like this.

"Has Crew been good?" Gray looked up at me, avoiding Crew's tongue as he scampered around, wagging his tail in excitement.

"If you call eating my new boots good," I teased, wondering if my admission would annoy him.

He glanced at my sneaker-clad feet, giving Crew one last pat. "You need to teach him manners."

The familiar shadow covered his face inch by inch as he rose to stand, the muscles in his shoulders tight.

My shoulders dropped at the return of the Dr. Stanton I'd met in the exam room. "That's why I'm here."

"You can stand over there." His words short, he pointed to the spot next to an older woman and a rambunctious lab.

I sighed, disappointed he was back to his usual self. I took my spot. Something told me getting close to him would be like sidling up to a porcupine. I wondered if I could find a way to push the needles down, would he be soft underneath? I wasn't interested in a relationship since I just moved here and was starting a new business, but I was intrigued by him.

Gray introduced himself, his voice was mesmerizing as he talked about the clinic, why the clinic offered obedience classes, and how important it was to train your dog early so you didn't run into behavioral problems later.

I wondered if the dog that had been hit by a car was doing okay. I made a mental note to ask him after class.

He ran through basic commands like sit and stay; then he taught us a little about heeling. Reading about dog training was different than seeing it in person. I listened with rapt attention.

When it was my turn to work with Crew, I was a little nervous trying to mimic the commanding tone of Gray's voice. Crew wasn't cooperating. Instead, he pulled on the lead to get closer to the other dogs, and he barked at the squirrel running up the tree. As frustrating as it was, I knew training a puppy would be challenging.

Gray walked around the group, issuing soft-spoken suggestions until his gaze landed on us. Crew took that moment to bark at Gray, pulling on my arm to get closer, his butt wiggling with everything he had. Crew obviously thought Gray was a good person. I already suspected Gray was better with animals than people if our meeting in his exam room was any indication.

"He needs a firm hand. May I?" Gray held his hand out for the leash.

My face heated at his words, my mind going to a completely different place before I recovered. "Of course."

I offered him the leash, his hand brushing mine,

sending awareness through my body. He stepped close. I smelled leather and man, making it difficult to draw a deep breath or think about anything else. I forced myself to focus on his words.

"You're going to want to use your body language and your tone to assert authority over Crew. You want him to respect you as an alpha."

"Okay." He'd mentioned the same to the class. I wasn't sure how to put that into action.

Gray stepped in front of Crew, holding up a hand, and then issued a firm command to sit.

Crew's butt was on the ground within a second of the words leaving Gray's mouth. Gray offered him a treat, praising him.

Of course Crew would listen to him.

"He's a good dog. You just need to be consistent." He patted his leg, encouraging Crew to stand before handing the leash back to me.

I nodded, feeling a little discouraged. I wasn't sure I could replicate what he'd managed to achieve.

"Now, you try."

He was going to watch me. The added pressure tensed every muscle in my body as I attempted to use the same tone Gray had used when I asked Crew to sit. Crew looked back and forth from me to Gray trying to determine who was in charge.

"You need to be convincing."

I stepped assertively in between them so that all Crew saw was me holding up my hand in a stop motion before saying clearly and succinctly, "Sit." I willed him to sit. He hesitated a few seconds before his butt slowly lowered to the ground.

I stood straighter, pleased he'd complied.

"Good. That was better." Gray's hand rested on my shoulder briefly. All the hair on the back of my neck stood at attention, the warmth spreading through my jacket.

Before I could say anything, he'd moved away, giving instructions to a woman whose dog was ignoring her repeated commands.

Disappointed he'd moved on to someone else, I watched Gray for a few seconds, impressed by his ability to work with the dogs. There were little moments when I thought there was more to Gray Stanton than his gruff exterior suggested. I wondered who the real Gray was, the man who exuded confidence around animals or the brusque man in the exam room.

He ran through the rest of the lesson without spending any extra time with me. It shouldn't have bothered me. I barely knew him.

Crew improved slightly as the lesson went on, giving me hope that I was capable of training him. Gray ended the session by reminding us to practice during the week and to make sure the dogs got plenty of exercise.

I waited while one of the men talked to him about theories of dog training before I approached.

Gray raised one brow when he saw me.

"I just wanted to make sure the dog you operated on was doing okay. You know the one that got hit by a car?"

"Athena? Yeah, she's going to be fine." He tilted his head, studying me.

Would he think I was being nosy or tell me it was none of my business?

"Did you find a home for her?" I wasn't sure why it was so important to me, but it was. I hadn't been able to stop thinking about the poor dog's situation since Crew's appointment.

He shook his head, his forehead wrinkled. "Not yet. I talked to a local rescue to see if they have room for her."

Could I take her? I didn't like that she was homeless. However, I had my hands full with Crew. "It's so sad the family didn't want to keep her. Does that kind of thing happen a lot?"

"A couple of times a year. I don't like being asked if I can put a healthy dog down because they don't want to pay for surgery or whatever care they need. I offer payment plans and pet care insurance, but sometimes people are too proud to ask for help. Other times, they don't believe in spending a large amount of money for a dog's care. Surgery's expensive."

I sucked in a sharp breath. "I don't know how you do it."

"I refuse, offering to find the dogs a home when it

happens. The owners are usually relieved. They don't want to kill the dog; they just don't want to care for it anymore. It's probably for the best. Then the dog can go to a home where they can afford to care for them." His tone was matter of fact.

I could see being put in that position bothered him deeply.

"Still, I can't imagine giving up Crew because he was hurt." I couldn't imagine asking a vet to put Crew down because he needed surgery. There had to be organizations out there who could help so the dog didn't need to be re-homed or put down.

Crew jumped around us in a circle, eager to get moving.

Gray started walking toward the parking lot. "People don't realize how expensive dogs are."

"Yeah. That's true." I fell in step with him, Crew between us.

I was acutely aware we were alone. I was happy because it would give me an opportunity to get to know him better. When we reached the lot, the other vehicles were leaving.

I tilted my head slightly, wondering how I could help him. "Who pays for a dog's surgery if the owners can't, or won't?"

He glanced over at the clinic before meeting my gaze. He seemed reluctant to tell me. "I do."

"Wait, you mean you're paying for the surgery, not the clinic?" His frustration when we met that I'd gotten a dog with no prior experience came back to me. He was worried I'd taken the decision of getting a puppy lightly. It was presumptuous, yet understandable, given what he'd been through that morning.

"That's right."

"Why?"

"My hands are tied. I want to help, but I don't own the business." He opened his mouth, then closed it without adding more.

There was more. He was holding back. I waited patiently for him to continue.

He stuffed his hands in his pockets, lowering his voice. "I'm afraid my boss will tell me to comply with the owner's wishes. I can't put down a dog with survivable injuries."

This man, who seemed so grumpy at Crew's examination, had a heart of gold, at least when it came to animals. "I think that's amazing."

Gray's lips twitched. "I'm not sure Ed would think that. He thinks his client's wishes come first."

I placed a finger over my lips, trying to think of some way I could make things better for him. "I could put up a sign at the shop asking people to donate money to pay for Athena's care if you want."

"That's not necessary," he said each word slowly, seemingly surprised I'd offered.

"The offer stands." Crew pulled toward my SUV, so I picked him up, placing him on the back seat. When I turned, Gray had taken a few steps back from the vehicle.

I wished he'd take a step toward me, asked me something about myself. The idea was ridiculous. He wouldn't want to know me if he learned about my past.

I'd gotten a brief glimpse into Gray's personality this morning. It left me wanting more.

I opened the driver's side door, settling inside as Gray waved, turning to head inside the clinic.

Gray was unlike anyone I'd ever met. No one in the crowd I hung around with, including the show's employees, would pay for a dog's surgery, putting their own job on the line in the process. They were usually out for themselves, or what they could gain from any given situation. What Gray was doing was heroic, even if the life he was saving was an animal's.

CHAPTER 4

Gray

$\mathcal{S}$unday night, I drove down the long lane leading to Henry's family home, Rigby's Ranch. I tried to make their weekly family meals whenever I could because I loved home-cooked meals. My apartment was uninviting, so I tried to spend as little time as possible there. Because it was a rental, I didn't take any pride in it. I certainly didn't see it as a home.

I ran my fingers through my hair. Ed's concerns about me were valid, forcing me to challenge the solitary life I'd led the last four years. Ed wanted me to prove I planned to make Telluride my home. It was something I'd never considered until now.

With Elle, I *could* blame my irritation, that first day,

on what happened with Athena, but it wasn't true. My attraction to her threatened my uncomplicated life. When she approached me during the obedience training class, her beauty struck me in the middle of my chest, sharp and potent. Her hair fell in waves around her face, her cheeks rosy from the cold, and her eyes shone bright with excitement as she looked up at me from under long, black lashes. When she realized who I was, her smile dimmed. As much as I liked her looking at me like that, nothing good could come of it.

Henry's mother, Rose, had been hinting at both Henry and me to settle down. We always laughed her off. Henry wasn't ready to settle down for different reasons. He had things in life he wanted to accomplish first, with the ranch, whereas I had nothing to offer a woman.

I stepped onto the porch of the Rigbys' log farmhouse, knocking on the door. It was different than the traditional farmhouses in Maine. Different enough that living here didn't bring up any memories of my childhood.

Mrs. Rigby opened the door. "Gray, how many times have I told you that you don't need to knock?"

"It's never enough, Mrs. Rigby." I stepped inside, muscles relaxing as the smell of roasted chicken and fresh-cooked bread reached us.

"And it's Rose."

I smiled, not acknowledging her words. The hardwood floors were covered in area rugs; every inch of the walls had western-style pictures or family photos. My gaze caught on one of Henry standing next to me. As much as I enjoyed spending time here, it made me ache for what I didn't have. I followed Rose into the kitchen.

Henry came into the room. "Good. You're here."

"I wouldn't miss it. It's my best meal all week."

Rose smiled with pride. "And don't you forget that when you meet some nice young woman. You won't have time for us anymore."

"Yeah, that's not happening." I exchanged a smirk with Henry before Elle's face popped into my head. At first, my excuse was that I was young. At thirty years old, I wasn't that young anymore.

Henry smirked. "I heard the owner of the new barbershop is smoking hot, and that she was at the vet clinic with her new puppy."

Elle. Panic shot through me. "Christ. The gossip in this town is unbelievable."

Rose looked up in exasperation. "Watch your language."

I winced. "I'm sorry."

"Piper's working there now. She wanted a change from the salon. She said she met Elle a few months ago when she was renovating the shop. I guess Piper asked if she was hiring, then invited her to the bar with us. Elle must have left before I showed up because I never met her."

"Yeah, I met her." I had been attracted to her even

then. What I remembered was that she kept her head down, her hair covering her face as if she didn't want to attract attention. She seemed more open now.

I followed Henry to the family room. It was a sunken room with large windows showcasing the fields, the vastness of their land. There was wood paneling on the walls, a braided area rug, and a lamp in the corner that gave off a warm glow. The design was different than the home I'd grown up in. Though the feelings of safety and belonging were the same.

"Where is Piper?" It seemed like she tried to avoid Sunday dinners as much as I wanted to be here.

"Who knows? I think she told Mom she has knitting club or something."

I wrinkled my nose. "Knitting club?"

"Lame, right? It's either the worst or the best excuse."

"It sounds like something she made up. Anyway, I'm going to go check it out this week." Henry sat in the armchair by the large screen TV, pointing the remote at it to turn it on.

I sat on the couch across from him. "Check out what? Knitting club?"

Henry flipped through the channels until football players filled the screen. "Smoke & Mirrors, the barbershop. I want to see if the owner is as hot as people are saying."

I'd forgotten the name of the shop was Smoke &

Mirrors. I wondered if it had any meaning for her. "Her name is Elle Carmichael."

He looked from the TV to me. "So, you did meet her?"

I shifted, uncomfortable with his scrutiny. I didn't want Rose to find out. If she did, I'd never hear the end of it. "She was at the bar months ago. It was probably when she was renovating the shop. I saw her again at the clinic when she brought in Crew."

At Henry's raised brow, I added, "Her puppy."

I hoped he wouldn't ask any follow-up questions about the night I ran into her. Touching her was a jolt to my system, shocking me out of my solitary existence. The moment only lasted a few seconds, but I'd wanted to give into temptation, my fingers easing from steadying her balance to wanting to be closer, lowering my head, imagining the feel of her lips under mine.

I ignored my strong desire for self-preservation, giving into baser needs. I wanted more time with this woman. Would she be up for one night? Right before our lips touched, she was the one to jerk back, easing out of my grip. With an apology for running into me, she'd taken a step past me, disappearing. I didn't know she owned the barbershop. I didn't think I'd ever see her again.

"What's she like?" Tourists looking for a good time were plentiful, so I wasn't sure why Henry was so fixated on her when he usually went for the ones that were only in town for a short time.

"I don't know much about her except she's from California, she opened the shop, and she has a puppy."

Henry's face fell in disappointment. "Is she hot at least?"

I didn't want to admit it to him. I didn't want Henry to lay claim to her. "She's pretty. If you like the down-to-earth, natural look."

For reasons I couldn't quite place, I hoped he didn't.

Henry sat on the armchair, cradling a beer in his hands. "I usually go for high-maintenance women. Maybe I should go after something else."

Something about his interest in a woman he hadn't met yet, irked me. "She's not your type. She's here to stay, a business owner. She's not a tourist, here for a few days then gone."

"That's true. Although, you seem really concerned about me dating her. Are you staking a claim?" His tone was infused with incredulity.

"What? No. What are we, teenagers?" We hadn't worried about staking a claim on anyone since Henry's high school sweetheart cheated on him our junior year of college. He found out when he went home with an engagement ring intending to make things official. Humiliated by her betrayal, he'd hit the bars more often. We'd matured since then, discovering we liked different people. He went for the confident women who were tourists visiting town and usually came on to him. I was generally distrustful of people, so I liked to do the pursuing.

"No, but I won't go after a woman you're interested in." What he'd left unsaid was that it was rare for me to take any interest in a woman.

I had short relationships, thinking I could offer something more. It was inevitable I'd freak out when they asked too many questions. I tried to avoid anything serious. The words stuck in my throat on the way up. I managed to choke them out, "No claim."

His expression was thoughtful as he took a long sip of his beer. "How's work going?"

I settled deeper into the couch, thankful he was letting it go, my eye on the football game on the TV. "Ed finally mentioned drawing up papers so I can buy the business."

"That's great news."

"The problem is, he's not convinced I'm going to stay." I'd been on edge since the conversation with him. It felt like an ultimatum: Prove yourself, or you're not going to get the business. How could I prove I intended to stay when I lived like I could pick up at any time to start over?

Henry shifted in the chair so his attention was on me. "I got the impression you don't want to go back home."

I shook my head, leaning my elbows on my thighs. The place that once had been a sanctuary, turned on me. "I don't."

Henry rubbed his forehead. "You don't want to live anywhere else, do you?"

The one thing I appreciated over the years was that Henry never pressed for more information than I was willing to offer. That's why we remained friends for so long, even when I'd distanced myself from other people.

"I don't." If I moved, I'd be starting all over again. That, I couldn't stomach. At least here, I knew a few people. It was as close to home as I'd ever get.

"Then how are you going to prove it to him?"

Henry wanted me here. It felt good that he had my back, even if I didn't trust anyone one hundred percent. "Buy a house, date a local."

Henry shook his head, chuckling. "You might as well get married and pop out a few kids."

An image of Elle popped into my head, long brown hair curling around her shoulders, wearing a thick sweater over leggings with fuzzy socks on her feet, curled up on my sofa with a steaming mug of cocoa in her hands. It was simple, domestic.

The picture was everything I'd avoided. I had to remember nothing was what it seemed. She was no exception. Even if you got comfortable with someone, thought you knew them, they might turn out to be someone else in the end. "Yeah, that would probably do it."

Henry shook his head, turning in the chair so he faced the TV again. He was quiet for so long I didn't think he was going to comment on it further. At the next commercial break, he said, "Why don't you?"

"Why don't I what?"

His expression was pensive. "Why don't you buy a house? You said yourself you're not planning on leaving."

Every muscle in my neck stretched taut. Being tied down to a place meant it hurt that much more when it was gone. "What if he doesn't offer me the business? I'll probably want to go somewhere I could open my own practice or buy one."

My stomach churned at the idea of leaving. It was something I thought I could do if I had to, but I didn't want to.

"I don't know. It's easier than finding someone willing to marry you quickly. You could sell the house if you had to." Henry shrugged as if it wasn't a big deal.

I sighed, leaning back into the cushions. I couldn't expect Henry to understand when I'd never told him about my past, at least not all of it. He knew my parents were divorced, and that I visited my mother occasionally. I never spoke of my father. Opening up to someone was difficult. A woman I was dating would want to know things about me, my family, my past. "That's true."

"Would it be so horrible to put down some roots, maybe buy some more furniture, get a good gaming system so I can come over?"

I picked up the nearest pillow, throwing it at him.

It smacked him in his face because his attention was

on the game. He shot me a disgusted look. "Hey, that was uncalled for."

"So was what you said. There's nothing wrong with my apartment." What I didn't say was that I couldn't have a home as much as I might want one. Buying things made me feel uncomfortable. It had a permanent sort of feel when nothing was guaranteed. Things could be taken away. People left.

"It doesn't even look like you live there. You're either working, hanging out with me, or sitting in that depressing as shit apartment."

I shrugged. "I don't know. Buying a house is so permanent. Your family has lived on this property for generations. It's assumed that it will always be in your family. You'll always have a place to call home."

My heart cracked, breaking open. It was the first time I'd spoken anything close to the truth since the day I went to college. I'd run from everything that was taken from me, never wanting to be in that position again. If I didn't have a home, it couldn't be taken away. If I didn't fill my apartment with things, I could leave quickly. If I didn't get close to anyone, they didn't have power over me when they left.

Henry focused on me. "You never talk about your family or why you don't go back."

I stayed silent as my teeth ground together. I knew the day would come when he'd want answers to the blanks I'd left in my story. Why I didn't talk much about my family; why I was never eager to return home. Why questions made me uncomfortable.

He shook his head, sighing. "I'm just saying, it might be time to make a change. Maybe making a home here won't be so bad. Maybe it will be the best decision you've ever made."

"Dinner's ready," Mrs. Rigby called from the kitchen.

"Think about it." He got up, leaving me alone.

Following behind him, I rubbed my neck, trying to erase the itch that started when he gave his opinion.

Mr. Rigby came in the house, pulling off his shoes, and washing his hands in the mudroom. When he finally entered the kitchen, his gaze landed on me. "Oh good, you're here. Would you mind looking at Blaze before you go? I don't like the way he's limping."

"Of course. You want me to check him out now?" I always kept a bag in my truck in case of emergencies. It was easier than running to the clinic each time. Plus, I liked helping the Rigbys out. They'd done so much for me.

"No. Eat, then I'll take you to him."

I nodded, accepting a dish piled high with food from Rose. The food was delicious like always. I appreciated that after my first visit, the Rigby family never asked why I spent so much time at their home, seeming to accept I was too far from my family to visit often. I never said that; I just let them believe it.

The conversation inevitably turned to talk of the

progress on Henry's cabins. He had visions of turning a few rustic cabins on the far end of the Rigbys' property into rentals. He was in the process of renovating them. I was trying to convince him to build a lodge for group events with a condo for himself on the top floor. It sounded amazing. Lodging in Telluride was at a premium. I knew it would be a success.

After dinner, I grabbed my medical bag, following Mr. Rigby to the stable. After leading the horse out, I could see what he was talking about. Blaze dropped his hip to the right. I offered him an apple before petting him slowly, talking softly, soothing him. I crouched down to run my hands along his leg, checking for heat, swelling, or any source for his lameness. Finally, I picked up his hoof. There was a foul-smelling, black discharge.

"It looks like thrush," I said to Paul.

"That's what I was thinking."

He held the reins, patting Blaze's nose while I carefully cleaned out her hoof. When I finished, I said, "You'll want to clean it out daily with diluted iodine, and keep him in a clean, dry stall."

"I know the drill." Paul led Blaze into the stall, securing the door while I cleaned up.

I shouldered my bag, ducking into the house to kiss Rose on the cheek, thanking her for a good meal, and saying a quick goodbye to Henry. Then I headed back outside, falling in step with Paul, heading to my truck.

"I heard a rumor you're finally going to buy Ed's practice."

I'd gone to the bank to start the process; word must have gotten around. "That's the plan."

"Good." We came to a stop by my truck door.

As a pseudo-parent to me, Paul's approval felt good.

"He's not going to give it to you easily, is he?"

"No. He wants to make sure I'm staying here, that I'm making permanent roots. He's worried his clients won't like the change." Speaking to him about Ed's expectations made everything more real than when I spoke to Henry.

"And are you?"

"Am I what?" Even though I knew exactly what he was talking about, I wanted to hear his opinion, yet I dreaded it at the same time. If Paul agreed with Ed's assessment, it made what I had to do more real.

"Are you making permanent roots?"

"I've lived here for four years, ever since I graduated from vet school."

Mr. Rigby crossed his arms over his chest, widening his stance. "Listen, I hope you're going to stay. I don't want Ed's practice going to anyone else. Henry likes having you here."

"I don't know if I can do what Ed wants. I work hard." I almost never had free time. I took over most of the emergency calls, working six to seven days a week. I didn't have a family or anyone I needed to make time for, so it worked perfectly.

"He just wants to see you settled here. House, marriage, kids."

I chuckled without any humor. "Yeah, but that's impossible. I'm not even dating anyone."

"What about buying a home, a small farm or something?"

The pain of losing my childhood farm was still strong, twelve years later. I grabbed the back of my neck, squeezing it before I responded. "I saved money to buy the practice. I don't know. I'll have to think about it."

"I hope you can convince him. You deserve it."

"Thanks."

Paul said goodbye, heading back toward the house.

He was the closest person I had to a father since I was eighteen. His concern was appreciated. I just wasn't sure how to convince Ed I was serious about Telluride, that I had no intention of leaving when I'd avoided anything permanent over the years.

I sensed I was on the cusp of something big. I couldn't keep going like I was. Buying a home was a tangible way to prove I wanted to stay. It was a huge commitment, especially if the deal with Ed fell through. The thought of signing a contract, putting money into something like that, made my heart pound and my chest tight. It was overwhelming, making it difficult to draw in a deep breath. The feeling was suspiciously similar to the panic attacks I'd experienced before I left home.

CHAPTER 5

Elle

We had a slow, steady stream of customers the first week, but it wasn't enough to pay the expenses for the building. I had enough money to get by for a few months until it was profitable. I hoped that would be sooner rather than later.

"It'll get better," Piper said when we closed the door Friday night, turning the sign from open to closed.

"I hope you're right." Success didn't happen overnight. I hoped for enough customers to at least break even the first month. Coming here felt right. Telluride was an escape from Los Angeles. I hoped it would become a haven. I'd avoided people for fear of being recognized. The only person I talked to with any regularity was Piper, and she was my employee.

My phone buzzed in my pocket. Looking at the screen, I saw it was my sister, Alice. Smiling, I said to Piper, "I'm going to take this in the back office."

"I'll finish cleaning up then head out."

"Thanks, Piper." I'd thanked her a billion times for giving me a chance. It would never be enough. Her working here gave my business some legitimacy with the locals. If she trusted me, they could too.

I hit speaker as I entered my office, closing the door behind me for privacy. "Hey, sis."

"Hey. I miss you." Her usual cheerful voice came over the line.

"I miss you too." I'd asked Alice to come with me, to help open the shop. She'd declined, loving life in LA too much to leave.

"When are you coming home?" Alice's voice brought me back to the conversation.

My family seemed to think I'd fail, coming home sooner rather than later. My parents still owned the beach home we grew up in. There was nothing there for me but bad memories. I was determined to make Smoke & Mirrors a success so I didn't have to go back. "I bought a building and opened a business. I have no plans on leaving."

Her sigh filled my small office I was so proud of.

"You could come visit." I wanted to show her what

I'd done, not just in pictures. I wanted her to see the business I'd built.

"I don't want to leave LA. Everything's here."

Alice followed me there, living with me while I filmed the spin-off show, the one that followed us after high school as most of us attempted to go to school and figure out what we wanted to do with our lives. It was mostly throwing parties, watching us fight over guys, and shopping. When I was filming the show, I tried to keep her away from it as much as possible. I wanted to shield her from it.

"There's nothing there for me anymore." Moving here was the right decision. While filming, the cameras followed me relentlessly. I felt like I never had a moment of peace. Even when the show wasn't following us, members of the paparazzi were.

My one attempt at working at a salon was a disaster. People in LA would never forget the person I'd played on TV. They'd never forgive me or acknowledge it was a role, not reality. There was nothing for me in LA except Alice.

"You could have the barbershop show. The producers wanted you to open it here. They would have given you money to do it, too."

Pressure from Alice to go back on the show felt like a betrayal. She knew how much I disliked it. Acting like someone else, someone who wasn't a good person, slowly chipped away at my soul.

"I wouldn't have owned the business. The studio

wanted to dictate the name, the look, who I hired, how I ran it." I would have been continuing my role as the show's villain, a person who stabbed her friends in the back, who stole other people's boyfriends. I got a sick feeling thinking back to that time in my life.

When we started out, the producers convinced us it would be a good acting opportunity. We could use the experience to get more roles. Unfortunately, the show was sold as reality, following rich teenagers with nothing but time on their hands. When the shows went off the air, the producers finally came out with the truth. By then, no one believed it was scripted or that we were talented.

I was a naive sixteen-year-old who believed whatever the producers said. My parents loved the idea of me being on TV. They told me it was an amazing opportunity. I believed them. To be fair, I don't think they thought the show would be as successful as it was. That my reputation would forever be marked by my actions, directed or otherwise.

"It's easy money. Emily said she wanted to hire me as the shop's receptionist."

Emily was the producer who was with me the most. At first, I thought she was a friend. When I'd gotten older, I realized she only cared about ratings and keeping her job. She wasn't my friend. I didn't like that she was trying to manipulate Alice too. "You don't have any experience at a salon or barbershop."

"You know as well as I do, it's a role. I can play the

part."

"It's so much more than that, Alice. I don't want that for you. It didn't lead to any acting opportunities for me. That's a line they feed you to get you to sign on."

"What? My picture on every gossip site? Look at the amazing opportunities you guys had. Lillian has her own fashion line now. You were offered a spin-off."

I was sad that any friendship we might have had was ruined by filming, but I am happy for her. Lillian, one half of the popular sweetheart couple on the show, had a better reputation than me. As far as the public knew, I stole her boyfriend from her. I was the bitch in that situation. I only kissed her boyfriend, Chad, on camera. Nothing happened otherwise. "That opportunity came with strings, very real implications for my reputation and my future. I don't want that anymore."

I wanted a place to call my own. I craved privacy, that cozy, comfortable feeling you got when everything was yours. Nothing would be shown to someone else, dissected or talked about. I didn't want to live in a snow globe anymore, one the producers could shake up at will, upending my life, changing the trajectory of my future.

"We're young. We should be having fun." Alice's voice was whiny.

"I'm twenty-four. I'm tired of clubs, cameras, and gossip columns. If I never see a member of the paparazzi again, I'll be happy." I wasn't friends with my castmates. I didn't keep up with what they were doing.

I wanted a clean break. I wanted to figure out who I was without the cameras and the people prodding me about what to say and do.

"I'm only twenty-two. I deserve this opportunity. It's not fair they chose you. They never wanted me."

I ground my teeth at her entitled tone.

"Alice, be happy they didn't. You were way too young. Your reputation wasn't tarnished. Mom and Dad will pay for college wherever you want to go. You have options." I wish I could go to college without being known as the bad girl, or the life of the party. I would have liked to have that experience.

"I don't want to go to college."

"Trust me, Alice, the show isn't what it seems. The part I played will haunt me forever. Anyone can look up my name, see the articles, the comments, the stupid things I did." I lived in a constant state of awareness that someone could recognize me, judging me for who I was then.

"I wish you'd change your mind."

"I'm not going to. Please don't tell Emily I will." If she did, Emily would be on a plane, coming here to convince me to go back. Knowing her, she'd probably bring a camera, filming it for attention. All it would accomplish would be to ruin my reputation here, destroying any chance of starting a new life.

"If you wait too long, they'll move on to something else." Her voice was pleading, almost desperate.

Guilt filled me that I was here, and she was there

alone, handling sharks. How many times had we been told if we didn't do what they wanted, we wouldn't be popular, no one would watch us? We had to keep the show interesting, ratings up, and people clamoring for more. It was all at our expense. "I want them to move on to someone or something else."

I didn't want that someone else to be Alice. Growing up, it was her and me. My parents were busy working. They worked in LA, only coming to the beach house on some weekends. We had a nanny, but her involvement was minimal. We had money, time, and a huge house at our disposal. I saw the show as an escape.

I wanted better for her. "I wish you'd come here, let me show you the town."

"I've been there, remember? It's boring. I don't like the cold."

She'd always been a California girl, loving the warm weather and sand. LA was exciting, the possibilities endless, the downside devastating. I had no idea it would alter my reputation forever. Hopefully, with distance and time, people would forget.

"Be careful, Alice."

"I will. Talk to you later, sis."

On the show, the producers quickly pegged me as the villain. I played the jealous girl who came between the fan-favorite sweetheart couple. I had no idea how that description would plague me when I tried to get a real job.

I wanted to save my sister from that life. If she was determined to experience it for herself, I wasn't sure there was anything I could do to prevent it.

CHAPTER 6

Gray

"Your next puppy ate raisins," Sheila said as I grabbed the folder, seeing *Crew Carmichael* at the top.

My heart rate picked up, moving quicker as I pushed the door open. For a brief second, I hoped Elle was overreacting, but Crew sat on the metal exam table, his head bowed, drooling, showing clear effects of toxicity.

Elle lifted her head from Crew's back, her eyes shiny with tears. "Can you help?"

Seeing Elle like this, scared and crying, tore at my heart, unraveling it like a ball of yarn, one strand at a time. In these situations, I was efficient, calm, and cool under pressure. I knew what to ask, what to do. Yet today, at the sight of Elle wiping away the tears on her cheek, the panic laced in her voice, I felt sluggish. "Has he thrown up?"

Elle's brow furrowed. "No."

"Did you try to induce vomiting?" Experienced owners knew to feed their dogs hydrogen peroxide, making them throw up, before driving to the vet. Elle probably didn't know that trick.

She shook her head slowly. "No, I don't know how to do that."

Panic rose in my throat, squeezing it. Saving Crew's life was vital. Something told me Elle wouldn't survive it if something happened to him.

"How many raisins did he eat? How long ago did he eat it?" I glanced at the clock, ready to calculate the number of raisins in his system, and how long they had been there, to determine if I could save his life, or if there was too much for his small system.

Elle let go of Crew to rifle through her purse, holding up a red raisin box. "He got into this. It was in my purse."

"How full was it?" A few raisins weren't a big deal. The whole box, however, was dire for a small puppy.

"It was new. He ate all of it. I'm not even sure when he ate it. He was already drooling when I found the empty box." Her tone was defeated.

It was the worst-case scenario. A large number of raisins in his system for an unknown period of time. I'd do anything I could to save him, hoping we weren't too late.

I looked at his eyes and mouth, quickly probing his body for any other injuries. "We're going to take him in the back to induce vomiting. Then we'll administer activated charcoal to get it out of his system. We'll need to keep him here for observation for a few hours, if not overnight."

Elle nodded, the motion jerky, more tears welling in her eyes.

Elle gave Crew a quick pat on his head, her fingers shaking as she kissed him. She murmured something to him I couldn't hear.

When Elle stepped back, I called for Sheila to come and get him. When Sheila gathered him up, leaving the room, a small sob erupted from Elle.

She covered her mouth with her hand, her shoulders hunched. "I don't know what I'd do if anything happened to him."

I wanted to go to her, eliminate the space between us, and assure her everything would be fine.

"Will he be okay?"

Flexing my fingers, I resisted the urge to touch her, to hug her. I barely knew this woman, yet I wanted to relieve her pain, her worries. "I hope so. It depends on how long ago he ate them, how much he ate, and how much his small body can take." Hating how impersonal my voice sounded, I softened my tone, "I'll do everything I can to save him."

"I knew chocolate was bad, but not raisins. I'd forgotten those were even there." Her tone was laden with guilt and shame.

I stepped closer, standing in front of her. I wanted to reach out and move a strand of hair out of her face. Standing this close to her made it hard to breathe. My chest felt tight and my ears were ringing.

She looked up at me through wet lashes, her lips parted slightly.

I wanted to soothe the ache in my chest and the pain I saw in her eyes. I had no business offering her comfort by touching her or pulling her tight against me. She was a client. Crew was my patient. The only thing I could do was promise her I'd do anything to save him. "I'll keep a close eye on him and call you with any updates."

Elle stepped closer, her hand squeezing my forearm lightly. "Thank you, Gray."

My eyes followed her movement, the warmth of her hand seeping through my doctor's coat. My resolve weakened at the touch. I cleared my throat. "You're welcome."

Elle removed her hand, picking up her purse.

She wasn't any more neglectful than most owners. Not all dogs dug through purses for food, but some did. I pulled out a business card, writing the directions to induce vomiting on the back, along with my personal cell phone number. "Buy hydrogen peroxide. Next time this happens, mix it with some yogurt or whatever he'll eat. It will make him throw up. Then bring him to me. It's best to get it out of their system quickly."

She chewed her lip. "Okay. I can do that."

"If you have any questions, please call." I handed her the card, wondering if I'd been too forward by giving her my number. She had to know I didn't do that with my other patients.

"I'll do that. Thank you so much."

I hoped leaving Crew with me eased her stress. I wouldn't let her down.

I suspected Crew was holding her together. If something happened to him, she'd unravel. I understood that. I felt that same desire to have a pet. But I'd never been able to get one of my own, no matter how much I loved animals. The thought of something happening to them was overwhelming.

"I'll do everything I can for him." Seeing the appreciation in her eyes, I turned away to wash my hands so I wouldn't say anything else to her. I'd never felt this overwhelming need to help someone, to take away their pain.

When I heard the door click closed, I carefully dried my hands, taking a deep breath to clear my head. I couldn't get the look on her face, this morning, out of my head. Tear-streaked cheeks, red and puffy eyes, all because she cared about her puppy.

Elle Carmichael was deeper than I thought. If I were a different man, I might want to get to know her better, ask her out on a date, find out why she'd moved here, why she needed a dog to survive. But I wasn't that man.

I was a shell of who I was supposed to be. I had no interest in connecting with another person outside of the Rigby family. It hurt too much to put yourself out there, to allow someone else to have control, the power to betray you, or walk away.

* * *

I KEPT a close eye on Crew that afternoon. I was concerned about all the animals under my care, but I didn't want to deliver bad news to Elle.

When Sheila came into my office during a break between appointments, I asked, "How is Crew?"

"He's doing good. Do you want me to call his owner to pick him up?"

Relief poured through my body, easing the taut muscles in its path. "No. I'll do it."

Sheila paused. "You will?"

"Yeah, I had something I need to talk to her about." I wanted to hear her voice. I needed to be the one who told her he was okay.

Sheila looked confused, probably because I almost never called clients unless there was a problem, or I was updating them on the outcome of a surgery. Then she saw the book on the desk in front of me, *How to Care for Your Puppy.*

"Do you want me to leave that at the front counter for her?"

I wanted to hand it to her. I pulled it as an excuse to see and talk to her, to assure her everything would be okay.

"Um, yeah. That would be great. Thanks." I handed her the book, my stomach sinking that I wouldn't have an excuse to see her. It was probably for the best. Women like Elle wanted the house with a white picket fence. Not one you purchased to prove something.

Sheila walked out. I pulled Elle's phone number up on my computer screen, calling her.

"Hello?" Her voice came over the phone sounding husky.

My dick twitched in my pants. "Elle Carmichael?"

"Gray? Is that you? Is Crew okay?" Her words were rushed, lined with stress.

"He's fine. I was calling to let you know you can pick him up."

She exhaled, the sound drifting over the line. "Oh, thank God. I thought you were calling with bad news."

I could imagine her placing a hand over her rapidly beating heart, her shoulders sagging in relief. I didn't admit that this wasn't a call I ever made. That was probably what Ed was talking about. I was generally impersonal with clients, letting Anne handle them once they left the exam room. "I left something at the front desk for you. A book. Read it."

"Thank you, Gray."

My heart turned over in my chest at the sound of her saying my first name, soft and full of appreciation. Pride filled me that I'd been the one to help her.

"You're welcome." This soft exchange snagged the old wound in my chest, ripping it open. Feeling like an idiot, I hung up. I didn't know what I was doing or why I was attracted to this woman. What was different about her?

There was something in her eyes, in her desperation to make sure her dog was okay, that reminded me of myself.

I was discussing a surgery with another pet owner in the lobby when Elle walked in looking more put together than she had this morning, the tension I'd held in my body all day easing. She wore a puffy jacket open over a flannel shirt tied at her waist, exposing a sliver of her stomach above skintight leggings and boots. She didn't look like any California girl I ever envisioned. She looked more like a Colorado girl, one who was up for anything life had to throw at her. I liked that.

I refocused my attention on the dog owner standing in front of me, answering his questions about the aftercare for his dog following surgery, telling him to follow up if the incision site was still red and bumpy after a few days. I was eager to speak to Elle.

I should have walked to the back, cleaned up for the day, and checked the patients who'd stay overnight before I left them in a vet tech's care. Instead, it was like there was an invisible line pulling me to the counter.

As I approached, Elle pulled out her credit card, handing it to the receptionist. The book I'd left for her sat on the counter in front of her.

"Oh, Dr. Stanton left that for you," Anne pushed it toward her, taking the card to the other end of the counter where the credit card machine was.

Elle picked up the book, a curious expression on her face.

I searched my brain for something intelligent to say. I could ask if she was here to pick up Crew, but that was obvious. I settled for what I wanted to know, "How are you?"

Elle startled, spinning to face me, the book clutched in her hands. "Oh, you scared me."

"Sorry." I reached out a hand to touch the small of her back to steady her, comfort her, at the same time grounding myself. Her ponytail swished behind her as she held the book out to me.

She smirked. "You think I need more dog training?"

A smile played on my lips as the old flirting techniques I'd used when I'd first moved here came back to me. I moved closer to her, anchoring a hand on the counter. Time slowed as I watched her eyes darken at my proximity. "You *did* bring your dog in with a life-threatening emergency just this morning. So…"

I let my voice trail off, tilting my head slightly.

A blush tinged her cheeks. "Are you flirting with me?"

The confidence I'd felt a minute ago evaporated now that she'd voiced it out loud. Stepping back, I said, "Yes. No."

Did she want me to?

She looked down, shaking her head slightly.

Seeing her that torn up over her dog made me long for that attention on me. It was stupid. It was childish, but I couldn't help how I felt. I wanted more of her. I wanted to touch her hair, to test its weight. I wanted to touch the sliver of her belly that was on display. I wanted to move closer, tilting her chin up while I watched her eyes darken with desire for me.

Maybe it wasn't crazy. Maybe we could have a one-night stand. A no-strings fling. If only she'd be up for that. Anything more was too risky. A woman wanting a relationship would ask questions about my family and why I rarely visited home.

Her tongue darted out to lick her lower lip, her teeth followed up with a delicate bite. I almost groaned out loud before I realized where we were.

"There you are, Ms. Carmichael." Anne thrust the card between us, bringing me back into the moment.

I took a step back, shooting Anne an apologetic look. "Crew looks good. Keep an eye on him tonight. If he seems lethargic or starts drooling again, call me. My number is on the card I gave you."

Nothing that was happening was usual or made

sense. When Elle looked up at me, her warm brown eyes appreciative, everything seemed to fall into place. It felt right to offer her help. I wanted to reach out a hand to tuck a wayward strand of her hair behind her ear. I wanted to ask her out on a real date, but Anne's gaze was heavy on us.

"There's your receipt. Call us, or *Dr. Stanton,* if you have any issues. I'll get Crew for you."

Anne wasn't used to me flirting with anyone, much less a client. It was probably her way of asking what the hell I was doing.

Anne walked to the back leaving us alone. Elle looked at me, questions swirling in her eyes.

She swallowed, my attention drawn to the line of her neck, the beat of her pulse. "What are you—"

"Go out with me."

"I'm sorry?"

"I like you."

Her eyes widened in disbelief. "That's straight-forward."

"I'm nothing if not honest." I wanted to say, 'you get what you see,' but that wasn't true. I wasn't even particularly honest if you considered the fact that no one, not even my best friend, knew anything about my life before college.

"Somehow I doubt that." She tilted her head slightly, a playful smile on her lips as she considered me.

Anne walked back to the lobby, the scrape of Crew's excited paws on the floor filled the air. The tension between us dissipated as Elle dropped to her knees on the dirty floor, opening her arms to her puppy. Crew pulled at the leash until Anne let go. Elle giggled as Crew placed his paws on her shoulders, licking her face. "That's my boy. I'm so glad you're okay."

I wanted to say, 'I'm happy you're okay. Not Crew. You. Elle Carmichael. The new girl in town.' The desire to change my lonely existence was strong.

"I'm going to get the files ready for tomorrow. The front door is locked." Anne walked away without waiting for me to respond.

It hadn't escaped my attention she never answered me about a date. She clearly loved animals. Maybe this was a way to draw her in, in a way that was nonthreatening to her. The word *date* evoked so many things she might not be ready for. I wasn't either. "I have to make a house call to check on a horse. Would you like to come with me?"

She patted Crew's head, taking his leash before standing in front of me. Her lips curved in a small smile. "You make house calls?"

Was she considering my invitation? The muscles in my shoulders tensed in anticipation. "It's a horse, so it's part of the job. I have a few clients that aren't as mobile. I like to make sure they can keep their pets. I do whatever I can to make things easier for them."

Her eyes softened. "You're a mystery, Gray."

"A good one, I hope." I ignored the trepidation in my belly. I wasn't a good mystery, but she never had to know. We could have a good time, a diversion from the boring life I'd led in Colorado so far.

"I'd love to go with you. Do you mind if Crew comes?"

Joy filled my chest, filling the hollows, smoothing the jagged edges like water slamming on rocks. "Of course. Let me grab my things. I'll meet you by my truck. It'll be easier if I drive. I can drop you off here afterward."

"Okay."

I left before she could change her mind. My pulse pounded in my ears. What was I doing? Why was I creating a relationship when I could pursue something physical with no strings attached with someone else? Elle wasn't the type of girl who'd want a one-night stand, but I wanted her any way I could get her, even if it meant pursuing a relationship with her though it went against every instinct in my body.

I hung my white coat on the door, grabbing my heavier jacket I wore in the field, one I didn't mind getting dirty.

CHAPTER 7

Gray

*O*n the way out, I waved to Anne, not stopping for the questions I knew she had. I never answered her questions, but that didn't stop her from asking them.

Stepping outside, Elle was walking the perimeter of the parking lot. Light from the parking lot illuminated her face as I approached. Her face was welcoming, her full lips sexy and inviting. I didn't deserve her, but I sure as hell wanted her.

"Are you ready to go?" I stopped in front of her, my hands in my pockets.

"Yeah. This your truck?" She gestured at the black truck that had seen better days.

It was a used one I'd bought from Paul when I moved here. A truck was necessary living in Colorado, but it wasn't so pretty I worried about dirtying it up.

Opening the passenger side door, I helped her into the cab, thinking Elle Carmichael could use some dirtying up. Would she let me be the guy to do it? Closing the door firmly behind her, I rounded the hood.

I didn't know what I was doing. I didn't have a plan. I was dormant for years waiting for something, or someone, to wake me up. Climbing into the truck, I made sure Elle buckled her seat belt, with Crew curled into her side before I backed out.

I don't know why I ever thought she was flighty or had gotten Crew for the wrong reasons. I wanted her to be exactly as she seemed.

I had so many questions about her life, her past, and why she was here, but those questions invited reciprocal ones I wasn't ready to answer. Instead, I went with something germane, "You like Telluride, so far?"

"I love it. It's exactly what I needed." She settled back in the seat.

I didn't want to interrupt her to ask her what she needed: peace, tranquility, or an escape? Colorado was that for me. I wasn't wrong when I thought we were kindred spirits, that there was something in her calling out to me.

"It's been that way for me too." My voice was quiet in the cab, the blare of the heat the only other sound.

"Yeah, how so?"

I felt her gaze on the side of my face. My heart rate picked up. I hadn't meant to open the door to her asking questions, it was just so easy to talk to her. "I had nowhere to go after I graduated from vet school. My best friend from college, Henry, told me about the opening at the clinic. He encouraged me to apply, said I'd love it here. That it would be exactly what I needed."

"Is it?" Her tone was soft.

For some inexplicable reason, her being here gave me more reason to want to stay. "I hope so."

"Me too. I have everything riding on this business. If it doesn't work, I don't even want to think about the alternative, going back to LA."

I could tell by the slight grimace on her face, going back to LA wasn't really an option. It was too early to ask why that was. "I'm sure the business will be successful."

She tilted her head considering me before I turned my attention back to the road. "Are you going to let me cut your hair?"

I cleared my throat, imagining me sitting in a chair, her standing close enough to run her fingers through my strands, her breasts at eye level. "My friend's sister cuts my hair."

She nodded, smiling. "Ah. You're not pretentious."

"I'm the opposite of pretentious." At least now that I'd learned an important life lesson. Nothing was certain. Nothing was guaranteed. Nothing was permanent.

"I like that. I've had too much of that in my life."

Being from LA, that made sense. The pressure to be perfect must have been heavy. I wondered if that was what she was running from. "Is that how you were?"

"Not by choice." Her tone was bitter.

Had her parents held unrealistic expectations for her? Was it a boyfriend? I wanted to know everything there was to know about her, but I couldn't voice that sentiment out loud. It was too soon for intense conversations, even if this seemed like the most meaningful one I'd ever had.

I turned into the driveway under the wooden, rustic ranch sign with the words Rigby's Ranch on it.

"This is beautiful." She gazed out the window at the expanse of property, the mountains in the distance, her lips slightly parted in awe.

I tried to remember what I'd thought about Colorado the first time I'd visited with Henry. The terrain of Colorado, the majestic mountains surrounding the town, so different from the rolling hills and trees of my childhood town. "This is what I love about Colorado."

"Do you live on a farm like this one?" she asked as we pulled up to the house. You could see the large barn with stables behind it.

"No. I live in an apartment." For the first time, I was embarrassed to admit I was thirty and living the life of a bachelor. I shifted in my seat, grabbing my bag from the back.

"That's a shame. I figured you'd own a pack of animals as a vet."

I placed the bag in my lap, something cold shifting in my chest. Every answer was highlighting my barren existence. "No. No pets."

She looked at me as if I'd said something unbelievable. "A vet who doesn't own any animals."

"I'm too busy taking care of everyone else's, I guess."

I got out of the truck before I said anything closer to the truth. I'd had a home, a family, a dog, and a girlfriend. It was all taken in the middle of the night. When you lived life as if nothing bad could happen, you set yourself up to lose things.

I opened the door for her. She held Crew's leash as he hopped out, nose to the ground. "I'd leave Crew on the leash so he doesn't get lost."

"I was planning to. I can't take any more emergencies today." She placed a hand over her chest.

"At least you're with a vet this time if anything goes wrong." My tone was light.

She smiled. "That's true."

Paul opened the door. "Gray. You here to check on Blaze?"

He glanced at Elle, his brows raised in silent question.

Maybe I shouldn't have brought her. I didn't want Paul

or Rose getting their hopes up that we could be a thing. Not only was it too early, but it was also fairly unlikely she'd like me after she got to know me. "That's right. I brought a friend along to see your horses if that's okay."

"Never a problem, Gray. This is your home too." The sentiment was one he'd said often, but I never allowed myself to believe in the myth. I'd carefully numbed myself to the words, remembering nothing was mine.

Paul stepped closer, holding his hand out to Elle. "I'm Paul Rigby."

"Elle Carmichael. Nice to meet you."

He rocked back on his heels, his hands pushed into his pockets. "You're new."

I could practically feel Paul questioning what she was to me when I'd never brought anyone here, much less a woman.

"Yeah, I own the new barbershop in town. Smoke & Mirrors." Her tone was tentative like she couldn't believe it was hers.

"My daughter, Piper, works there. A spa for men or some nonsense."

Elle smiled. "Oh, right. I should have realized Piper is your daughter. It's a traditional barbershop with reasonable prices. I wanted men to feel like they had a place to go that was a small break from their day. A luxury."

"I live on a farm. I don't need luxury, but I might try

it out one day. I've heard good things." Paul's tone was admiring.

"I think you'll do well with the tourists. Some of them are too busy to get cuts back home when they're working all the time." I touched her shoulder briefly, offering support. Many of the locals might find her shop frivolous or a waste of money.

Paul nodded before stepping toward the barn. "That's true. I think the tourists will like it. The season should be picking up soon."

I saw the curve of her lips grow, her eyes shining with excitement. "That would be nice. I could use something to look forward to."

I wanted to grab her hand, squeezing it to reassure her things would be okay. I didn't because I wasn't here for that. Instead, I took Crew's leash from her, tying him to the fence post just outside the stable.

"Dogs don't always like horses and vice versa," I said by way of explanation.

Elle crouched down, patting Crew's head. "Stay here. Away from the horses."

Her tone was light, almost baby talk. The gaping hole in my chest grew wider to see her so open with her love for Crew. She was opening me to things I hadn't allowed myself to feel in years.

Paul let us into the stable, stopping in front of Blaze's stall. "I'll lead him out for you."

"Appreciate it." Then to Elle, I asked, "Have you ever ridden a horse?"

She laughed. "No. I grew up in a small beach town. Not much opportunity for horseback riding, although I loved horses as a little girl."

"I could see that." Hair in braids as she jumped from one adventure to another, I pictured her young and fearless, the whole world in front of her, waiting to be conquered. The image was so strong, I was momentarily stunned by the intensity.

She was casting a spell on me, making me want to be in her sphere. No one had ever done that. Not even my high school sweetheart who walked away when things became too much for her. She hadn't stood by me. She'd believed the rumors and speculation.

I blinked away the memories, focusing on Blaze who stood in front of us.

"Can I touch him?" Elle asked tentatively.

"Sure, you can. Stroke him like this." Paul held Blaze by the harness, showing Elle how to touch his nose and the side of his neck.

I grabbed two apples, throwing one lightly in the air and catching it. I demonstrated how to hold her hand out flat, letting Blaze eat from it. I was surprised when she took the second one from my hand, mimicking my pose. I'd expected her to be afraid. Horses could be intimidating.

She was fearless. She laughed when Blaze sniffed her hand, eating delicately from her. "He's so sweet."

"As long as you know how to handle him, he is. You have to be careful, though. Horses are a lot stronger than us." My words came out harsher than I intended, reverting to the way I'd talked to her in my exam room. I didn't want her to get hurt.

"I know, Gray. I'll be careful." I liked the way she'd said my name. Her voice soft, her tone almost affectionate.

I moved to Blaze's rear end, needing to create space between us, wanting, but not quite ready for the intimacy of being close to her. Lightly touching Blaze's leg, I bent it, examining the hoof. "It looks great. You're doing a good job cleaning it. You're putting iodine on it?"

"Every day."

"Good." I dropped his hoof to the ground.

"Thanks for coming out. Do you want to stay for dessert? Rose made a peach pie," Paul said.

I wanted more time with her. I wanted her to say yes.

"Oh, I'd love to." Elle's response was immediate, her smile genuine.

It only made me like her more. We waited while Paul put Blaze back in his stall. On the way to the house, I unwrapped Crew's leash, handing it to Elle.

Did she realize this was very date-like? Showing her a horse, eating pie with friends...

We walked in the back door, kicking off our shoes in the mudroom, and washing our hands in the basin. The smell of warm peaches filled the air, reminding me of my mom's home. "You can let Crew loose in the house."

Elle unclipped his leash, tucking it into her back pocket. I trailed Crew and her into the kitchen.

"You have a beautiful home, Mr. Rigby," Elle said when we stepped into the large kitchen where Rose was pulling the pie from the oven.

"Call me Paul. This is my wife, Rose."

"This is Elle Carmichael. She's opened the barbershop." Paul told his wife.

"Oh, how amazing. I'm so excited when new things open up here. Piper said it's the cutest place. You give out toy cars to the kids."

"Yeah, and lollipops."

"What a cute idea. A nice addition to the town."

"Thank you." Elle looked pleased.

It made me wonder if she wasn't used to compliments. I had no idea she gave out cars to the children. I thought she was catering mainly to men. "I bet the kids love it."

"They do. The moms do too."

Rose cut generous slices of pie, adding vanilla ice cream on the side. "Here you go. Why don't you sit on the back porch? It's a beautiful night to watch the sunset. I'll keep an eye on your pup."

I took the plates without arguing. I led the way outside, sitting on the swing. The setting was intimate.

Elle placed the glasses of water on the end table,

sitting next to me. "Do you ever get used to the view of the mountains?"

I looked out over the fields, lush green giving way to mountains. "No. I've been here for years and I'm still in awe of them. I can't imagine living anywhere else." It was the first time I'd admitted it to myself. The mountains had been my constant over the last few years, a reminder the world was vast. That no one would find out about my past, or if they did, they wouldn't care.

I handed her the plate.

Taking it from me, Elle said, "This smells amazing."

"Rose is a great cook. I come here when I need a home-cooked meal."

"That's nice." She took a bite, closing her eyes. "Mmm. That's good."

I swallowed hard when she moaned, her tongue darting out to remove a crumb from her lip. I had to look away, focusing on my own pie.

I knew I'd have to reciprocate when I asked a personal question. I still wanted the answer. "Did your mom bake?"

She laughed. "Our nanny cooked for us. She didn't do much baking."

I looked at her in surprise. I didn't have the perfect family growing up, but I had two parents in my life, even though they were divorced. That probably made what happened in the end, worse.

Elle shrugged. "My parents were always working. It

was the same with most of my friends. What about you?"

"My mom loved to bake." The comforting memory came back to me.

I hadn't thought about her, or the kitchen I grew up in, for a long time.

"Nice. So, you have good memories."

"I do have good memories of living with my mom. When I was a teenager, I thought it would be cool to live with my dad." It was until it wasn't.

"Oh, your parents were divorced?"

"Yeah, they divorced when I was young. I don't really remember them ever living together." There was something about eating pie and talking about our childhood that was comforting. I'd never allowed this level of intimacy with other women. I never brought them here, only to a bar or my apartment. Introducing them to the Rigbys was like introducing her to my family. I hadn't intended tonight to be that. It sure felt like that now.

I finished the last bite, stacking my plate on top of hers on the table. Then I pushed off the porch with my foot to slowly rock us. The subtle creak of the swing and the sounds of the night were all we needed to fill the air.

"I love it here. I loved the sound of the beach where I grew up, but not the horns, traffic, or people in LA."

"I bet. I couldn't live anywhere that wasn't in the country." Even though it would be easier to disappear in the city, I enjoyed the country air and the open spaces as well as taking care of large animals, along with dogs and cats.

"You grew up somewhere like this?"

"I did." I wasn't willing to delve any deeper into my past than I already had. An uncomfortable feeling slid down my spine. Too much of a good thing was bad. "Are you ready to head back?"

She looked up at me in surprise, but she didn't call me out on my abrupt change of subject. "Sure. Let me thank Rose and grab Crew."

I followed her inside, waiting while she thanked the Rigbys and clipped the leash onto Crew's collar. I kissed Rose's cheek, promising to come back for Sunday dinner.

Rose grabbed my arm, holding me close to whisper, "Bring her again. She's welcome whenever."

I smiled tightly, nodding in agreement even though I wasn't sure I would.

After we were alone in my truck, Elle asked, "You come to dinner every Sunday night?"

"Usually. Henry comes too, so we have time to catch up."

"That's nice." Her tone was wistful.

"Piper tends to miss them for one reason or another." I never understood why. From where I stood, her family seemed perfect. I wondered what dinners were like at Elle's house. Did she eat in front of the TV after the nanny made the meal? Did she sit at the table with her siblings to talk about their day, like I did with Mom? "Do you have any siblings?"

Elle smiled. "I do. One younger sister, Alice."

I was glad she had someone. "Where is she now?"

"She's trying to figure out what she wants to do with her life. It's not a sob story. My parents will pay her way, but she doesn't want to go to college, or a trade school like me. She wants easy money, maybe become an actress." Her tone was tinged with disgust.

"Acting is a tough road."

"Tell me about it." Then she snapped her mouth closed as if she'd disclosed more than she meant to.

Was she an actress? She didn't seem like the type. I wanted to ask more questions, get to know her. The problem was, she'd want to know me.

"Do you have life figured out, Dr. Stanton?"

I'd thought so until Ed made me rethink everything. "I think so. I want to buy the vet clinic when Ed retires."

"Is that happening?"

"He mentioned it the other day, but he has reservations about it." I was still mulling over the ramifications of buying a home. I couldn't obtain anything I wasn't willing to lose.

Her brow furrowed. "He doesn't think you'd be a good owner?"

"His clients are loyal. When I first moved here, it was difficult to convince some of his longstanding clients to see me if he wasn't available." I spoke carefully, thinking things out in my head, to see if there was a way for me to get the clinic.

I glanced over at Elle in time to see her nod with a knowing smile. "Ah. I can see that. People can be set in their ways. Surely, that's improved over time."

One thing that had bothered me since my meeting with Ed was his criticism of how I talked to clients. I was intentionally brief with them, not wanting to establish connections with anyone. I hadn't realized how that might affect me being a good business owner one day. It was something Elle didn't have to worry about. She was inherently likable. "Ed said I can be cold —not to the animals—but to people."

She was quiet, not acknowledging my statement.

My stomach dropped. "You think so too."

"You were a little cold when we met in your office." She shrugged like it was no big deal. "But I get why. You're better with animals."

Appreciating her honesty, I winked at her. "Being good with animals is an important quality when you're a vet."

She sucked in a breath. "It is, but your clients are people."

I tightened my fingers on the wheel, focusing on the road. "True. I'll try to do better."

"If you let people see this side of you, the one I saw tonight, I think you'd prove Ed wrong."

"Yeah?" Was I that different tonight than when I was in the office? I tried to be clinical with clients, giving them the facts. I thought that made me appear to be more confident, more knowledgeable. I thought they'd respect me more.

"You were more open. You're good to the Rigbys."

My heart pinched at her assessment of me. "Ed wants to know that I'm here to stay. That I'm not going to leave."

"Are you planning to leave?" She shifted in the seat to face me.

I felt her gaze on the side of my face, the intense focus on my answer. Did the answer matter to her? "If he sells me the practice, I won't. I can't rule it out otherwise."

"That's fair. You have nothing keeping you here? No family?"

"The Rigbys are my family." It wasn't a lie. It was the truth.

"They might as well be family. They're so welcoming."

Happy she saw what I saw, I agreed. "They're great people."

"How are you going to prove to Ed you're serious about staying?"

It felt good that she was concerned. I missed someone being invested in the decisions I made, my future. "Short of buying a home, dating someone, and getting married, I don't know."

She was quiet for a few seconds as she mulled over

my response. Finally, she asked softly, "Are you dating anyone?"

I wasn't sure how to answer. I wasn't, but the more I was around her the more I wish I could be with someone like her. She was too good for me. The type that wouldn't be mine for long. "Not currently."

"That seems like an easy thing to fix. You asked me to go to the Rigbys. We ate pie together. That was similar to a date."

I shifted in my seat. She hadn't answered when I asked her on a date, yet she was quick to call this one. I wasn't sure where I stood with her. "Are you saying we should date?"

She blushed, looking down at her hands in her lap. "It's probably not a good idea. I just moved here. I want people to respect me and my business. I probably shouldn't be jumping into anything personal. People might gossip, ask questions."

I wondered why she was worried about people asking questions. Was she hiding something? Was there something in her past she wasn't proud of? If so, we had something in common. "If your business fails, will you go back to LA?"

I hated to insinuate there was a possibility of her business failing, but I had to know what her plans were. I'd avoided taking any risks. Starting something with someone who could leave had me on edge.

"Thanks for the vote of confidence," she said dryly.

"But you're right. I have nothing keeping me here either."

The rest of the ride to the parking lot was quiet. No matter how attractive she was, there was no future for us. She wasn't looking for anything, and I'd sworn off relationships because people always left.

I pulled into the lot, parking next to her SUV.

"Thanks for inviting me. I enjoyed meeting the Rigbys and spending more time with you."

She made no move to open the door. I wasn't sure if she expected me to say something more. I enjoyed spending time with her too. I didn't think it was a good idea to tell her what I was thinking, that I wanted something with her. I wanted more of the feelings she evoked when she was around—comfort, desire.

"What are your plans for the clinic if Ed sells to you?"

Should I share my dreams with her? "I don't have any immediate plans to change anything. The one thing I've always wanted to do was add a rescue. We have this huge lobby with room to expand the kennel area. We could work with another local rescue to house more dogs so they aren't in kill shelters."

I held my breath as I waited for her response. I'd never told anyone, not even Henry, what I wanted to do with the clinic. Saying things out loud meant believing in them, knowing they'd happen when I was never sure of anything.

"Have you told Ed that?" She shifted in her seat, her eyes trained on me.

I sighed, a little embarrassed that I was afraid to voice my thoughts. Things that came so easily for other people, talking about their hopes and dreams for the future, were difficult for me. "No. I'm not sure how he'd take it. I'm worried he wouldn't like it."

Elle bit her lip. "Or he might see it as your commitment to staying. Are you the kind of guy who walks away from something you start?"

"Not usually." The intimacy in the cab of the truck reminded me of dating Aubrey in high school. Sitting in my truck with a pretty girl, wondering if she'd accept my advances. Being with Elle was familiar, easy. Her scent filled the cab, overwhelming my senses. The gentle curve of her lips drew me in.

"Maybe he'll see this as a way for you to show you're invested in the community and the clinic. It doesn't hurt to try."

I tried to focus on what she was saying instead of how good it felt to be with her. I weighed the risks of being upfront with Ed about my plans. He might decide I wasn't the right person to take over the clinic, or it might sway him in my direction. "You might be right."

She smiled then, her gaze on me. Her hand covered mine. At her touch, I lost any interest in talking about the clinic. I licked my suddenly dry lips, my heart racing. I wanted to lean closer, eliminating the space between us, and drop a kiss on her lips.

But I wasn't ready. One kiss with Elle would mean something to her. She'd want a relationship, intimacy, honesty. I wasn't sure I could have that anymore. How could I open myself to someone when I hadn't done that since high school?

Instead of leaning in closer, I gently pulled my hand from hers, averting my gaze. "Thanks for coming tonight."

I kept my voice soft, hoping she wouldn't take it as a rejection. I wanted her. I just wasn't sure I could have her. I could feel her gaze searching my face. I refused to meet her eyes.

"Thanks for inviting me. I had a good time."

The words hung in the air between us, ripe with expectation. I couldn't acknowledge it. If I leaned over, I'd kiss her like I wanted to, passionate and unrestrained. Instead of burying my hands in her hair, I curled them into fists. Making a move wouldn't be fair to her.

"I have to open the shop tomorrow, so I'd better get going." She wasn't looking at me anymore. She pushed open the door, urging Crew to hop out. "Good night, Gray."

I didn't respond. I couldn't. I was afraid I'd ask to see her again. I was afraid I'd touch her, pulling her in for that kiss; that if I started, I wouldn't want to stop. It would be too easy to fall into her, into a relationship, a life. I didn't want to see the disappointment on her face when she discovered my past. I didn't want her to think less of me.

She shut the door, easing into her vehicle before I could respond. I wanted to push her away. So why did I feel like I just kicked her puppy?

CHAPTER 8

Gray

*E*lle's suggestion that I speak to my boss about the rescue tumbled around in my head as I drove home. Maybe Henry and Elle were right. I'd been merely existing, staying in the same apartment, making plans for the clinic, and not doing anything about my future. I was in limbo waiting for Ed to decide when he wanted to retire and to feel comfortable selling. I'd only envisioned the things I'd do after all of that happened. If I acted on some of those plans sooner, maybe Ed would feel more confident handing the practice over to me.

The idea of being proactive was unsettling. The decision to go to school on the other side of the country, to move here and work for Ed, had all been carefully calculated moves. Buying a home and dating a woman seemed impulsive when I didn't know what the future held.

I needed to ask Ed if he'd be open to boarding more dogs for local rescues. If he was against the idea, he might not want to sell to me. But what if he liked it? The thought of having more control over the business and more room to make improvements was heady. I'd been taking the easy route since I graduated from vet school. It was past time I did more to secure the future I wanted instead of waiting for it to happen.

* * *

WHEN I WOKE up the next morning, I felt restless with nervous energy. I took a quick shower, grabbing a to-go mug of coffee before heading to work. Inside the clinic, I paused at the receptionist's desk to talk to Anne.

Rapping my knuckles on the counter, I asked, "Is Ed in?"

"He's going to be in a little later this morning. Why?" Anne's brow furrowed as she looked up from her computer screen.

"Can you tell him I need to talk to him?"

Her shoulders relaxed. "Of course."

"Thanks." I rapped my knuckles on the counter

again, moving to walk away. "Oh, can you send me the list of rescues we give discounts to?"

"Sure." Anne looked like she wanted to ask follow-up questions, but she didn't. "I'll email it to you."

"Great." I headed toward my office with renewed purpose. If Ed were on board, I'd check with the rescues to ascertain needs for boarding before drawing up plans to renovate.

I didn't want to get too far ahead of myself. Now that I'd made the decision to move forward, my mind was full of possibilities for the practice.

I ran through my morning appointments, getting more nervous about my upcoming pitch to Ed. I almost found myself hoping Crew ate something or got into another minor mishap so I could see his owner. I wanted her sweet optimism to wrap around me, buoying me for the conversation I needed to have.

Ed popped his head into my office at lunch. "You wanted to see me?"

Was I making a mistake in being honest with him? What if he hated my ideas? I wiped my sweaty palms on my pants. "Yes. Please shut the door. Have a seat."

"You went to the bank?" Ed sat across from me.

I relaxed slightly, knowing this piece was taken care of. "Everything's in order. The business was valued, and the bank approved me for a loan."

I'd be using a large chunk of my savings to buy the clinic, but it's what I intended to do with the money.

Secure my future. Buy something that couldn't be taken away from me.

Ed nodded in approval. "Great."

I took a deep breath before telling him my plans. What I had to tell him could change everything. "I've thought about the possibility of opening up boarding to local rescues. We could add more kennels with more staff on nights and weekends to care for the animals. We'd take care of the dogs until a foster home is found, allowing more to be brought into the rescue, getting them out of the shelters before their time is up."

Voicing my ideas out loud made me feel vulnerable. Putting them out there gave him the power to reject them, reject me. My body was rigid waiting for his response.

Ed rubbed his chin thoughtfully. "Why do you want to do this?"

"I realize it's minimal profit to us. We'd be offering boarding at a reduced cost to the rescue, increasing our staff costs, but I think it would be nice for the community. We'd be working with local rescues, keeping in close contact, figuring out what they need."

"It's not a bad idea."

I relaxed my shoulders, breathing easier knowing he was at least receptive to my suggestions.

"You have anything else going on in that head of yours?"

I shifted in my chair, excited that he seemed interested in hearing more. He'd been receptive to my idea for the kennels, maybe he'd be open to the mobile vet clinic, the idea I'd had since vet school. "I've thought about offering a vaccine clinic. I could have a mobile van and take it to communities who don't have access to vets or can't afford to pay their vet bills."

"You'd be offering that at a reduced cost?" He leaned forward in his chair, his thoughtful gaze focused on me.

I was aware that some business owners were purely about profit. I hoped Ed was more open-minded than that. Keeping myself distanced from people, especially Ed, put me at a disadvantage in not knowing how he'd react. "I'd like to offer them for free."

He leaned back in his chair, crossing his arms over his chest. "It's an interesting idea. How do you propose we pay for this?"

I channeled Elle's enthusiasm from last night. "We can ask for donations from the community, or we could get high school volunteers to help. Many students have service hours to complete before graduation." I placed my elbows on my desk, trying to contain my excitement that Ed seemed open to my plan.

"I love the idea of partnering with the community, strengthening our presence, our ties. My only caveat is you're in charge. You talk to the rescues, inquire with other vet clinics who offer a mobile unit, see if it's feasible. I'll look into the finances to see how much we can afford."

Pride filled me that he liked my ideas and wanted

me to take the lead on it. This was what I wanted, to be in charge and implement my ideas. "If we don't have the funds for the mobile unit, I can take my medical bag with me to administer the vaccines. We'd just need a spot to set up, maybe a local community center."

Ed steepled his hands, considering me. "I like your initiative. How long have you been sitting on these plans?"

"For a while now. I was hoping to implement them if I became the owner," I said my words carefully, wondering how he would take my admission.

"Hmm. What happens if you decide to leave? Who runs it then?"

My heart sunk. We were back to his disbelief I'd stick around. "I told you before, I don't have any plans to leave."

"You buy yourself a home yet?"

I bit back a groan. "I'm thinking about it."

The thought caused my neck to prickle with worry, my palms to sweat. It was a huge decision. It would take a sizable chunk of the trust fund I'd carefully added to over the years.

"Good. I'd like to see you settled before I retire. Not planting your roots here makes it seem like you've never viewed Telluride as your home." He stood, opening the door to leave. He paused in the doorway. "I think you need to give it a chance."

After he left, I turned my attention to my computer screen. I was ready to start over if word got out about who I was. It had been twelve years since everything imploded. The corruption ran deep, spreading from local businesses to deputies, making national news, shaking our small community.

Being honest with Ed made me feel vulnerable, so I did what I usually did when that feeling crept in, I sifted through the articles from the initial raid, the hearings, trials, and the sentencings for anything new to reassure myself nothing had changed. Relieved there wasn't any news, I closed it out, clearing my search history. The last thing I needed was for someone to use my computer, find the article, and recognize my last name.

I made the obligatory calls to my mother during the holidays, even visited occasionally. When I went home, the old feelings resurfaced. She'd never traveled outside of our small town, so I didn't worry she'd come here.

I finished out the rest of my appointments for the day, happy there were no emergencies. I closed the clinic, wondering if I should text Henry to ask him to meet me for dinner. I wasn't ready to go back to my empty apartment. I needed a friendly face right now. I needed someone who made me feel good in their presence. An image of Elle's face in my truck last night filled my vision. She was the one I wanted to talk to about this.

I didn't know what I was going to do. I drove into town, parking my truck on the street. I told myself I was just going to walk by her barbershop to see if it was open, to see if she was okay. Her shop was on the corner with two bay windows facing the sidewalk. They were filled with fall decorations, pumpkins, and small scarecrows. I saw her standing behind a man seated in her chair talking to him in the mirror. He turned, their eyes meeting. I imagined he was flirting with her, asking her out. Why wouldn't he? Elle was new to town. She was young and beautiful, clearly successful.

I pulled open the heavy wooden door before I could think it through. The bell over the door signaled my arrival.

"Hey." Piper tipped her head to the side.

I had forgotten she worked here. "Do you take walk-ins?"

"We do, but I could have cut your hair at the ranch." She pointed to a clipboard resting on the counter between us.

I signed my name in the blank box, avoiding her gaze. If I said I was here to see Elle, she'd know I was interested in her. "I thought I'd check this place out."

Piper eyed me warily. "You can have a seat. I'll get my station ready."

I hesitated, not following her gesture to the waiting area where a flat-screen TV hung on the exposed brick wall surrounded by black leather chairs and a shelf of bound books. I swallowed, wondering if this was the worst idea I'd ever had, if Piper would know immediately what was going on in my head. "Is Elle available?"

Piper stilled, then smiled knowingly, like she had a secret. "If you don't mind waiting a few minutes. She's just finishing up with a client now."

I glanced back at Elle. Wearing a form-fitting dress, her back was to me, her brown hair tinged red under the lights.

Her client stood. Elle stepped into his space, using a lint roller to brush off the stray hairs from his shoulders. She paused, saying something that made him throw his head back, letting out a loud guffaw. Her eyes twinkled with amusement; her lips tilted into a pleased smile.

I wanted to be the one to make her smile. I went to sit in the waiting area, nervously running my fingers through my hair, wondering what she would think when she saw me waiting for her.

I kept my eyes trained on the TV, a home improvement show playing as I strained to hear the exchange between them, relaxing when she said, "Have a good night."

Finally, she stood in front of me, her hands clasped together. Her forehead wrinkled in confusion.

I wanted to reach out to touch her, connect with her like we had in my truck before I'd backed off.

"Gray? Piper said you were here for a cut."

"Yeah, she said you take walk-ins." I stood, realizing too late the move left only inches between us.

"I thought Piper usually cuts your hair?"

I wanted to smooth the wrinkle between her brows. I wasn't sure how to answer.

I was walking by, wanted to make sure you were okay. I walked in because seeing you with your customer made me tense. My jaw ached from clenching my teeth. I shifted on my feet. "I wanted to see what all the fuss was about."

A small smile played on her lips. "Piper could have helped you."

Was she teasing or was she searching for validation after I'd pulled away from her last night? I wanted to set things straight. "I wanted you."

Her eyes flared at my unintended double entendre for a second before she carefully schooled her features. "Okay. If you'd like to take a seat, I'll be there in a minute."

Relieved, I moved past her, her shoulder brushing my chest. I leaned closer, inhaling her scent, something citrusy mixed with the masculine scent of leather and shaving cream.

I sat in the oversized maroon leather chair with its old-fashioned metal footrest as I scanned the walls. There was a wooden sign proclaiming it to be a man cave and a wall of badges honoring the local police departments. It was classy. I loved what she had done: made a place where men could feel comfortable, pampered even.

I wasn't focused on the ambiance. I was hypersensitive to where she was in the room, how close her hands were to touching me, the way her dress rippled around her, highlighting her curves.

She appeared behind me, gazing at me in the mirror, her hands on the back of the chair. "What were you looking for?"

I gestured at the unruly mess on my head. I was overdue for a cut. This time, my procrastination worked in my favor. "A trim."

She smiled.

I loved being the one who made her smile.

"Would you like a shampoo first?"

The thought of leaning back, her hands on my scalp, massaging as she worked in the shampoo had a shiver running down my spine. "Yes."

I shouldn't be here. I shouldn't be getting a shampoo. It was one thing to regret how I pulled away from her last night. It was another thing to let her touch me.

I discretely adjusted myself as I stood, following her to the chair in front of a basin. Piper was nowhere to be seen. I was worried she'd tease me in front of Elle for requesting her, so I was glad she was giving us space.

Music played softly on the sound system as I sat in the seat she indicated. I leaned back as she turned on the water. "Tell me if it's too hot."

With her fingers in my hair, her nails lightly scraping my scalp, I closed my eyes, imagining we were in the shower. The warm water ran over my hair as her fingers deftly wet each strand before adding shampoo. I wanted to groan at the arousing sensation of her fingers massaging my scalp. I imagined her kneeling between my spread legs, her hair tickling my thighs, her fingers working my cock as she sucked me into her mouth. Her eyes looking up at me from under lowered lashes.

I opened my eyes, trying to remember where I was —in Elle's place of employment—getting my hair shampooed. I wasn't in the shower with Elle. She wasn't on her knees. This wasn't a fantasy, no matter how much I wished it were. The idea that this fantasy could be a reality, if I were honest with her, had my cock twitching in my jeans.

She rinsed my hair, taking care to avoid my ears. She wrapped a warm towel around my head before walking around the counter to stand next to me.

"I'm going to dry your hair."

I nodded, unable to speak with my throat dry. She used the warm towel to squeeze excess water out of my hair, rubbing my scalp, then tossed the towel in a bin.

"You ready for a cut?" She placed her hands on her hips as if she expected me to walk out at any second.

I didn't blame her for being wary after last night.

"Sure." I followed her, walking stiffly to the chair.

She smiled, our eyes meeting in the mirror. "You trust me?"

I scanned her face. I didn't trust easily but I wanted to make up for last night. To show I did trust her, or at least I wanted to. Starting with something simple like a haircut would be a good first step. "I do."

"That's good. I'm not going to do anything drastic. I like your hair long." She moved to grab her scissors, my eyes dropping to her ass clearly outlined in that dress, not a panty line in sight. Was she wearing a thong or was she commando?

Realizing she'd admitted to thinking about me, I asked, "You do?"

Her arms stilled, her chest close to my shoulder. "Yeah."

"So, what you're saying is I don't need a cut?"

"You will eventually, or it will fall in your eyes." She moved her hands deftly around my head, cutting this way and that. I couldn't see any pattern. I should have been nervous about surrendering control to her. Instead, I felt taken care of.

The shop was quiet, only the soft croon of music filtered through the air. I looked around to see if there were any other customers. "Is Piper gone?"

"Yeah, she left while I was cutting your hair. You're my last client." She nodded toward the front door where the sign facing us said open, meaning the side facing the street said closed.

We were alone. No one could interrupt us. I was glad Piper left, giving us time alone. I just hoped I wouldn't screw things up like I had last night.

"What do you think of the shop?"

"It's classy yet cozy." The words were out of my mouth before I could censor them.

She paused as if she was surprised by my words. "I love that description. Who knew you could be eloquent with words?"

She moved away from me, placing her scissors on the counter. Grabbing a hand mirror, she spun my chair so I could see my reflection. "What do you think?"

"It looks good." I wasn't looking at my hair, I was looking at her. Open. Honest. Vulnerable. If I wanted to be close to her, if I wanted to keep her in my life, that's what I had to be.

She spun the chair again, so I faced the mirror. She stood next to me, one hand on the back of the chair.

"I'm sorry about last night." My eyes locked with hers in the mirror.

She toyed with the chain of her necklace which dangled suggestively over her breasts. "What are you sorry for?"

"For pulling away from you. I wanted to—"

"Thank you." She unhooked the smock, throwing it in a bin beneath her station. "You're good to go."

She was still distancing herself from me. I didn't like it even though I'd done the same thing to her last night. I needed to voice what I wanted, not push her away. I needed to be upfront and honest with her.

"Can we be friends?"

She flitted around her station, tidying, doing a

whole lot of nothing, probably to avoid meeting my gaze. Finally, she braced her hands on the counter, her back to me. "You want to be friends with me?"

I stood, my heart beating hard in my chest. I wasn't sure what I'd do if she said she didn't want to be friends with me. I'd gone years without needing or wanting anything from anyone. Admitting my feelings felt like taking a step off a cliff. Exhilarating, yet terrifying. "Yeah."

She turned to face me, her eyes conflicted. "Why?"

"Because I like being around you."

She sucked in a sharp breath. "I don't know, Gray. I'm very particular about my friends. I prefer they be friendly, not hot one second, cold the other."

I winced at her accurate assessment. "Being open with someone is difficult for me. I can't say I won't push you away again when you get too close, but I'll try hard not to."

She finally nodded.

Relief flowed through me. I knew I'd have to show her I meant what I'd said. I wanted to tell her about my day. "You were right, by the way."

She tilted her head. "Right about what?"

Pulling in a deep breath, I said, "Ed liked the idea of helping local rescues. He was even open to my idea of a mobile vet clinic."

"That's amazing, Gray. I'm so happy for you." Whatever walls she'd put up last night were lowered. She smiled, seeming genuinely happy for me. She stepped into me, wrapping her arms around my waist.

I stiffened before relaxing in her embrace, wrapping my arms tentatively around her shoulders. The warmth of her body, the tickle of her hair against my jaw, grounded me, reminding me how good it felt to be with her.

When was the last time I'd been hugged? I'd forgotten how good they felt when it was done by someone you cared about. Of course, I'd never had Elle Carmichael in my arms before.

CHAPTER 9

Elle

*S*till feeling the warmth of his arms around me, I waved Gray off when he tried to pay. Cleaning up, I found cash at my station he must have left when I wasn't looking. Smiling, I tucked it into my pocket.

I'd been a little annoyed after he'd left things the way he had in his truck. I'd felt a connection to him at the Rigbys' farm. We'd even talked a bit about our pasts while on the swing, eating pie. It was nice. A part of me thought it had been too much for him too soon, so he'd pushed me away. I appreciated that he showed up tonight. It didn't seem like something he would normally do, which endeared him to me even more.

After everything I'd experienced growing up, then on the show, I thought I would be attracted to someone who was straightforward, the what-you-see-is-what-you-get type. That was not the case with Gray. He pulled me in one minute, with his gentle manner around animals and the Rigbys, then pushed me away the next. I felt like I was in front of the stage during a concert, caught in a mosh pit. Every time I tried to make my way to the edge of the crowd, he'd suck me back to the middle. I was powerless to resist him.

Gray Stanton probably wasn't good for me. So, why was I giving him a second chance? I closed my eyes, remembering the joy on his face when he told me Ed's reaction to his plans, the feel of his arms around me, his breath coasting over the shell of my ear. When he was like he was tonight, I could fall so easily into him.

I couldn't forget that his moods ebbed and flowed according to whatever was going on in his head. Whatever it was, he might not confide in me. Was that something I was willing to put up with?

I finished cleaning the shop, double-checked the locks, then took the narrow steps in the back up to my apartment. Crew's claws scratched the tray in the crate, excited I was coming home. It was nice to have someone not only waiting on me to come home but excited to see me.

Crew's whining greeted me when I opened the door. Releasing the latch on Crew's crate, he flew out, running in circles around my feet. "Are you ready to go out, bud?"

I leaned down, petting the soft fur on his head, dodging his kisses before grabbing the leash off the hook next to the door. Locking up, I jogged down the steps then out the back door of the shop to the small strip of grass that came with the property.

The evening was cool. A few people were walking to restaurants and bars, enjoying the fall weather. I felt safe in Telluride, far away from the cameras. It was exactly what I was searching for, but I hadn't expected to feel so lonely. I thought once I removed toxic people from my life, I'd meet genuine friends. It wouldn't happen organically. I'd need to make an effort.

My phone buzzed in my back pocket. I pulled it out seeing Piper on my screen.

Piper: You want to go out tonight?

Piper had invited me out a couple of times since the shop opened. I'd always said no. Staying in was intentional. For the first time in my life, there were no producers telling me to go out every night so they had footage. It was nice to have choices.

Maybe it was time to meet some of the residents, be open to the possibility of making friends. It would also be a good opportunity to spread the word about Smoke & Mirrors.

Elle: Sure.

I fed Crew, playing with him for a few minutes before I got ready to go out. Unsure what to wear for a night on the town in Colorado, I put on my tightest skinny jeans, heels, silky shirt, and a jacket. I felt bad leaving Crew by himself for a few more hours, but I needed to meet some people in my new town.

The Last Dollar Saloon's sign hung over the door in maroon and gold lettering. I took a deep breath before stepping inside to the narrow space. The bar was rustic with worn, wooden floors. A long bar was to the left with liquor stacked on backlit shelves. Seating was to the right with a stone fireplace, and old-fashioned chandeliers hung from the ceiling. I scanned the room relieved to see most people wearing flannel and jeans. Piper waved at me from the bar. Some of the tension eased from my shoulders at seeing a familiar face.

I crossed the room, weaving between tables until I reached her.

She hugged me. "Hey, I'm so glad you made it."

I eased onto the bar stool next to hers. "Me too. I've been here for a few months, and I haven't had a chance to meet anyone."

"I'm excited to introduce you to everyone."

"What can I get you?" The bartender braced his hands on the bar between us.

Piper waved a hand at him. "This is Sebastian. Sebastian, this is Elle Carmichael."

Recognition flitted through his features. "You're the new owner of Smoke & Mirrors." Sebastian inclined his head toward me. "The barbershop is all anyone's been talking about lately."

A rush of excitement shot through me that people had been talking about us. "That's good to hear."

"Is it okay if I send tourists in your direction? You okay with walk-ins?"

"Of course. I'm not turning down any customers." This was exactly why I needed to come out tonight. I wanted friends, to find my place in the community. If the locals knew me, they'd be more likely to recommend my business. Being aloof would have the opposite effect.

"What can I get you?" Sebastian repeated.

I glanced at the beers on tap, asking for the one that said it was a local favorite.

"You got it." Sebastian grabbed a glass, filling it as he talked to another patron.

I turned to face Piper.

Two women approached Piper wearing skinny jeans and booties, one with a tight long sleeve shirt, the other with a flannel tied at her waist. I felt out of place in my silky shirt, dressed for a casual night in LA, not Telluride.

Piper gestured at me. "This is my new boss, the owner of Smoke & Mirrors, Elle Carmichael. Elle, these are my friends, Reagan and Angela."

"It's nice to meet you." We smiled, shaking hands.

"You want to grab this table?" Angela gestured at a nearby high top that was recently vacated.

"Sure." We slid off our stools, following them.

I sipped my beer, listening to them talk about whatever guys they were dating. I couldn't keep all the names straight, but I enjoyed the easy camaraderie. There was none of the posturing and pretense that I'd seen in LA, bragging about the latest handbag or club you got into.

"Hey." A man stood at the end of the table, his broad shoulders filling out his shirt, a beer in his hands. His blue eyes were on me as if he were waiting for an introduction.

Piper eased under his arm for a side hug before introducing me. "Hey! This is my boss, Elle Carmichael. Elle, this is my older brother, Henry."

I shook his hand. He had the same stocky build as his father. "It's nice to meet you."

Gray sidled up next to Henry. He'd said he was close with the Rigbys, so I shouldn't have been surprised to see him, but I was. "Hey, you want to grab a table or sit at the bar?"

My heart beat rapidly in my chest. We'd hugged not more than an hour ago before he left the shop. Would he treat me with the same intimacy he had at the shop, or would he create space between us, pretend we were just casual acquaintances?

Henry raised his glass to the full tables. "The place is packed. I was just talking to Piper."

Gray's gaze traveled around the table, nodding at Piper before resting on me. His eyes widened slightly.

A rush of heat flowed through me, making my knees weak. I hadn't expected to see him again so soon.

I thought I'd have time to separate myself from the time we'd spent together in the shop.

He dipped his head. "Elle."

When I stepped in front of him to dry his silky hair with a warm towel, his legs splayed wide and his eyes hooded, it would have been so easy to straddle his lap, kiss him, and run my fingers over the scruff on his chin. I crossed my legs to suppress the throbbing in my core at the memory.

Piper smirked. "How was your cut?"

Henry leaned an elbow on the table, shooting a surprised look at Piper. "Wait, you didn't do it?"

Piper raised a brow. "Gray asked for Elle."

I glanced around the group, noticing Angela was looking at something on Reagan's phone, neither of them paying attention to our conversation. I waited for Gray's reaction, wanting to collect nuggets of information, putting them in a jar to take out, unfold, then analyze later.

Gray's expression was unreadable, his tone defensive. "I wanted to check her place out."

I wanted to ask if the cut lived up to his expectations. At the same time, I didn't want to bring up that moment because it was something between the two of us. If I had, everyone at the table would know how he affected me.

"What did you think?" Piper asked.

Gray braced his elbows on the table, looking at me

when he answered, "I'm impressed. It's inviting, classy, and comfortable."

Pride filled me. His gaze caught on mine. Before someone realized there was something there, I blurted out, "He took me to check on a horse."

Piper's gaze darted from me to Gray. "You took Elle to check on one of the horses?"

"Yeah, Blaze had thrush." Gray's shoulders relaxed. Even though he was at ease talking about animals, he might not want to talk about me being at the farm.

"It's a beautiful farm. Your mother's an amazing baker." Words flowed easier now that we weren't talking about what happened in the shop.

"My mom fed you?" Piper asked, bewildered.

"Rose had just taken a pie out of the oven when we arrived." I shrugged as if it was no big deal when it was. Eating pie with Gray on the porch swing was sweet. It was a glimpse of him, one I suspected he didn't reveal to too many people.

Piper blinked slowly, her mouth opening then closing like she didn't know what to make of this.

Henry grabbed a stool from the bar area. "Sorry man, there's only one."

"That's okay. I can stand," Gray shifted closer to me to give him room, my neck prickling with awareness.

Each time someone walked past, Gray moved closer to me to give them space, brushing against my shoulder, pressing against my back. I sucked in a breath, only able to focus on his proximity and the smell of the shampoo I'd used on his hair, reminding me of massaging it into his scalp.

"I enjoyed the shampoo. I've never done that before," Gray's words moved strands of my hair. I shivered at his proximity.

The others were joking about some prank from high school.

I looked up at Gray, a little surprised he was talking about something so personal, something I hadn't fully processed yet.

"The massage was—" his Adam's apple moved up and down. "Relaxing."

"It's meant to be." What it wasn't supposed to be was arousing. I wondered if he'd felt the same way. If he'd imagined me washing his hair in the shower, our bodies naked, my nipples rubbing against his skin.

He took a long sip of his beer, placing the empty bottle in front of me. He leaned one hand on the table, one on the back of my stool, precariously close to my ass. I wanted to shift closer to him, to feel his touch, but we were surrounded by people even if the moment felt intimate.

"It was so—"

My mind filled in the space with the word *sensual.*

"Your hands—"

His struggle to describe the sensations brought me right back to that moment. His eyes met mine. "It was like nothing I've ever felt before."

I was warm all over from the longing and desire I

saw in his eyes. I couldn't look away, I couldn't respond. I was afraid I'd agree with him.

I finally tore my eyes from his to break the moment. "You'll come back sometime then?"

When I finally raised my eyes to his, he smirked.

I got an impression of who he might have been when he was younger. He looked almost impish with that expression and his artfully messy haircut. I wondered if he was a troublemaker in high school.

"I'll come back if you're the one cutting my hair."

"That can be arranged." The words fell out of my mouth before I could stop them. Heat pooled in my core. Who was this Gray? The one who said what he meant? Was it the alcohol? Was it my touch in the shop?

I didn't want him to revert to being gruff. I wanted this Gray. This one had the power to dip below the surface of my skin, bringing my deepest secrets to the surface, getting to the heart of me. This Gray was dangerous.

He raised one perfect eyebrow as if considering the veracity of my statement.

The air between us was so thick with tension, it was palpable. I wanted to reach out and touch it. I wanted to bottle it up, opening it in the privacy of my bedroom so I could live out a fantasy with him. There was more to Gray than he showed people: his life before Colorado, his family, his wants, fears, and dreams. He kept everything close to his chest. I wanted in with a fierceness I'd never felt before.

Letting him make the moves was safer. Because this man and whatever his secrets were—his demons—had the power to eviscerate me. It was like knowing sweets weren't good for me but wanting them anyway. The more I abstained, the more I craved them, craved him. I knew I'd have to indulge, gorge myself until he was out of my system. But like with any good binge, I'd either feel satisfied I'd taken the journey, or I'd feel emptier than when I'd started.

"Any news on the clinic?" Henry asked Gray.

I braced myself for his response, wondering if he'd be as excited to tell his news as he was with me or if he would be more reserved with Henry.

Gray's eyes flicked from mine to his. "I told Ed some of my ideas for the clinic."

Henry sipped his beer. "What's that?"

"I wanted to expand the kennel area to help out local rescues. I want to purchase a van to use as a mobile vet clinic, offering free or discounted exams and vaccines. He liked my ideas."

"You think it will make a difference?"

Gray sighed. "He didn't say. I hope he sees I'm serious about staying."

"I think it would. It shows you're making a commitment not only to the clinic but to the community and local organizations." Henry's tone was serious.

None of his ideas would necessarily bring in extra

money. I wasn't sure how Ed felt about that. As a woman who wanted some good in her life, I loved it.

"I hope so. I have everything riding on this. If he doesn't want to sell to me, I don't know what I'll do." Gray winced when the words left his mouth. Maybe he hadn't meant to be so honest.

My heart squeezed at his vulnerability. These moments were the reason I gravitated toward him.

Henry placed his empty beer bottle on the table. "You could keep doing what you're doing, start your own clinic."

"I don't think I could stay if Ed doesn't think I'm capable of running the clinic. It's the logical next step. It's what I've always wanted. It wouldn't make sense to have competing vets in the same town. It wouldn't be right."

My stomach turned at the idea of Gray leaving town. I'd only been here a short time, but I'd connected with him.

"Gray Stanton is a total softie. Who would have thought?" Piper smiled at him before giving me a pointed look.

Did she know there was something between us? Was it because he'd asked for me to cut his hair, or was my attraction to him that obvious?

I wondered if opening up about his dreams was new. If so, was I the reason for the change? I liked to think so. I wanted to be the one who could get a reaction out of him, bad or good. I never met a man more in need of a shake-up than him.

"You've come a long way since college," Henry lowered his voice, speaking only to Gray.

Gray's shoulders tensed; his jaw tightened. I quickly averted my eyes when I realized Henry hadn't meant for me to overhear.

What was he like in college? How was he different? I could only guess he was even more closed off. Or he rebelled.

I'd never had that experience because my parents hadn't instilled any rules or structure in our lives besides a nanny. We were free to make whatever decisions we wanted. Even signing on for the show was more my decision. My parents approved, saying the decision was ultimately mine. In high school, I thought it was cool. My parents should have known putting their child's life in the spotlight was a bad idea. They were going to make the same mistake with Alice.

When Piper asked if I wanted to go with her to the bar to get another round, I readily agreed. I needed some space from Gray. Having his body rub against me each time someone walked past kept me on edge.

Piper ordered another round, then turned to face me, lowering her voice. "What's going on with you and Gray?"

"What? Nothing's going on." I hoped I sounded sufficiently surprised by her question. I hadn't realized the tension was obvious to anyone. After years of my relationships playing out in the spotlight, I wanted whatever was brewing to remain between us.

"The chemistry between you guys is off the charts."

I shrugged, ignoring the way my heart beat faster in response to her words, my gaze sliding away from her. "He's a good-looking guy, but—"

I wanted to be friends with Piper, sharing information about dates and guys, but I wanted Gray for myself. I didn't want to dissect what we had. It would lessen its intensity.

Piper nodded. "I agree. He has too much baggage."

I burst out laughing at the image. "It does seem like that. He's grumpy one minute, correcting my dog parenting skills, then sweet and caring the next, wanting to work with rescues and run a free vaccine, mobile vet clinic. He sounds like the perfect guy, but there's something else. It's like he's a book written in invisible ink. I can ask him a question, but the answer might be the truth or some version of the truth. I'll never find out what's on every page."

The realization saddened me because I wanted to know Gray. He was a book I wanted to savor, reading slowly, one page at a time.

She shook her head. "I've known him for a while. He is quiet, nice. He never talked about his family. He'd just say it was too far to travel home. I'm not even sure he ever said where home was exactly. I don't know if he has brothers, sisters, or parents."

"If he was an orphan, he'd say that." A chill ran

down my spine. He could easily lie about his past. Was he telling as much of the truth as he was able?

"Here you go, ladies." Sebastian handed us the drinks. "It's busy tonight. I'll talk to you later."

Piper smiled her thanks before turning back to me. "He's an enigma. I'd be careful with him. If you do go into something with him, go in knowing you won't ever know the real Gray. He keeps that shit locked up tight."

Maybe Piper felt that way because he was her brother's friend. It was unlikely he'd open up to her. Maybe it would be different when he was dating someone.

Following Piper back to our table, my mind was reeling with possibilities about his past, the last one worse than the one before.

When I arrived at the table, Gray took a couple of the bottles from my hands, smiling down at me. It seemed like he was happy to see me.

My heart tripped before picking up the pace.

At Rigby's Ranch, he'd talked about his childhood, his mother. Was that information he told everyone or was I different? Was Piper wrong about him? Maybe he hadn't met the right person yet, the one who made him feel like he could trust them with his secrets.

"You were gone a long time."

I tipped my head toward the bar. "It's really busy. We were talking."

"What about?" He leaned down to speak into my

ear, his voice low and seductive. Or maybe I was imagining it.

Should I tell him the truth, or should I play it off? Did I want to get to him, or did I want to pretend that everything was fine? If I wanted to know Gray, I'd have to take a chance. "You."

He scoffed, straightening. "Why would you be talking about me?"

Would I be revealing every single thought in my head by telling him the truth? "Piper said no one really knows who you are, even Henry."

His lips straightened into a thin line; a muscle twitched in his jaw. "I don't like talking about my past."

I stilled, my heart pounding in my ears, worried I was taking this too far. "Why not?"

"It's not something I'm proud of. When I moved to college, I wanted to start over, make a new life for myself." His jaw was tight, his tone deceptively smooth, as if his words were the litany he said whenever anyone asked about his past.

"Were you a troublemaker in high school?" I teased in an effort to lighten the mood.

"No." His expression was cold.

My skin turned cold. I had pushed him too far. "I didn't really think that. I was teasing."

He didn't respond as the muscle continued to twitch in his jaw.

"I'm sorry, Gray. I didn't mean to make you uncomfortable." I reached out my hand touching his forearm, his skin warm under my fingers. His muscles tensed. "I hope you know you can trust me. I won't betray you."

Something flashed in his eyes before he carefully masked it. It made me think he'd been betrayed by someone important to him. It had rocked his world, sent him on this course where he didn't take risks. In reality, he was careening out of control if one question could tilt him this far off balance.

I looked away from him, trying to focus on the conversation around us. It was a bad idea to be attracted to someone so closed off. Something about what he was going through, what he wanted to accomplish, made my heart ache for him. On some level, he thought he was a bad guy, maybe even undeserving of love. In that way, we were exactly alike.

CHAPTER 10

Elle

*J*olting awake, I sat up in bed. My heart still racing, my breath came in quick pants; I closed my eyes. I slept fitfully last night. My mind was full of thoughts of Gray—his proximity, his voice, his scent. It was torture. My brain knew he was a bad idea, my body didn't. I didn't want a man who'd be resistant to opening up. I wanted a guy who knew exactly what he wanted and went after it.

When Gray talked about ways to get Ed to sell him the clinic, needing ties to the community, I hadn't thought it applied to me, but it did. It wouldn't hurt for me to do the same, to prove to the community that I planned on sticking around. This wasn't a whim I would abandon in a couple of months to head back to Los Angeles.

Gray warned me that first day that the locals could suss out someone who wasn't genuine. I needed to prove I belonged. The only question was, how did I do it? Should I partner with a local organization? If so, which one? I could hang a bulletin board on the wall, encouraging businesses to advertise their wares. Before I opened, I'd called the local fire and police departments asking for patches to hang on the wall. Maybe I should go one step further, offering discounts as a gesture of goodwill.

I flew through my morning routine, showering, then walking Crew around town. I'd never tire of the ever-present view of the mountains. Mornings were quiet in town with people getting ready for work. I stopped at the window of the vintage trailer that was The Coffee Cowboy, grabbing coffees and pastries for us. I dropped Crew off in my apartment before heading downstairs to open the shop.

Piper was already there, getting her station ready. She must have walked in when I was putting Crew upstairs.

"Morning. I have coffee." I wanted to be friends with Piper. I wanted Telluride to be my home, to make the shop a success, to see Gray again. The last thought had my heart beating faster in surprise. Gray was front and center in my head. I glanced around the shop, my gaze pausing on the chair he'd sat in last night when I washed his hair. The familiar desire coiling in my belly.

Piper headed straight to me, not responding until she'd taken a large sip of the coffee I had offered her. "Thank you."

I smiled. "You're welcome."

"You brought food too?" Her tone was hopeful.

I offered her the bag of pastries. She sat in her chair, pulling out a muffin before taking a bite. She chewed thoughtfully for a few seconds, considering me.

I bounced on my toes, vibrating with energy. I'd been so wrapped up in Gray, I'd forgotten about myself.

"Why are you so chipper this morning after being out last night? Did something happen?" Her words were tinged with disbelief.

I gave her a disbelieving look. We'd parted outside the bar last night, all going our separate ways.

"Not exactly. I had an idea, an epiphany of sorts." The caffeine was flowing through my veins making me jittery.

She arched her brow. "Oh, yeah?"

I glanced at the clock. We had ten minutes before our first appointment. "Gray was saying how he needed to prove to Ed he was here to stay. I do too. I need to make ties to the community; prove I'm not going anywhere."

"Okay. How are you going to do that?" Piper drew out her words.

"First, I'm going to make a flyer saying we're offering discounts to first responders and veterans, then hang them around town."

"I like that idea."

I sank into the chair across from her, realizing my ideas were kind of low-key. "My other brilliant idea, that doesn't sound so exciting in the light of day, is hanging a bulletin board for other businesses to advertise community events. That's all I have. It's something but not enough."

Piper touched her chin with her finger. "You could partner with a local organization that needs donations or funds. It could change through the year, like collecting toys for needy children at Christmas, or food for the homeless shelter another time."

"I like that." I liked the idea of being the place people needed to stop in to drop off donations, then remembering they needed to make time for a haircut.

After being on the show, I was used to second-guessing everything I did. I never wanted to be viewed the same way I had been back then. "Do I sound completely selfish with these ideas? I'm helping the community to bring in new clients."

"You want to connect with the community. You want people to like you enough that they'll want to support your business. Yeah, you have a bit of an ulterior motive, but your desire to fit in here is real. I don't think you sound selfish or self-serving." Piper stood, brushing the crumbs off her lap.

She handed me the bag with the remaining pastries. "I'm going to wash up."

I hoped she was right. I wanted to fit in when I never had anywhere else. I thought I'd come here for peace, to figure out who I was. Maybe I was really searching for somewhere to belong.

The bell rang, signaling my first customer. A three-year-old, his blond hair falling into his eyes, who didn't want to get his hair cut. He crossed his arms when his mom tried to pull off his coat.

I turned on a cartoon, encouraging him with lollipops and a kid-friendly smock. When I patted the booster I'd placed on the chair, his mom reached for him, but he bolted for the door.

His mom pleaded with him to come back.

I smiled at his mother before crouching next to him. "Hey, buddy. I know it's scary, but I think you're brave. I think you can climb on that booster chair and get your hair trimmed like a big boy, am I right?"

He considered me for a few seconds before nodding with a solemn expression. "I'm a big boy."

"Exactly." I smiled at him as the satisfaction of convincing him settled in my chest.

His mother smiled at me, her shoulders lowering.

He clambered onto the booster seat, waiting patiently for me to put the smock around his neck. I cut his hair as quickly as I could, worried he was going to decide halfway through that he wasn't as brave as he thought. When his cut was done, I offered him a toy car.

He was so excited about the toy, I knew he'd beg his mother to come back. Maybe things were going to work out here. I just had to stay positive. I'd win people over one customer at a time. It wasn't just enticing people to try us out, it was giving them an experience they'd want to repeat.

When I was cleaning up, his mother approached with a generous tip. "Thank you so much. You were so great with him."

"You're welcome."

"I'm going to tell everyone in my moms' group how you're giving cars out to the kids. It's such a great idea. He'll want to keep coming back just for the toy."

"That's so great to hear." The good feeling from that appointment stuck with me the rest of the day. I was confident the ideas I'd voiced to Piper earlier would help. If not, I'd come up with something else.

"I told you the cars were a good idea."

"You were right. Thank you, Piper. I don't know what I'd be doing without you."

"You'd be doing all right on your own. It might have taken you a while longer, but you would have gotten there."

"Thank you." I paused from sweeping up the clippings on the floor to look out the window. I wasn't used to people being confident in my abilities. This town was charming, people standing in line for coffee at The Coffee Cowboy, going in and out of the bookstore. It was nothing like where I grew up. It was the opposite of LA, yet it was starting to feel like home.

A woman walked by with her dog, reminding me that Gray paid for Athena's surgery. "Gray mentioned he pays for surgeries for dogs that are abandoned out of his own pocket."

"He does?" Piper asked, sounding distracted.

Glancing from the window to her, her attention was on the computer screen.

"Yeah. We could help raise money, put a picture of the dog at the front counter, and a jar to collect money. Would Gray be okay with that? Should I talk to him first?"

"Probably."

"Last time I offered to help, he said no, or at least, I think he did. I definitely got the impression he didn't want help." His reluctance to accept help made me want to do more for him.

"That's Gray," Piper said wryly.

"So, maybe I should just do it." I resumed sweeping.

Piper finally looked up from the computer. "How are you going to get a picture of the dog? You need the name too, find out how much money you need to raise, so there's a goal."

"That's true."

Piper focused on me finally. "Are you doing this for the dog or to get closer to Gray?"

I wanted to help him. I wasn't purposely trying to

get closer to him, or was I? "What? No. Why would I want to get closer to Gray? You said yourself it's an impossible task. He doesn't let anyone in."

"You think you'll be different." Her tone was matter of fact.

My heart sank in my chest. Maybe I did think that.

"I know I'm not different." My impression was that he'd been betrayed.

I was hiding something from people. My past was easily discoverable. No one had connected the dots yet. When Gray found out, would he think the same way about me? Would the townspeople? Or would they believe I was the person they saw on TV?

My stomach churned. I didn't want people approaching me here, calling me a bitch for what I'd done on the show. I liked being anonymous here. I worked hard, tried to be a good person. Would it matter in the end? Would my past always be a part of me?

All I could hope for was that people liked me enough to overlook my past, to give me the benefit of the doubt. I pushed back my uneasiness, the thought that my peaceful existence was a ticking clock. It was only a matter of time before it imploded in my face.

In the meantime, I was going to fully embrace being the Elle who cared about the community, being the person I was meant to be all along. Armed with my new ideas, I formulated a plan to talk to Gray, approach him about helping with the dog's fees.

At lunchtime, I told Piper I was going to grab something to eat and would be gone for an hour. She distractedly smiled at me before continuing to chat with her client.

I slipped out, grabbing a couple of sandwiches from Baked in Telluride, before heading to the vet clinic. Pulling into the lot, I grabbed the bags, heading to the receptionist's desk.

"Elle. I don't have you down for an appointment. Did Crew get into something again?" Anne asked.

My face heated as I held up the bags. I hadn't accounted for the small-town feel, where everyone wanted to know what was going on, or would formulate their own ideas. "No. I brought lunch for Gray to thank him for his help last week with Crew."

"He's in his office." She smiled knowingly, pointing down the hall. "Second door on your right."

I followed her directions, pausing at the doorway to knock softly, wondering if I'd made a huge mistake coming here. My stomach knotted. Would people gossip about me bringing him lunch? Would it get back to the shop before I did? Would Gray see it as a friendly gesture or something else? Did I want this to be more?

The sight of Gray, seated at his desk, white button-down shirt rolled up over his forearms, glasses on as he read something on his computer, stole my breath. He was sexy in ways I hadn't noticed before.

He looked up when I knocked again, louder this time. "Elle. What are you doing here?"

He pushed back from the desk, standing, a slow smile spreading over his face.

I smiled; my heart pounded in my chest. "I brought lunch."

He placed a hand on his stomach. "I'm starving. Perfect timing."

Heat radiated through my chest because he was happy I was here.

He cleared off a space on his desk, grabbing the bags and opening them.

I placed the iced teas on the table, pulling up one of the guest chairs.

Gray walked behind me to close the door. "This is a nice surprise."

I bit my lip, worried he'd see through my thinly veiled excuse of bringing him lunch. Would he assume I was here because I was attracted to him? "I wanted to thank you for your help last week with Crew."

He waved me off. "That's my job."

He sat, taking a big bite of his sandwich.

I unwrapped mine, trying to figure out the best way to broach the subject of raising money when he'd shut me down the first time. "I also wanted to talk about possibly raising money for Athena. I was thinking it would be good to place a collection jar by my front register with her picture, and a little description about what happened."

He clenched his jaw. "It's not necessary. I covered it."

"I know you want to help local rescue organizations, but if you're taking dogs in, paying for their care then finding them a home, aren't you a rescue?" I was relieved I'd thought of this argument on the way over. Piper was right. He wouldn't accept help easily.

He took a sip of iced tea. "I suppose. I never thought of it like that."

Maybe if I made it sound like he was doing me a favor by doing this, he'd agree. "I'm not asking for purely altruistic reasons. I need ties to the community, too. People need to believe I'll stay so they'll invest in my business."

Pulling on his earlobe, he asked, "You think this will help?"

"It's a small thing, something that shows I care about the community. I have a few other ideas too." I picked up my sub and took a bite, preparing for the inevitable pushback.

"I think it's a good idea. It will bring attention to a problem as well. People getting pets or giving them as gifts when they don't understand the responsibility."

A fluttery feeling erupted in my belly. "I agree, it will make people more aware."

"I'll need to look into creating a nonprofit so the money goes directly into a fund for future dogs." Before I could argue the money should reimburse him, he continued, "What are your other ideas?"

"Ideas for what?" The heat radiating in my chest

spread through my whole body, leaving tingles in its wake.

"To get the community to accept you."

Not tell them about the reality show I starred in during my late teens through my early twenties. "On the way over, I was thinking of offering a daddy-daughter class where dads could come with their daughters. I can teach them how to take care of and style their hair."

"You cater to men." He sounded confused.

"I used to work at a salon, so I know how to style women's hair. There might be men who are single dads or just dads who want to style their own child's hair. I can help."

His eyes shone with admiration. "It's a cool idea."

His praise made me feel lightheaded. "Really?"

"Yeah. I don't know how many guys you'll get. I agree it's unique."

I let the good feeling wash through me. "I'm offering discounts for veterans and first responders too."

"That's a great start. Have you noticed we're both trying to ingratiate ourselves to the community? Prove we're here to stay?"

I laughed because it was exactly what I was thinking. "You kind of gave me the idea last night."

He was quiet, finishing his sandwich before he said thoughtfully, "We should work together."

"On what?" My only skill was cutting hair. "I can't

groom dogs."

He laughed a full-body laugh, his head tipped back.

It was so surprising, I forgot to laugh myself. When his gaze settled back on me, I tried to recover, wiping my face with a napkin to cover my shocked expression.

"We can work on the rescue and the mobile clinic together. You obviously love animals; you have a heart. You're probably good at planning stuff."

I tilted my head. No one had ever described me that way before. Maybe pretty or fashionably dressed, but not kind or smart. "And what? You're not?"

He had a glint in his eyes. "I could use the help. I'm busy as it is with the clinic."

When I remained silent, surprised he was asking for help, he continued, "You're the one who pushed for this. You wanted me to talk to Ed. You thought it was a great idea."

"I did, didn't I?"

He nodded. "You kind of owe me."

"Fine." I rolled up my wrapper, surprised time passed so quickly. I was worried we wouldn't have anything to talk about, that the meal would be awkward, but the more time I spent with him, the more I liked him.

An older gentleman in a white coat similar to Gray's jacket, walked in when I stood to throw out the wrapper. I tensed, not wanting to get Gray in trouble if he wasn't supposed to have lunch guests.

"Sorry, I didn't mean to interrupt." The name in

script above his pocket read Edmund Bester. That name was on my invoices. He must be the owner.

"You weren't. We were just finishing up." Gray gestured at me.

I smiled, sitting back down. "I dropped by with lunch."

Ed looked from Gray to me. "And who might you be?"

I held my hand out. "Elle Carmichael. I own the new barbershop, Smoke & Mirrors."

His eyes shown with respect. "I've been meaning to stop by there. My friends love it."

"If you love a good old-fashioned cut and shave, it's the place to go." I was a little uncomfortable selling my business to people. If I wanted it to be a success, I'd have to get used to it.

"I think you're going to do well here with the tourists who like swankier digs."

"I hope so." I had to cover my smile at Ed's attempt at slang.

"Swankier digs? Really?" Gray, a smile playing on his lips, leaned back in his chair, letting it rock.

Ed leaned a shoulder on the doorjamb. "I don't know whatever word you young people think is cool these days. I think you've got a good idea there."

"Thank you." That was twice today someone had complimented me on a business idea. It wasn't something I was used to. It was a good feeling. It solidified the idea I'd made the right decision coming here.

"Elle's going to be helping me with possibly forming our own rescue to pay for animals that get dumped here as well as with the mobile clinic." Gray's appreciative gaze rested on me as he talked.

My face heated at the attention.

I wasn't sure Ed knew about Gray's propensity to cover abandoned dogs' medical care. "A dog was hit by a car a few weeks ago. The owners abandoned her, so Gray paid for her surgery. I'm raising money to reimburse him, but he wants to start a nonprofit to help future dogs."

"I didn't know you were doing that. As a businessman, you're going to have a hard time making money with all the free stuff you're giving away." He paused, considering Gray. "As a man, I'm proud of you. This is exactly what I was talking about the other day. You should be upfront about what you're doing. You can't hide your involvement." Ed's tone was tinged with respect.

I shifted forward in my seat. "He's got a point. If you want the community to embrace you, you need to be a bit more vocal about what's going on. Take credit when you do something amazing."

"I'd rather fly under the radar." His smile disappeared, his jaw set.

We hit on the exposed nerve he tried so hard to cover. As much as I felt bad that I'd upset him, it was these moments, when someone got too close, that I saw the real Gray. The one he hid from everyone.

I wanted to know why he felt that way. Even if Ed wasn't here, we didn't know each other well enough for that.

"I have an appointment. I'll catch you later. Nice meeting you, Elle. I hope to see you around more often."

There was no mistaking his implication. He hoped something more was going on between us. I liked the idea that Ed thought I was good enough for Gray. "He's sweet."

"Lately, he's been meddling in things a bit too much for my liking," Gray grumbled, but I caught the affection in his tone.

I looked down to hide my smile. "I think he wants to make sure you're settled before he retires."

"What do you mean?"

"He wants you to be happy."

Gray snorted.

"Why is that so hard to believe? You've worked here for how long?"

"Four years."

"Surely you've developed a relationship with him. He sees you as a son or his mentee. He feels responsible for you. He sees you not living life to its fullest. He wants to make sure you're on the right path before he leaves." I was starting to wonder if Gray was oblivious or just downplayed the important relationships in his life.

Worried I'd crossed a line in our tentative friendship, I looked up in time to see Gray's expression. It was a mix of awe and respect. He cleared his throat as if he wanted to respond but he didn't.

"I'd better get going. Let you get back to work." I walked to the door, placing my hand on the frame as I looked over my shoulder at him. "I'd like to work with you on the rescue stuff, even the mobile vet clinic. Whatever you need, let me know. You already have my number."

He'd given me his number when Crew ate the raisins. I'd originally put it in my phone so I'd have it if Crew got sick again. I'd never admit it to him, but I pulled his contact information up occasionally to stare at his name, wondering if he liked to text or if he was more of a phone call kind of guy. He seemed like a man who eschewed whatever was trendy.

I walked away, my heart beating loudly in my chest. It was either the dumbest decision I'd ever made or the best. Ed saw something in Gray. Whatever he was hiding, whatever made him reluctant to reveal himself to others, couldn't be anything too bad.

There was a man in there waiting to break out and live life to his fullest. My heart ached for whatever he'd been through to make him think he didn't deserve accolades for his plans.

I wanted him to see his worth. I wanted the town to realize how amazing he was. He wasn't the most personable, but he meant well. Underneath his posture was a man I wanted to know.

CHAPTER 11

Gray

Something warm and tingly skidded over my skin when Elle said she wanted to help. Even if the thought of seeing her more often was appealing, nothing would come from it. At some point, she'd want to know more about my family. She wouldn't like what I had to say.

I hadn't let anyone in since my high school girlfriend, Aubrey, dumped me. We were high school sweethearts. We had plans to go to the same college, continue dating, maybe get married eventually. She'd walked away as if I meant nothing to her. It wasn't even that she walked away from our relationship. She'd walked away from me. I'd careened from having a support system to weathering the storm alone. There was speculation and gossip, and no one on my side.

With maturity, I could see the odds were against us having a long-term relationship. We were so young. We had no idea what life would bring us or how we'd react to it. I couldn't blame her. Her parents saw me as a criminal, an extension of my father. No one wanted their teenage daughter embroiled in controversy.

Elle wanted to help because she needed the same thing I did: respect from the community. She hadn't expressed any interest in me as a man, even if I felt like a live wire being near her, sparking and crackling; feeling more alive than I'd felt in a long time. Spending time with her was the only break I had from the monotony of my life. One I hadn't realized I needed until she showed up in my exam room.

I'd accept any help she was willing to offer because I needed her. I'd seen how Elle was at her shop. Maybe she could teach me how to be warmer, more understanding with my clients.

If I wanted the clinic, I needed to step outside my comfort zone. I needed to be different than how I'd been in the past.

Between appointments that afternoon, I called my contacts at the rescues to outline my plans, getting an idea of how much room they might need for boarding, their budgets for medical costs, and their plans for intake. Most of the rescues were excited at the prospect of taking in more dogs from shelters they normally had to turn away because they didn't have any room for them.

It sounded like the older dogs with increased health issues were overlooked more often than not. If we could raise some funds, maybe we could help with some of those costs.

Then I called a contractor to discuss expansion costs, emailing my proposal to Ed in between my appointments for the day. Thankfully, there were no emergencies that got in my way.

At the end of the day, I ran a hand through my hair. The next project I'd tackle would be the mobile clinic. I'd need to call other vets who had the same service to inquire about cost and feasibility. That one might be a long-term project. It never hurt to have a business plan ready. It would show Ed I was serious about my plans for the clinic. I was serious about this community.

I ignored the nagging thought that he wanted to see me settled with a girlfriend when a home was more permanent. You couldn't just abandon or walk away from a home.

My phone buzzed with a text from Elle. My heart rate picked up. I'd programmed her in my phone the first time I called her, not as a client or Elle Carmichael, but Elle. No other description was necessary.

Elle: Why don't you have a pet?

I leaned back in my chair. I tried to remember the

guy I'd been when I was dating Aubrey. I was less serious, more easygoing.

Gray: Why would you think I don't? Maybe I've gotten one since we talked last.

I could almost envision the narrowing of her eyes as she read my message.

Elle: So, you do have a pet?

I chuckled.

Gray: I didn't say that.

Elle: Has anyone ever told you how infuriating you are?

Avoiding questions was a specialty of mine. Right now, I was enjoying this playful banter with a woman.

Gray: All the time.

My phone rang with an incoming video call from her. Glancing at the clock, it was seven. The staff had left for the day. Ed had said goodbye on his way out, thirty minutes ago, warning me not to work too late. I wondered what Elle would think of me still being at work. Would she tell me I needed to get a life? Why did it bother me what she thought? I answered after the fifth ring. "Hey."

My eyes were busy scanning the screen, soaking in everything about her. She was in a kitchen, maybe her apartment, bustling around. Was she was cooking or baking?

"Are you at home?" I asked the same moment she asked, "Are you still at work?"

We both laughed.

"Yes, I'm at work. I was working on my proposal for the new kennels, researching the possibility of the mobile vet clinic."

"I'm impressed. You work fast."

I was excited about my plans, eager to get started on them. Lately, I felt like I had nothing to go home to. That had never bothered me before. Consistency and routine made me feel safe in the past. Now it felt lonely.

"If you had a dog, you wouldn't be working so late. It would make you more approachable."

She picked up the phone, dropping to her knees as Crew filled the screen. He was wiggly, nudging the phone with his nose, his soft snuffling noises coming through the line.

What would it be like to come home to Elle and Crew?

"See, wouldn't a soft, cuddly guy be a nice addition to your cold, sterile office?"

I cleared my throat as she stood, her face filling the screen. Her face was devoid of makeup, her hair up in a messy ponytail, an old sweatshirt falling off one shoulder. She was relaxed, casual, *sexy*. "Um, yeah. That would be better."

My voice cracked. I wasn't even sure what the question was, I just knew everything was better with her.

Her face lit up, triumphant from my answer. "See. I told you. You should get a puppy."

My brain scrambled to keep up. "I'm sorry, what?"

"You should get a puppy. How do you think it looks that the town vet doesn't have any pets?"

She leaned a hip on the counter, taking a sip of what looked like red wine. "It's weird, am I right? I looked at your website. Ed has a ton of animals, including chickens and goats."

"He lives on a farm. I live in a small apartment." The excuse sounded weak.

"But why?" Her nose scrunched adorably as she set the phone on the counter, propped against something as she gathered ingredients and mixing bowls. When she leaned down to get something from under the counter, I caught a glimpse of the top of her breasts.

I swallowed over the sudden dryness. "Why what?"

She straightened, her eyes narrowing on me. "Are you paying attention to me?"

"Yes." I was paying very close attention—to her expression and the way her body moved. Blood pumped through my body. I wanted more.

"I asked why you live in an apartment. It seems like the easiest solution to your problems with Ed would be to buy a house and get a pet or two, be domestic." She waved a hand at me as if she were exasperated.

The thought made it difficult to draw in a deep breath. What if there was a fire, what if I couldn't afford to pay the mortgage, what if the dog got out? I couldn't handle those unknowns. "It's better this way."

She'd dumped some ingredients into a bowl. "It's not."

"What are you making?"

She smiled. "Cookies."

"Is there a particular reason why you're making cookies?" Why was she calling me when she was making cookies? Was she planning to invite me over for a taste test? Desire shot through me thinking about eating cookie dough off her skin.

She winked at me. "I had a craving for them."

Her wink was like a lightning bolt to my heart. "You know you could pick up pastries at Baked in Telluride."

She put her finger in the batter, sucking it off before looking at me. "What would be the fun in that?"

My dick twitched. My eyes fixated on her lips. I had this sudden urge to be with her. I'd wrap my arms around her from behind, kissing her bare shoulder while she pushed her ass against my crotch. I could practically feel the warmth of her body pressed against mine.

Her head tilted slightly, her gaze focused on me. "Are you okay?"

I shifted, adjusting myself in my pants. Why had she called to torture me, sucking batter from her finger, leaning over so I got a glimpse of her breasts?

"I'm fine. Why were you calling again?" I desperately wanted my mind off getting her naked.

She turned her attention to mixing the batter. "I said I'd help you."

"I thought you were helping me with the rescue."

"No. I want to help *you*." She emphasized the word *you*.

"Why?" An unfamiliar sensation trickled down my spine. No one offered to help me. Not even Henry tried. I liked to think I exuded confidence.

She braced her hands on the counter, looking directly into my eyes. "Because I like you, Gray Stanton. I think you deserve that clinic. I think you're a great addition to the community. I want everyone to see what I do."

Overwhelmed with emotion I wasn't used to feeling, I struggled with how to respond. No one had ever said something so nice about me, not since I was a kid. Why was she so focused on saving me? "What about you?"

"What about me?"

"Don't you think the community deserves to know you?"

Something cold passed over her face before she ducked her head as if looking for something.

She was avoiding me. "Are you going to answer?'

She finally lifted her head, her face pinched. "We're talking about you, not me."

"You want the same things I want, remember? Maybe we can help each other." I could introduce her to people, help her make friends. The problem was, making friends hadn't been my specialty since I've moved here.

"What you're saying is, you're going to vouch for me?"

I smirked, my rusty flirting skills coming back to me. "Are you worth vouching for?"

Something flashed in her eyes. "You don't have to do that. I think my association with you, especially after we rehab your image, will be enough."

I wanted to ask why she didn't think the community should like her. Ed was impressed in the few minutes he talked to her. Maybe she had low self-esteem, even though it didn't seem plausible. She was a hard worker. She was brave to start her own business in a new town, knowing no one.

I'd let her think she was helping me while I tried to figure out what her deal was. I'd let her off the hook for now. "What kind of cookies are you baking?"

Her shoulders lowered, the muscles in her neck relaxed. "Chocolate chip."

She spooned the batter into balls on a cookie sheet.

My stomach rumbled. I hadn't eaten since lunch with her. I wanted to be with her, caressing her skin with my fingers, kissing her neck while the smell of freshly baked cookies surrounded us. I could almost hear the hitch of her breath, the soft moan, her arch into me. I wanted her to invite me over with an intensity I hadn't ever felt for a woman. "I want some."

Her cheeks flushed. Whether it was from our conversation or the heat of her oven, I wasn't sure. "I can bring you a few, tomorrow."

I grunted in acknowledgment. I wanted to be in her kitchen sucking the dough off her fingers.

"I'll save you some. I promise." She looked at me, her brown eyes flashing with humor.

I wanted to ask her if she could teach me how to bake. I wanted any reason to be in the same room with her. My attraction for her was reeling out of control. She didn't even know. How was I going to control my overactive imagination when it came to her?

She picked up the cookie tray, bending over to put it in the oven. I had an up-close shot of her ass in tight as hell pants.

She didn't seem like any LA girl I'd envisioned. She was laid back, low-key, and casual. Down to earth— that's what I'd thought when we'd met.

"Hopefully they turn out. I've never baked without help before."

"You baked with your nanny, right?"

"She did if we begged her. She cooked because she had to. The extra stuff, being our stand-in mother, wasn't in her job description." Her tone was bitter.

My heart twinged at the thought that she'd wanted her nanny to be her mother. As much as I felt like I got the short end of the stick with my parents, they'd been relatively normal for a divorced couple, until my dad was arrested. After that, everything spun off the rails. The only way I could right myself was to get out of there, move as far away as I could.

She smiled wryly. "Don't feel sorry for me. I was a

spoiled rich girl who had too much time and money on her hands."

"I didn't say that." Why did she think so little of herself? Had someone described her that way? Nothing about her shouted spoiled rich girl. Maybe independent and lonely. Beautiful and intriguing.

She shot me a pointed look. "You were thinking it."

"I wasn't."

She cocked her head. "You don't know me."

Her voice was so quiet, I almost couldn't hear her. I didn't press for answers because she didn't know me either. Maybe we're drawn to each other because we saw something similar in each other. A desire to be someone different, to hide where we came from.

"I intend to."

Her lips pursed.

"I can't wait to taste your cookies." My face heated, imagining being between her legs, devouring her while the smell of freshly baked cookies hung in the air. I had this strong, overwhelming feeling of contentment. "I'm sorry, I didn't mean to sound like an asshole just now."

To my surprise, she burst out laughing. "I knew what you meant. The look on your face was worth everything. You're so uptight. I like loosening you up."

"How do you propose to do that?"

She crossed her arms over her chest, a smirk on her face. "Have you ever snowboarded?"

I paused for a few seconds, surprised by her sudden change in subject. My mind was warm and fuzzy, filled with visions of her soft skin and the smell of cookie dough. "No."

"Skied?"

"Not since I was a kid."

"Why not?"

My throat dry, a persistent tic caused me to cough. Reaching for my water, the cool liquid soothed my throat. I carefully considered how much to tell her. "It was something I did with my dad."

She didn't ask any follow-up questions, like *why can't you ski with your dad anymore*? Relief flowed through me. She must have sensed I wouldn't respond. "Let's go snowboarding."

"How is this helping me get the clinic?"

"Trust me, it is. You need to loosen up."

I clenched my teeth. "I don't know."

"Do you trust me?" Her expression was innocent. She'd picked up the phone, holding it so close I could see the freckles on her nose and the blue of her eyes. She was real. Going on this outing with her would be allowing myself a luxury, a connection with someone. My fingers flexed with the desire to grab onto her, never letting go.

"I do."

"Perfect. Let me know your next day off so we can plan something."

"Sunday." Elle Carmichael wasn't like anyone I'd ever met. She was in a league all her own. She should have been sophisticated, but she wasn't.

"I have obedience class with Crew, but I can miss one, right? You could probably teach me independently."

I'd only taught the first class. The instructor had returned for the second one. I almost wished he hadn't so I could spend every Sunday with Elle. I couldn't wrap my mind around her wanting to invite me to go snowboarding, seeking me out, wanting to spend time with me. She knew nothing about me, not the stuff that mattered.

I wasn't going to turn her away though. I was going to ride out this thing between us, seeing where it went. For the first time, I was going to do what I wanted, no matter the consequences.

The timer beeped on her microwave. She leaned over again to pull the cookie sheet out of the oven. Her nose scrunched adorably. "A little overcooked. I'll have to reduce the time on the next batch."

I wanted to say, *I wish I was with you. I'd boost you up on the counter while we were waiting for them to cook, music playing softly in the background while I explored your mouth. I'd take my time, my hands cradling your face, drawing out the anticipation while I stepped between your legs.*

"I'm going to throw in another batch. I'll talk to you later?"

I blinked, the vision evaporating into thin air. "Oh, yeah. Sure."

She hung up then. I looked around my office feeling

alone, bereft. I wanted her. It was more than wanting a one-night stand or no-strings sex. This was Elle: unique, beautiful, and with a hint of vulnerability underneath the brave.

If I pursued something with her, it would mean something. I hoped I was ready for that.

CHAPTER 12

Elle

 *W*ho knew baking could be so hot? I felt the intensity of Gray's gaze as he watched my every move. After I leaned over to put the cookies in the oven, his eyes darkened. I wondered if he was thinking naughty thoughts about me. I might have spiced things up by sucking cookie dough off my finger, but I couldn't have anticipated his reaction. He'd leaned forward, every muscle in his body tense. It was like he was lost in a fantasy in his head. I'd never felt more desired.

I had to get off the phone before I said or did something completely out of character, like ask him if he wanted to come over to eat cookie dough off my body.

The more time I spent with Gray, the more I wanted to indulge. I wanted all that intensity focused on me. Somehow, I knew he'd be hot in bed. Nothing like the boys I'd dated before, the hangers-on to the show who wanted to say they'd been with me, trying to stir up shit so they could be part of filming. I'd acted like it didn't matter even though it hurt to be treated like a trophy then tossed away for something better.

The second batch of cookies came out gooey. I took a bite of the sugary goodness just as my phone buzzed with a text from Gray.

Gray: Good night. I'm looking forward to snow-boarding on Sunday.

Happy he'd answered the thoughts I was having, I finished the cookie, brushing the crumbs off my fingers before sipping my wine. His goodnight message was sweet. His second statement was a little formal yet revealing. I'd have to miss Crew's obedience training class, but it would be worth it.

I wanted to unbutton that starched shirt he always wore, shove it off his shoulders, and push him back on the bed. I wanted to shake him up. I dropped my head back, a little buzzed from the alcohol. I was just horny because I hadn't had sex in a while. Not being able to trust someone's motives puts a damper on sexy times.

It was nothing a vibrator wouldn't take care of. I ignored the voice in my head telling me it wasn't a substitute for the real thing. Gray was a man. Being with him would be unlike anything I'd experienced before. He had this air of secrecy around him. I bet there was so much more to him than he wanted to reveal.

I finished baking, placing the cookies into separate cartons, one to take to work the next morning, and one to take to Gray. Ed and Anne would appreciate the gesture too.

I ordered a ski jacket, snow pants, and a helmet for the weekend before falling into bed, exhausted from the wine and my conversation with Gray. Something simmered under my skin, making it difficult to fall asleep despite my exhaustion. My eyes popped open when it hit me; I was excited to go snowboarding with Gray. Would he be as intense as he had been on the phone tonight? Would I invite him back to my apartment afterward? Was being with him a good idea when he knew nothing about me?

THE REST OF THE WEEK, I exchanged texts with Gray about the weekend and our plans for helping our respective businesses. We bounced ideas off each other. He asked if we needed to rent equipment and whether we should drive to the mountain or take the gondola. Without question, I wanted to spend the time in the gondola, taking in the views. Whenever I thought about it, there were flutters in my stomach.

I created flyers for my daddy-daughter styling event

and for the discounts for first responders and veterans, hanging them up around town in between my scheduled clients. Gray emailed me the information about Athena so I could print it. I taped it onto a jar I placed at the register. People seemed to sympathize with what happened with her, but so far, I hadn't gotten a lot of money for her. It was raising awareness, at least.

On Sunday, I woke up feeling tired. I'd tossed and turned all night. Unlike the time he invited me to the Rigbys' ranch, this outing was carefully planned. Gray wanted to go snowboarding with me. There wouldn't be anyone telling me what to say or do. I was on my own.

I'd never had a date that wasn't a part of the show. When the show ended, I wanted to be on my own, figure out who I was as a person. I hadn't met anyone, until Gray, who intrigued me enough to want more.

I needed to be myself, not the puppet I was on the show. I gathered the cold weather gear that came in the mail yesterday and drank my coffee as I waited for Gray to pick me up.

He texted when he arrived since no one could get to my apartment without walking through the shop. Nervous to see him, to spend time with him, I patted Crew on the head, saying "Behave," then locked my door. My heart beat loudly in my ears as I walked down the narrow wooden steps through the shop, expecting him to be waiting in his truck. Instead, he stood by the shop door holding two coffees.

His hands were covered in gloves, a wool hat was on his head, and he wore a bulky ski jacket. He looked casual and happy to see me. The flutters in my stomach turned to bolts of electricity, awareness of him skidding across my skin.

I opened the door, unable to stop the smile spreading across my face. "Morning."

"This is for you." He handed me the coffee.

"Thank you, but you didn't have to," I said as I took a tentative sip, the coffee warming me as I stepped outside into the cold.

"I stopped at The Coffee Cowboy. I thought you might like some too."

His gaze traveled down my body, taking in my puffy jacket, pants, and boots. "You have gloves and a hat?"

I held up my other hand.

"Perfect." He led me to his truck parked on the curb, holding the door open for me.

He boosted me in because I was barely able to move in the puffy ski pants.

Closing the door, he walked around to the driver's side and got in, making sure I was buckled before pulling from the curb. He drove toward the rustic-looking barn at the base of the mountain where the gondolas picked up passengers. I was able to admire the strong set of his jaw as he drove.

Parking, he held his hand out to me, helping me down from the truck, keeping hold of my hand as he led me inside the barn. We waited in line, getting a gondola to ourselves.

Settling inside, the car lifted us up. The view was white-covered mountains. It was impressive, quiet, and peaceful. "This is beautiful. I'd forgotten what it was like to be up here."

Gray moved our still-joined hands to his thigh. "How long has it been since you've been snowboarding?"

"We stopped coming after—"

He glanced over at me. "After what?"

I shook my head. I'd almost said after the show started shooting. The near-miss had me shaky. "When we were in high school."

My heart ached. Not for the first time, I wished I'd never done that stupid show—that there wasn't gossip online about me.

What were the odds he'd give me the benefit of the doubt because I was an impressionable sixteen-year-old without parental guidance? Would he believe producers told me what to do to get the most viewers, telling me the fate of the show depended on me creating compelling drama?

"Everything okay? You're quiet."

I smiled weakly. "I haven't been snowboarding in a while. I'm a little nervous, I guess."

His hand patted my knee for a second, my gaze following the motion in disbelief. My heart skidded to a halt the second his glove connected with my pants. I couldn't feel any warmth between the layers, but the sentiment behind his touch wrapped around my heart and squeezed. "We'll be fine. There's nothing to worry about."

"I'm supposed to be reassuring you."

He glanced over at me, a smile playing on his lips. "It will be an adventure."

I settled into the seat more at ease than before. I wondered when the last time he'd tried something new. I wondered if he'd be a natural athlete on the board or if he was uncoordinated.

I was glad he was doing this with me.

The gondola entered the barn at the top of the mountain. Gray exited first, helping me out of the slow-moving car.

I couldn't resist placing a hand on his hard stomach as I passed him. Touching him, even through our layers of clothes, felt good. It eased the turmoil inside.

"Let's rent some equipment. Then we'll head out."

After renting our equipment and changing into boots, Gray held both boards and his helmet. "Where to next?"

I pointed to the lift. "Are you ready to go down the mountain?"

"You'll tell me what to do?" His tone was uncertain.

It was endearing.

"We'll do a green hill. I'll tell you what to do on the way up." Snowboarding was fairly simple to explain. It was just a matter of getting on the board to feel it out.

It was trial and error. I was confident I'd still be able to do it after so many years.

Gray tensed. He wasn't the kind of guy that let loose easily, so I wasn't sure he'd relax enough to have fun. I wanted to show him he could, that there was a life outside of work. I was positive if others saw this side of him, they'd give him a chance.

We headed toward the lift. I stopped Gray when we got close, demonstrating how to strap his lead foot onto the board, leaving the other free. "To move, push off your back foot like you're on a skateboard. When the lift comes, just sit like you're sitting on a chair."

"You make it sound easy."

"It is." We were covered head to toe in bulky gear. It wasn't a romantic date, yet it conjured emotions in me. He was out of his element, unsure of how to snowboard, yet trusting me to help.

When it was our turn for the lift, we moved into position. I grabbed his hand as the bench slid behind us, lifting us in the air. Holding his hand felt comfortable, right. I'd always found the snow to be quiet. Up here it was more so.

Gray held on to my hand, moving it to his leg. "That was easier than I expected."

"It's so beautiful up here." Maybe I'd never really paid attention. When I was a kid, it was all about who had the best of whatever it was, whether it be gear, electronics, or something else. It was always a competition. We never stopped to admire the simple beauty of the mountain. I'd told Gray I loved coming here as a kid, but it was more the break I got from my life than an appreciation for this place.

As an adult, I could take my time. Appreciate the things I hadn't before. I glanced at Gray to find him watching me, a serious expression on his face.

I was a little surprised he was watching me when we were gliding through the air, our feet dangling, the mountain slowly passing us by.

"Are you going to tell me what to do when we get to the top?" His need for affirmation made me think he was nervous.

"Are you scared of heights or am I distracting you?"

He chuckled nervously. "A little of both, honestly."

My heart squeezed again. He'd admitted a weakness. One I hadn't realized he had.

"When the chair approaches the ground, drop down. As soon as you hit the snow, shift your weight to the front, then push off with your back foot." Getting off was trickier than getting on. I didn't want to tell him that and make him more nervous. I squeezed his hand tighter. My gaze shifted to the slopes where snowboarders and skiers were flying down the mountain in zig-zag patterns.

He pointed at the ones going straight down the mountain, gaining speed. "I don't think I'll be that good today."

"You never know. You could be a natural." He was

athletic looking, confident. He seemed like a guy who'd work hard until he mastered something new.

We were quickly approaching the top of the mountain. I felt Gray's muscles tense under my hand. "See the little hill? Go that direction then pause at the flat area. We'll strap in our back leg there."

"Gotcha."

Feeling his nerves building as we lowered to the ground, I wanted to distract him. Before I could change my mind, I leaned up, kissing his cold cheek. For one brief second, it was like time stood still. The feel of his cheek against my lips lingered. He looked down at me in surprise, then we were next in line to step off.

I didn't look at him, not wanting to answer any questions about the kiss. I wanted to get his mind off disembarking. I also wanted to show him affection. I wanted him to know he wasn't alone. I was here for him. "Here we go."

We hopped down, letting our hands drop. I pushed off with my back foot, satisfied to see him doing the same. It came back to me quickly. I'd spent so much time here doing this.

We glided down the little hill to the area I'd pointed out on the lift. It felt good to be at the top of the mountain with the cold air, biting wind, and the familiar glide of the board over the snow. I had pleasant memories of being here as a child. I wanted Gray to have good ones, too.

"Okay. We should strap our back foot in. Do you

need help?" I looked down at my board, then at his, hoping he wouldn't ask about what I'd done on the lift. If he did, I was positive he would know it was more than a means to distract him or an impulse.

"What was that?"

"Hmm?" My face felt hot despite the cold.

"You kissed me."

I finally managed to lift my gaze to his, my heart beating loudly in my ears. "I wanted to distract you. It worked, didn't it?"

He held his body stiff. "I didn't have time to freak out about getting off the lift."

I smiled. "Good."

He shook his head. "I don't know what I'm doing with you."

Everything slowed, my heart rate, my breathing. The sounds of the skis and boards slicing through the snow dissipated. "You're having a good time. We have a full day of snowboarding and maybe some hot chocolate drinking in front of the fire lined up for us."

"I never thought I'd say this, but it sounds like the perfect day." His tone was wistful as if he hadn't thought about what a perfect day would entail for him, or he hadn't allowed himself to think about it, much less long for it.

I smiled wider, blocking the glare of the sun with my hand. "It does, doesn't it?"

He stepped closer.

My breath caught. Was he going to kiss me?

Instead, he dropped to his knees in front of me, maneuvering my foot into the bindings, strapping it in. "Is that right?"

I took a steadying breath. My heart thrummed with disappointment.

"It feels good." I was unsure if I was talking about the bindings, the kiss on the lift, or his nearness.

He shifted his attention to his own board. What just happened? It was like we'd crossed some invisible line on the chairlift. We were far above reality, the people small and insignificant. It was only us. No one could invade our bubble. Everything fell away until all I sensed was his nervousness, his fear, and the trust placed in me. I'd kissed him as a distraction.

I didn't regret it. It was the most unscripted thing I'd done in my whole life. Whatever happened today, it was between us. No one was watching. No one cared what happened. We weren't hurting anyone. Our actions couldn't affect anyone else. We were free to be ourselves, to do our own thing.

"Are you ready?" He stood.

His smile was as breathtaking as the view from the lift. He stepped closer, taking my helmet from my hand and placing it over my head in a thoughtful gesture. He was taking care of me as much as I was him.

"How do I do this?" He gestured at his board.

I took a deep breath, settling my nerves, pushing out thoughts of us. "First, I'm going to teach you how to go down sideways. Whatever you do, don't point your lead foot straight down the hill. You'll pick up speed quickly. You won't be able to control yourself."

"Okay."

"If you want to turn, shift your weight to one foot like this." I showed him how to shift one direction then the other, depending on where I placed more of my weight.

"It seems easy enough."

"As you gain speed, bend your knees, and keep your back straight. The best way to control your speed is to turn. That's why you see so many people going in a zig-zag pattern down the hill. Keep your weight on your front foot or evenly dispersed to both. Don't stay on your back foot."

His nose wrinkled. "How do I stop?"

"Make sure no one is bearing down on you before you put your board perpendicular to the mountain, then lean into the hill with your weight on your back foot. The more you lean, the more you will slow down. When you want to start again, point your board diagonally down the mountain, and shift your weight to the front foot." My parents hadn't been present with us on these trips. They'd sent us to ski school so they were free to do their own thing.

"You're a good teacher."

Pride filled me. "Let's not get ahead of ourselves. You haven't done anything yet. You want to try it?"

At his nod, I said, "Point your board a little, shifting some of your weight to the front. Remember to stop straight, your board leaning toward the hill, weight on your back foot."

He awkwardly shifted the board down the hill. Once he shifted his weight, his board picked up speed quickly.

I pressed my hands together, worried he was going too fast. "Try to stop."

He quickly turned his board, leaning toward the hill, falling over. He landed in soft snow. I wasn't too worried he was hurt unless his pride was. It would be interesting to see how he'd handle failure. Would he get back up and try again or would he be frustrated?

I laughed at this man who was always so stoic and confident, falling. I covered my giggles with one gloved hand when I made my way to him, holding out a hand to help.

"You think it's funny?" He grabbed my hand, pulling hard.

I landed in a heap on top of him. "Hey!"

He shifted me so I lay next to him, our boards making our position awkward. One gloved hand reached out to touch my chin, running a finger along my lower lip. I was mesmerized at the moment, the mountain not that busy around us; confident skiers and snowboarders would avoid someone who'd fallen.

If we weren't wearing helmets with shields covering the top part of our faces, I would have thought he was going to kiss me. Getting any closer was logistically impossible.

I sat up, breaking the moment. "It was a little funny. You're so confident in everything you do. It's nice to see you out of your element."

He propped himself up on one elbow. "I'm glad you're enjoying yourself."

The curve of his lips told me he was relaxed. I dipped my head, wishing we weren't wearing so many bulky clothes, and we weren't wearing helmets. I wanted to kiss him like I'd thought about when I was making cookies with him on the phone. Except instead of warm and cozy, his lips would be cold, yet unable to chill the heat that sparked between us. At the same time, it was comforting, almost freeing to know we couldn't act on whatever was building between us. I liked the anticipation, no one pushing me toward him, telling me what to do.

I stood waiting for him to struggle to his feet on his own this time. "I'm going to show you how it's done. Watch me."

I tilted my board, easily remembering the feel of the snow beneath me, turning first one direction then the other, reveling in the satisfying sound of the board slicing through the snow. I changed the direction of my board coming to a stop, knowing powder flew in a perfect arc behind me. As a teenager, I'd perfected this move.

His hands were on his hips as he called down to me, "I got this."

His lips were set into a straight, determined line.

Gray wouldn't let anything best him, even if he fell all the way down the mountain. He awkwardly made his way to me, mimicking what I'd done.

He skidded to a stop in front of me, managing not to fall this time. "How was that?"

I smiled, proud I was able to teach him. "Not bad for a first-timer."

"Let's keep going. I want to make it to the bottom before it's dark."

I laughed at his joke, happy I'd brought out this side of him. I liked to think only a few people, or maybe only me, got to him this way.

We headed down the mountain, starting and stopping as I directed him, giving praise, or helping him up when he fell. I was disappointed he didn't pull me down with him again.

When we finally made it to the bottom, I asked, "Are you ready to go again?"

"I think I need some food."

I couldn't contain my grin. An overwhelming urge to tease broke through. "Ah."

"Don't you dare say I'm a wimp."

"I wasn't going to say that. Food sounds great."

We left our gear in a locker. He held his hand out to me. I took it, a feeling of rightness flowing through me so strongly I had difficulty drawing a deep breath.

"Why don't you have a seat by the fire? I'll grab some drinks and food. Do you have any allergies?"

"No. Anything's fine."

He let go of my hand. I dropped into the over-stuffed leather chair by the roaring fire. My muscles ached already from using ones I hadn't in a long time. Gray was going to be sore tomorrow too, especially his butt. I closed my eyes, imagining giving him a massage later tonight, maybe joining him in a hot tub. Why had I suggested snowboarding when it was so romantic at the lodge with the fire and opportunities for hand-holding?

Remembering the night in the barbershop, I should have known nothing with Gray was friendly. It always felt like *something more.* His definition of flying under the radar probably made women think he wasn't lethal to their libido or their heart when he most definitely was to mine.

The smell of food hit my nose before Gray spoke. "I got a little of everything. I wasn't sure what you'd like."

I sat up in the chair, seeing a tray of wrapped sandwiches, chicken fingers, and french fries.

He handed me hot chocolate. "I put marshmallows in there."

"You did?"

"I thought you might like something sweet."

"Thank you." I opened the lid, blowing on the steaming liquid, feeling warm inside without drinking it yet.

Gray sat next to me, unwrapping his sandwich, taking a large bite.

The way the chairs were situated around the room,

it was like we were by ourselves. I took a tentative sip of the coffee, appreciating the taste of the chocolate combined with marshmallows. "This hits the spot."

I looked up to find his gaze locked on my mouth.

My tongue darted out to lick the chocolate.

Gray cleared his throat, shifting in his chair. "You should eat so you have the energy to go down the mountain."

"I don't think I'll make another run," I teased.

He handed me a sandwich. "This time you won't be able to keep up with me."

I carefully unwrapped the sandwich, enjoying this time with him. Moving here to open the shop was a calculated risk. Being with Gray was like hurtling straight down the mountain, gaining speed, a billion times riskier for his career and mine. He needed to prove to Ed he was here to stay. But I was an outsider, not a local. If anyone found out about my past, it could adversely affect his reputation.

I took a bite of the sandwich, curling my legs under me. I could stay here in this bubble forever, not letting anyone else in.

"How does your family feel about you moving here?"

I startled at his unexpected question. He rarely asked deep questions. I wondered if he was worried I'd ask some of my own. I finished chewing, giving myself a few seconds to consider my answer. "My sister wants me to come home. She feels like—" How could I explain the truth without revealing too much? "There are more opportunities for me in LA."

"What do your parents think?" He cleaned up his wrappers, throwing them on the tray on the coffee table in front of us.

I felt oddly detached whenever I thought about my parents. They'd been so absent it was like they were a nonentity. "They don't understand it. At the same time, they don't have an opinion one way or the other. We're free to make our own decisions."

"That's refreshing." His expression was genuine.

"It is." And it wasn't.

"Why do I think it's not?"

I was holding so much back from him. I wanted to give him a piece of myself. "They weren't there for us when we were younger and needed guidance and protection. It's not a surprise they're hands-off now. I would have appreciated them stepping in when we were kids." It would have been nice if they'd stepped in to handle the producers. I was a child dealing with adults.

"Did it make you more independent, though?"

"Unfortunately, it left me susceptible to other people's devices and opinions. I'm happy to say I'm independent now, but it was a journey to get here." I fiddled with the wrapper of my sandwich, suddenly not hungry. I'd revealed more to him than I had before. I'd told the truth, just not everything. I felt good about

LEA COLL

opening up but ashamed I couldn't be completely transparent with him.

I glanced at him to see his reaction.

His expression was pensive. "All that matters is where you are now."

My heart tugged then squeezed almost painfully at his words. I wanted his words to be right. I wanted my past not to matter. I knew it was asking too much. I couldn't help grabbing on to the hope he'd unknowingly floated in front of me. I'd hang onto it, and him, as long as I could. When my past caught up to me, I'd have to let him go no matter how much it would hurt. If I didn't, I was positive he'd walk away from me.

I covered my sandwich, throwing our trash out. "Are you ready to go again?"

He stood, smirking down at me as he flung a friendly arm around my shoulder. "Are you ready for this? I'm not holding back this time."

I placed a hand on his sweater-covered stomach, smiling up at him. "I should hope not."

We teased each other all the way to our lockers, pulling our gear on. Snowboarding was the best idea.

These experiences of normalcy, a life without cameras, were everything. He had no idea. I liked the person I was. I liked who I was with him.

For the rest of the day, flashes of my old life came back at me like reels of a movie film. I wished I could ignore my past while living in this world of pretending.

No self-respecting man who cared about his career

176

would entertain the idea of having me on his arm. I was forever the villain, the bitch, the woman who cheated to get what she wanted. Was it too much to hope that when it came out, he'd remember the woman he'd come to know?

CHAPTER 13

Gray

The day was unexpected. It had everything to do with Elle and her gentle instructions, guidance, and teasing. When she held her hand out to help me after that first fall, I couldn't help tugging her down on top of me. I'd felt freer than I had in years.

There were shadows in her eyes that popped up when I asked about her family. She'd revealed more to me than she had before. Enough to make my heart ache for the lonely girl she was. I was also so damn proud of her for striking out on her own and opening her business. She was badass whether she believed it or not.

Riding the gondola back to town, the lights of the town were just as mesmerizing as the view of the mountains on the way up. I wasn't ready for the night to be over. I wanted her to ask me up to her apartment. I wanted to lose myself in her. I knew it was wrong to get involved with someone like Elle. She was relationship—hell—she was *marriage* material. I couldn't get that close to someone, not with the past I carried around like a dark looming cloud threatening to drench everything with its strength and power.

Driving through town, I said, "Thanks for suggesting this. I had fun."

Her eyes snapped to mine as if she were surprised at my words. "I had fun too."

I parked in front of her building. The streets were quiet, the night clear. I didn't feel the familiar panic like I had the night I took her to the Rigbys'.

She paused, her hand on the doorknob. "Do you want to come up? Piper took Crew out a couple of times today, but I should take him for a walk."

"Of course." A thrill shot through me as I climbed out, jogging around the hood to help her. She was letting me in. The question was, what was I going to do about it?

I wasn't sure what to expect as I waited for her to unlock the shop door. Leading me through the shop, down the hallway, then up the narrow set of steps to her apartment, she unlocked the door, and let Crew out of his crate. She attached the leash to Crew's collar while he jumped around her legs.

I quickly texted Henry, telling him I wouldn't be at

his parents' for dinner, then shoved my phone in my pocket, taking the opportunity to scan her apartment. I could see a small kitchen, living room, and a hallway presumably leading to a bedroom and the bathroom. "There's no outside access to your apartment?"

"No. I thought it might be safer this way. I have a rope ladder in case of fire."

I nodded, wondering if I should offer to take Crew outside for her so she didn't have to walk him at night.

"I'll be just a minute if you want to wait."

"I'll come with you." I wanted to spend every minute with her I could.

"Okay." She smiled.

I took Crew's leash from her while she locked up again, leading the way outside.

"Are you sure you aren't too sore for a walk?" she teased.

"Oh, I'm sore. I could use a hot shower." An image of us in the shower, warm water sliding over our skin, her nipples hard pebbles begging to be sucked while my fingers parted her folds, easing inside, hit me. I could feel the heat of her body, the slickness, the taste of the water, and her skin, on my tongue. I subtly adjusted myself as we walked side by side, waiting periodically for Crew to sniff the grass, or a tree, before doing his business.

The simple act of walking a dog with her in this town we both called home was a balm to my soul. Today, we existed in this bubble I never wanted to pop.

When we returned to her shop, I was overwhelmed with the feeling of not wanting to leave. Her apartment was so inviting and cozy. The thought of returning to mine was unappealing when I could spend the evening with her.

She unlocked the shop door. "Did you want to order dinner, maybe watch a movie?"

The tension eased from my shoulders because she hadn't changed her mind. She wanted me to stay. "Yeah, I'd like that."

She smiled at me before closing the door to the shop behind us.

"If I haven't told you already, your shop is amazing. You should be proud of it."

Her smile was almost sad. "Thank you."

I wanted to know why praise made her sad. Was it what I said, or did it make her think of what she'd left behind? I followed her up the steps and into her apartment.

Elle paused in the middle of the room, spinning to ask, "What do you feel like? I can order pizza."

Crew tracked her every movement, waving his tail. He was probably hungry.

"That sounds perfect." I didn't want to leave to pick up anything. I wanted to stay in this apartment, never going back to the real world.

She turned her attention to her phone, presumably pulling up a menu. "Do you care what's on it?"

"I'm okay with anything."

"Grab a drink from the fridge. I'll be done in a second."

I followed her direction recognizing the kitchen from our video call the other night except everything had been cleaned up. My hand glided over the counter, the same one I'd imagined propping her on to kiss her.

My body flooded with warmth as I grabbed the waters before moving to the couch. I grabbed the remote to flip through her streaming channels. I paused on a popular movie from a couple of years ago. "Is this okay?"

She put down her phone on the counter, filling Crew's bowl with food before coming to sit next to me. Her couch was so small, her leg touched mine, the warmth seeping through my jeans, easing the something in my chest. "Sure."

She pulled off her boots, propping them on the table in front of us. "My feet ache."

"Did you want me to massage them?" I wasn't sure why I'd asked. It wasn't something I'd ever done for anyone else. It was so far out of bounds, I didn't recognize myself anymore. I wanted to touch her. I wanted to be close to her.

"Oh, you don't have to do that." She smiled softly.

I'd do anything to keep that look on her face.

"I don't mind." I maneuvered her leg so that it rested on my thigh, her back against the arm of the couch. I pressed a thumb into the arch of her foot, and she moaned.

"That feels so good." She relaxed further into the cushions, turning her head to watch TV.

I focused on relieving the tightness in her muscles, attuned to each soft sigh, content to be touching her. When the phone buzzed indicating the pizza was downstairs, I held up a hand, reluctant to leave but not wanting her to go downstairs to get it. "I'll get it."

She moved her feet off my lap so I could get up.

I headed down the steps, through the shop, and opened the door to pay the delivery man, then headed back upstairs. When I opened the door, she was pulling dishes out of the cupboard, placing them on the counter.

I couldn't remember the last time I spent time with a woman in her home, eating and watching TV. I usually spent my time in the bedroom, leaving as soon as it was socially acceptable. Assimilating into her life was risky. It broke all my carefully constructed rules. Letting people in meant them asking questions, wondering about the life I had before.

"Is everything okay?" Elle asked when I placed the box on the counter but didn't move to open it.

"Yeah, sorry." I grabbed a couple of beers from the fridge in case she preferred beer to water with pizza.

She plated a couple of slices. We sat back down on the couch to resume the movie.

We ate in silence. When the credits rolled, Elle got up to clear our dishes.

As much as I wanted to stay, I didn't want to pressure her or assume she was ready for that. "I should get going. I have to work early tomorrow morning."

Elle offered me a small smile as she stacked the dishes in the dishwasher.

I stood awkwardly in the kitchen, my hands stuffed in my pockets. I wasn't sure how to end the night. It wasn't a date, no matter how date-like it felt. The desire to touch her was acute.

Elle came to stand in front of me, her hands resting on my chest. "Thanks for coming today. I know it wasn't something you were comfortable doing."

Tenderness spread through my limbs at the uncertainty I saw in her eyes and the warmth from her hands. I wanted to erase her doubts. I moved her hair back from her face, my thumb brushing her temple. "I had fun. I'm glad you asked me."

She sucked in a sharp breath. "Is this—what are we—"

I focused on her lips, the room falling away, her words evaporating in the air. Blood pounded in my ears. I placed a kiss on the corner of her mouth, stopping whatever it was she was going to say.

She tipped her head back, her lips parted as I nipped her lower lip. She tasted like beer and the best decision I ever made. I stepped closer, forcing her head to tilt back further. I lifted her to sit on the counter, stepping between her legs, kissing her more firmly. Her tongue tangled with mine as her fingers gripped my shirt. My cock throbbed. This was better than my imagination.

Her fingers twisted in my shirt, pulling me closer. The pleasure of her thighs bracketing my hips, her lips on mine, and her fingers touching my chin shot endorphins through my head.

I didn't want to carefully consider each move, weighing whether this was a good idea. I wanted to lose myself in her, in this moment, not waking until I didn't know where I ended and she began.

"Bedroom?" I pulled back, noting the flush in her cheeks, the swelling of her lips.

She tilted her head toward the hallway. I took that as a yes. My hands went to her ass, lifting her so her legs naturally wrapped around my waist. She nipped my earlobe as we walked.

I growled as the sensation sent a tingle down my neck, pushing open the door to her room. It was small, with a bed in the middle and a dresser. The bed was rumpled. I dropped her on the bed so she would bounce. I didn't want tender. I needed to separate those feelings in the kitchen from sex to protect myself from falling into her completely.

I wasn't ready for that. I wasn't sure I ever would be.

I toed off my boots before pulling my shirt over my head, sending it sailing behind me. She sat up on her elbows, watching me. She licked her lips, crooking her finger at me. My cock jerked inside my pants.

185

I undid my buckle, shoving my pants down, leaving me in black boxer briefs. Her gaze dropped slowly down my chest to where my cock was clearly outlined under the cotton material. It hardened at the desire I saw in her eyes.

I placed a knee on the bed, bracing myself over her, meeting her lips. I'd never enjoyed kissing a woman like this before. I was getting to know her, her thoughts, her feelings, and her soul.

With Elle, I didn't want to break that connection. I wanted to shut my brain off, sinking into every new sensation—the softness of her skin, the silky feel of her hair, her fingers caressing my chest down the line between my abs to the spot above the waistband of my briefs.

Her touch was so light, I jerked when she firmly cupped me through my briefs. "Fuck, Elle."

I looked down at the challenge flashing in her eyes. Nothing about this girl was shy. She was confident in her sexuality. The combination coiled desire tight inside me, tensing my muscles until I was desperate for her.

When she gripped me again, I lifted her to pull her shirt off and over her head, unhooking her bra. She lowered her shoulders, letting the straps fall, revealing small perky breasts, her nipples hard, begging for my mouth. She braced her weight on her hands. The effect lifted her breasts as an offering to me. My mouth watered to taste her skin.

I watched her eyes as I lowered my mouth to one nipple, sucking it into my mouth, scraping it lightly with my teeth before soothing the sting with my tongue. Her eyelids fluttered as she moaned, arching further into my mouth. I moved to her other nipple, paying it the same attention.

Then she dropped down onto her back, shoving her leggings down over her hips in one jerky motion. I hoped she was as desperate for me as I was for her. I moved down her body, helping her roll them off along with her black lace thong.

I kissed my way up her calf and thighs, her muscles quivering under my lips.

"Gray. I need you."

"I know, baby." I kept my attention on the spot between her legs, not on the slip of my tongue. I'd never used an endearment in bed with another woman. With her, it felt right.

I slid my hands under her ass, pulling her to my mouth, determined to make her mindless, to make her forget what I'd said. I licked and sucked until she was writhing on the bed, her thighs squeezing my head. I ground my cock against the bed, wanting friction, sliding one finger, then two, into her hot, wet channel. Her hips lifted off the bed with each plunge of my fingers. She arched, her back bowing off the bed as she climaxed.

Her moans spurred me on as I wiped my mouth on the back of my hand, moving to grab the condom out of my wallet. She was chanting my name, reaching for me. That tenderness I felt earlier in the kitchen washed over me tenfold. I slid the condom down my shaft, lining myself up, pushing in slowly, inch by inch. I wanted to savor her tightness enveloping me for the first time.

It hit me then. Once would never be enough.

Her hands were everywhere, my shoulders, my chest, before settling for my face. I leaned down, kissing her as I slid in to the hilt. She felt so good, better than anything I'd ever felt. My heart was fluttering inside my chest, starting and stopping like a butterfly who hadn't learned how to fly.

Whether I wanted it or not, she'd eased under my skin, forcing me to feel things.

I slid out, almost to the tip, then drove into her again. When kissing became difficult, I sat up, watching the spot where I disappeared into her, my hands under her ass lifting her, changing the angle. The sight was erotic, urging me to go faster, harder.

When her moans increased, I knew I'd hit the spot I wanted.

She slid her hand down her body, between her breasts, until they circled her clit. I groaned at the sight. This woman had no inhibitions. No shyness. No pretense.

She clamped down on me. Tremors shook her body as her head tipped back in ecstasy.

I thrust one more time, growling my release into

her shoulder. The moment threatened to overwhelm my senses with the warmth of her skin, the brush of her hair, and the closeness I felt to her. I kissed her shoulder before pulling out, taking care of the condom in the bathroom. I took my time washing my hands, throwing cold water on my face.

I needed a minute to process what happened. I didn't regret what transpired, but it couldn't go any farther. Not unless I wanted her to know everything about me, and I didn't. I dried my face, telling myself not to fall for her. Maybe I should go home. Set the tone.

When I returned to the bedroom, she was on her side, her hands curled under her face, looking soft, peaceful, and sated. Unable to follow through with my plan to leave, I slid under the sheets, kissing her shoulder.

"Are you okay?"

"Yeah." She turned slightly so she could see me, a smile on her lips. "I'm just tired. Snowboarding then this."

"Will you stay?" she closed her eyes as if she couldn't keep them open any longer.

"Sure." That same tenderness I'd felt for her in the kitchen swirled around my heart in intricate loops. I couldn't tell her no.

She rolled onto my chest, my arm naturally going around her shoulders, holding her tight. Her breath evened out as she fell asleep.

CHAPTER 14

Elle

I woke early Monday morning with an arm banded tightly around me, my head resting on a firm chest, slowly rising and falling with each inhale. The relief was a physical, tangible thing.

Gray stayed.

I almost couldn't believe it. I was sure he would have left after what we'd shared last night. It had been intense, even for me. I'd never experienced anything like it. Gray was passionate and considerate. I'd gotten lost in the feel of his mouth, hands, and tongue, forgetting my past and how anything between us was doomed.

"Morning." Gray's voice was rough with sleep.

Crew's tail thumped on the comforter by my feet. He must have jumped up in the middle of the night. I'd need to get up soon to take him out.

"Good morning." I tipped my head back, admiring the scruff on his chin.

Was he regretting last night? He'd pulled away from me after we'd visited the Rigbys and last night was a hundred times more real.

He loosened his arm around my shoulders. "I have an early day."

I eased off him, already missing his arm around me.

He stood, the sheet falling from his body. He walked naked to the bathroom, his defined ass on display.

I lay back on my pillow, closing my eyes as he turned on the water for the shower. I suspected he'd back off after last night. Magic didn't exist in the light of day. In his mind, he was probably running through a list of ways to let me down easily.

I couldn't regret anything.

It was the easiest decision I'd ever made. I felt good with him. I felt cared for, respected. No one was pushing me to make a move. It wasn't for ratings or to create drama where there was none. It was as real as it got.

Him walking away, my past catching up with me, was inevitable.

A few minutes later, he opened the door, his chest glistening with moisture from the shower, his cock semi-hard. I licked my lips, regretting not tasting him last night.

"I have a surgery at eight." Regret tinged his voice.

I let the sheet drop so my breasts were visible, stretching my arms overhead. A part of me kept expecting him to run, to pretend last night was a one-time thing. "That's too bad. I had plans for this morning."

He surprised me by resting one knee on the bed, hovering over me with his minty fresh breath. I wondered if he'd used my toothbrush. The intimacy of that act tugged at my heart. "I'll have to take a rain check."

It wasn't a question.

He kissed me lightly, a promise of more. Hope bloomed, filling the empty cavity of my chest.

"Yes, please." Whatever he promised, I would agree to. I would enjoy the first private relationship I'd ever had. I'd never felt closer to someone after sex. He didn't want anything from me.

I propped myself up on the pillows as he tugged his jeans on commando, pulling a shirt over the smooth expanse of his torso.

It was on the tip of my tongue to ask when I'd see him again. I restrained myself, knowing that was a dangerous question the morning after. I needed to give him time to process last night, to decide if this—if I—was what he wanted.

He stood next to the bed, his gaze lingering on my

breasts, my nipples hardening under his scrutiny. "This is the hardest thing I've ever had to do. Leaving a beautiful, naked woman in bed."

Had I ever had a man talk about me this way? I wanted to retort with a—*so don't*—but he didn't have time. I didn't want to be needy. This thing between us felt precarious.

His finger rested under my chin, tilting it up. He kissed me hard. It felt more like a brand than a goodbye kiss. "I'll call you later. I'll let myself out."

I cleared my throat over the emotion I was feeling. "I'll go down to the shop in a minute and lock up behind you. I have to walk Crew."

He patted Crew's head on the way out of my bedroom.

I didn't feel the chill of the air until I heard the soft snick of the door closing. Would the regrets filter in through the day, creating distance between us, telling him we were a bad idea?

I eased under the covers, closing my eyes to relive the night before, every spine-tingling moment. He was intense, yet sweet and caring. My eyes popped open, remembering how he'd called me 'baby' in the heat of the moment. I wanted to think it was spontaneous, like he couldn't help himself from calling me an endearment.

He'd gone down on me as if he wanted to devour me, like he couldn't get enough. My face heated when I remembered touching myself in front of him. I'd never been that uninhibited with someone, chasing my desire without hesitation. With Gray, I could be myself, the person I was meant to be. Not the show's persona, Giselle, but Elle, the strong, independent woman, a successful business owner. The woman who knew what she wanted and went after it.

I finally got up, taking Crew outside. Then I eased under the hot water of the shower. The bathroom smelled like him.

Should I have told him who I was before we had sex, or should I hold on as long as I can before it all comes crashing down?

I hadn't even told Piper. No one in this town knew who I was. I couldn't imagine revealing myself at this point. Not when it would ruin everything I'd worked so hard for, and anything between Gray and me.

I pressed a hand against my chest, trying to ease the painful throb. Why was everything in my life affected by one horrible decision, compounded by many others? Why couldn't I start over, leaving Giselle behind, shedding her skin, and becoming a better person—one I could be proud of?

I deserved a successful business. I deserved Gray. For once in my life, I deserved real happiness, not manufactured, made for TV drama. I'd deal with my past when it came up. Until then, I wanted more snowboarding with Gray, more kissing, more touching.

I got dressed, taking Crew for a quick walk, grabbing coffees for Piper and me at The Coffee Cowboy. I brought Crew back to the shop, turning the sign from closed to open. I let Crew hang out with us in the mornings when it was quieter.

Piper walked in a few minutes later, pausing when she saw my face. "Did something happen?"

I looked around, wondering if something was out of place.

She pointed at me, coming closer. "No. You. Your face. You look more alive, happier or something."

Feeling slightly panicked, I busied myself organizing products so she wouldn't notice my reaction. I should keep whatever was happening between Gray and me between us, but I wanted to talk to someone about it. I was so used to protecting my sister from my life, I never talked to her about guys. "I had a lot of fun yesterday. I went snowboarding with a friend."

"Was it Gray? It looked like there was something between you at the bar."

There was nothing but genuine curiosity on her face. "It was."

She grabbed the coffee from the tray, sitting in her chair. "I didn't think Gray did anything other than work."

I sat across from her, cradling the warm coffee cup in my hand. Between waking up in Gray's arms and my burgeoning friendship with Piper, my heart was overflowing. "That's why I invited him. I thought it would be fun."

She shook her head in disbelief. "I don't even know how you managed to convince him to take a day off."

I put my coffee on a nearby table, pulling out my phone, scrolling through to find the selfie we'd taken last night by the bonfire at the lodge. He'd placed his arm around me. He looked relaxed and happy. I'd been looking up at him as he'd snapped the picture. I could almost hear the sounds of the snow-making machines, loud and comforting, the warmth of the fire on our cheeks, the feel of his arm around my shoulders. I wanted that feeling to last.

Piper looked over my shoulder. "That's a cute pic."

"Yeah. It was a great day." Looking at the two of us, the happiness on my face and the easy smile on his, dislodged something in my chest.

"Is it a thing? Are you together?" She got up, getting her station ready for the day.

"It wasn't even a date. Just a friendly outing." That ended up being a not-so-friendly evening. It felt good to keep that tidbit to myself.

"I've never seen Gray with a woman. Henry said he dates but keeps quiet about it. Once, Gray said, 'the longer you're with someone, the more they want from you,' when Henry asked why he'd ever had any long-term relationships." At her last statement, she turned to me, her eyes full of concern. "I'm not really sure what he meant, but I'm worried about you."

My heart sank a little at her statement. I wanted this thing to be the real deal. I didn't want to be another notch on someone's bedpost. "I'll be okay. I know this can't go anywhere."

"I'm not saying it won't. You just need to be careful." She emphasized each word.

I stood, giving her a hug. "Thanks, Piper. You're a good friend."

She'd quickly become a confidant, someone I trusted. She was nothing like the friends I'd had on the show. I didn't want to lose her, my shop, or this town. I especially didn't want to lose whatever was building with Gray.

CHAPTER 15

Gray

*H*enry walked into my office at lunch with a carry-out bag in his hand. "I come bearing lunch."

"I'm starving. Thanks." I held my hand out for the bag, pulling out a wrapped Italian sub. It wasn't uncommon for Henry to stop by for lunch from time to time.

He sat across from me, unwrapping his sub. "Where were you last night?"

Last night was family dinner night at Rigby's Ranch. "I'm sorry. I was caught up in something."

"One person missing isn't a big deal. You know that."

I took a large bite of the Italian sub, hoping he'd let his original question go.

Henry shot me a knowing look. "The question is, where were you that was so important you missed a home-cooked meal?"

I almost never missed dinner at the Rigbys' house unless I was out on a call for the clinic. "I went snowboarding."

Henry paused, his sub halfway to his mouth. "By yourself?"

"No." I shifted in my chair.

His gaze trained on me. "With who?"

"Elle Carmichael."

I took another large bite so I could avoid the next question for a few seconds. I rarely talked about women with Henry, other than to admit an attraction. This thing with Elle was personal, something I wanted to protect.

"Are you seeing her?"

It wasn't a secret I hadn't had a long-term girlfriend in the entire time he'd known me. Henry would think it was a big deal. It was. Normally I wasn't one to share, but I wanted advice. Remembering the way my heart clenched when I saw the picture on my phone this morning of us, I said, "I think so. We didn't have a conversation or anything, but it seems like that's where we're headed."

Waking up with a naked woman wrapped in my arms spelled relationship in my world. I never spent the night, I never cuddled, and I never let anyone below the surface.

"What makes her different?" Henry echoed the same sentiment ringing in my head.

I took the last bite of my sub, leaning back in my chair. I took my time chewing, drinking water before I answered, "It's a feeling I get when I'm around her. She's nice, cares about animals, and wants to help me. She's special."

Ever since yesterday, I had this warm, comforting feeling in my chest, encasing my heart like a warm sweater. It was something I hadn't felt since before everything changed.

"What you're saying is that she's willing to put up with you," Henry cracked.

I knew it wasn't easy being with me, but to hear Henry describe it like that was still a little off-putting. "She's convinced she can help me get the clinic."

When she said she wanted to convince the townspeople, and the community, of what she saw, a piece of the armor I'd worn broke off. She was slowly wearing me down, making me believe I deserved someone like her. Someone for the long haul, who'd be by my side no matter what.

"Are you going to tell her?" Henry stilled, his body tensed for my response.

"Tell her what, how I feel?" I was surprised Henry had mentioned feelings. This wasn't the sort of conversation we normally had.

"No. Tell her why you don't talk about your home life, your family, how you grew up."

The hair on my arms stood up. "I told her a little about my mom and my parents' divorce."

He stood, gathering up the trash and placing it in the bin by the door. "That's more than you told me. All I know is your parents divorced, you went to live with your dad, and you go back occasionally to visit. As far as I know, they've never visited here. We both know there's more. There's a reason you don't talk about them, a reason you never go home. You keep everyone at arm's length. I haven't pushed over the years. I thought you'd eventually trust me enough to tell me."

For the first time, I saw hurt in his eyes. I hadn't expected that. "I'm sorry. I never realized you—"

"You never realized I cared? We're friends, Gray."

Shame filled me that my one friend was hurt by my actions when all I'd ever wanted to do was protect the people in my life from what I'd experienced. "Close the door."

His eyes widened. "Seriously?"

I nodded. "Yeah, it's time."

My heart beat rapidly in my chest; my fingers drummed restlessly on the desktop. Here was the moment of truth. If he walked out disgusted by me and what happened, I wouldn't tell Elle. I'd take this as a foreshadowing of how she'd react. Henry had known me longer than she has.

He closed the door then sat across from me, his

hands clasped in front of him, his elbows resting on his knees.

I told him the whole story. Every detail I hadn't told anyone over the last twelve years.

As I talked, Henry's face softened. "I wish you felt like you could come to me. I wouldn't have judged you. I believe you."

I closed my eyes at his confident words. He believed me. What I would have given for someone to believe me then.

Henry whistled, indicating he understood the gravity of the situation. "I get it. I don't blame you for wanting to protect yourself, for wanting to start over. I just want you to know that I won't judge you, and my family sure won't."

I opened my eyes; every muscle in my body tensed. "What about Elle?"

He crossed his arms over his chest. "I don't know her that well, so I don't know for sure. If things between you are serious then you might want to consider telling her sooner rather than later."

It was a confirmation of what I was already thinking. Still, the idea made me nervous. Telling her was different than telling Henry. "I'm sorry I didn't tell you earlier. I was afraid you'd look at me in disgust and wouldn't want to be my friend anymore, and let's be honest, you're my only friend."

"You had your reasons. I just hope you're happy here, that you stay."

"I have no reason to leave." Elle was a big reason to stay. Being with her was like opening a curtain to my future. I could see us together so clearly, a home, pets, a family. Anything was possible if I opened up to her, if I took a chance.

"I'll let you get back to work. Thanks for telling me. It explains a lot."

I nodded, unable to say anything over the lump in my throat. I needed to focus on work. My next appointment was in a few minutes. I needed to figure out the best time to tell Elle when all I wanted was to bask in the afterglow of last night.

I felt lighter after talking to Henry and unloading my truth on him. It surprised me that he was more upset about me not telling him than what happened. He didn't doubt me, didn't accuse me of being involved; he supported me. It was more than I'd hoped for any time I'd imagined confiding in him. I hadn't expected it to feel so good.

He was right. I shouldn't wait to tell Elle.

CHAPTER 16

Elle

The vegetables were still hard. I'd put the food in the slow cooker around lunchtime and set it on low when I probably should have put it in this morning or at least on high. He'd messaged during the day asking me when he could see me again. I was already regretting inviting him over to test my first foray into solo cooking.

Worried the food wouldn't be done in time, I transferred the soup to a pot on the stove. While it was simmering, I rushed to my room to get ready, taking a quick shower. I also felt like I still had hair on me after working all day, even if I didn't.

Checking the soup, I heard a light knock on the

door. It was probably Gray because I'd told Piper to let him come up. Crew ran for the foyer, his claws skidding across the floor. When I opened the door, Crew darted out, jumping up on Gray's legs.

"Sorry." I was a little embarrassed Crew was jumping when I was supposed to be training him.

"He's a puppy." Gray crouched down to greet him, scratching behind his ears. "Hey, buddy."

His black button-down shirt was rolled to his elbows, exposing strong forearms. He wore dark wash jeans and stylish boots. He smelled good, like aftershave, leather, and something uniquely him.

I felt a little light-headed as I gestured inside. I didn't want Crew running out. He loved to escape down to the shop, grabbing whatever he could find. "Come in. It's almost ready."

It was hard to believe he was with me, that this was real when my past relationships had been anything but.

He stood, our eyes meeting. My breath hitched at the intensity in his.

Stepping closer, he placed his hand on the side of my face, lightly stroking my cheek. "I've been thinking about how I left you all day. The sheet pooling at your waist, your bare breasts, your hard nipples begging for my mouth."

My core clenched at the image, my nipples peaking at the hint of his wet mouth on them. My breath came in short pants. I loved that he'd thought of me all day. "Is it bad I like that?"

He kissed me lightly. "You're the best kind of distraction."

"Oh yeah?" I let a smile play on my lips because I liked this side of him, focused and intent on me.

He kissed me again, a little deeper, continuing what we started this morning. "I wanted to lose myself in you."

"Yes. Please." When had someone ever said anything like that to me? Sex had always been something quick. The guy usually saw me as a means to an end, not someone to lose themselves in. His sweet words made me think I could easily fall for him.

He cupped both cheeks, bending his knees slightly, increasing the pressure of his lips as if he wanted to ensure I wasn't going to disappear, guaranteeing I was going to stay.

His words, his hands, his lips, I'd never felt more worshipped. I blinked when he pulled back, over-whelmed with the feelings he was evoking in me. Feelings I'd never had with anyone else.

He stepped back, dropping his hands. "What are you making?"

I took a second to pull myself together after that greeting. Still a little flustered, I said, "Chicken tortilla soup. It seemed easy, but it wasn't cooking fast enough, so I transferred it from the slow cooker to the stove."

"It smells good."

"I hope it tastes as good as it smells." I busied myself

pulling avocados, cilantro, and green onions out of the fridge as well as tortilla chips from the pantry.

"Can I help?" His voice sounded close.

"Can you put these in a bowl while I cut up the veggies and slice some avocado? Salsa is in the pantry if you want some." I pointed out the cabinet with bowls for him.

I wanted to forget about dinner, take things to the bedroom, but I was a little unsure about his intentions. If he said he wanted a friends-with-benefits situation or that it didn't mean anything, I'd be crushed.

He dumped tortilla chips in the bowl, placing the salsa in a smaller one. He ate chips and salsa while he talked about his day, the pets he saw, the funny things they ate, and the owner who brought their dog in for every suspected ailment.

It was nice to hear about his day. I suspected he didn't talk to too many people like this, unguarded. I spooned the soup into bowls, placing it on the small two-person table I hadn't used since I moved in.

"Did you want a beer or a margarita?" I asked him.

Gray topped his soup with the extras I'd sliced. "A margarita sounds good."

I poured us each a glass, looking forward to relaxing. "Thanks for being my guinea pig. I've been wanting to experiment with cooking and baking."

"Is there anything else on your list?"

"I guess living on my own, no roommates." I hesitated, wondering if I should tell him I'd never dated anyone seriously. Would he even believe me? "I haven't been with anyone like this." I wondered if he'd think I was immature or anti-commitment in admitting that.

He glanced up from his soup. "You've never had a boyfriend?"

"Not really. Nothing serious. I couldn't trust most of the people in my life." Admitting that left me feeling vulnerable.

"I'm sorry." His expression was filled with regret.

I hoped his reaction meant he wanted something more serious.

"I trust you, so that's new for me." I was trusting him not to hurt me. I was certain he was nothing like the boys I'd dated in the past. He didn't want the limelight or some easy road to quick money. He worked hard to avoid scandal. I wanted to be worthy of him.

He shifted in his chair, running a hand through his hair. "I trust you too."

His actions belied his words. There seemed to be something on his mind, something he wanted to say. I hoped it wasn't something I didn't want to hear.

"This is really good."

I smiled, pleased it had turned out. "It's a fairly simple recipe. I don't know why I didn't think I could cook before."

"Maybe it's that you never tried."

"Yeah, maybe." Maybe I was good at being a good person, being honest and truthful. I could be a good girlfriend and a successful business owner. My past didn't have to define who I was now.

We finished eating in silence. Gray helped me clean up, putting the food away and placing the dishes in the dishwasher.

I turned to him about to suggest a movie, but his face was tight. Something was bothering him.

"Can we talk?"

My smile faltered. "Okay."

Had I scared him away by telling him I trusted him? Was it too much too soon? Had he felt obligated to say he trusted me too? I hated semantics or playing games. I wanted to be upfront with Gray, as much as I could, anyway.

He led me to my couch, sitting next to me. He took my hand, holding his forehead in the other as if he was searching for a place to begin. "I grew up in a small town in Maine. I told you my parents were divorced. I lived with my dad."

Still confused, I nodded.

He ran his fingers through his hair, sighing deeply. "What I didn't mention was that I lost my house and my father at eighteen, the summer before I went to college."

I pressed my free hand against my chest. My heart ached for him. "Your father died?"

He startled at my assumption. "I'm sorry. That came out wrong. The feds raided our house in the middle of the night."

My heart raced at the thought of what it would have been like to be woken up by the police. How scary would that have been? To have your home, the place you felt safe, invaded. I squeezed his hand, silently telling him I supported him, not wanting to interrupt.

His eyes were focused across the room. It was like he was reliving that night, his face filled with pain. "They handcuffed both of us, placed us on the couch so an officer could watch us while they rummaged through our things. I thought it was a mistake. I wanted my father to reassure me everything was going to be okay. He couldn't because they found millions of dollars of cash in his safe."

"Oh, Gray. I'm so sorry." I wasn't sure what his father was involved in. It must have been bad to have that amount of cash, to have the feds beating down your door.

He continued, not acknowledging what I'd said. "They arrested both of us that night, unsure if I was involved. I was held for questioning, but they finally let me go when they couldn't prove I knew anything. I was shocked and so confused by everything that was happening. Nothing made sense."

I wanted to move closer to him, wrap my arms around him, and comfort the boy whose world had been turned upside down. I wasn't sure he'd welcome it. He looked split open.

"They seized everything, our house, the property,

my dad's store, his savings. The only thing I had left was a trust fund he'd set up in my name."

"At the time, I felt like I didn't deserve that money because Dad might have acquired it illegally. My mom convinced me I should use it. Dad wanted to protect me in case something happened."

"He went to prison?" I asked tentatively, knowing this was painful for him to admit, maybe even embarrassing.

Gray lowered his gaze. "He's still there. It was a big deal, one of the largest drug trafficking operations in Maine involving sheriff deputies, local politicians, and several business owners. My father was at the center of it, laundering money through his hardware store. It made national news. I couldn't escape it. Reporters were hounding me. My girlfriend dumped me. My friends didn't want to be associated with me. It was too small of a town to keep my head down until it blew over."

I could imagine how horrible something like that would have been at a young age. It was so unlike what I experienced, it made me feel remorseful for thinking my past was horrible. It was nothing compared to what he'd gone through.

"I moved to Colorado to start over. I didn't want anyone to know. I went from having everything to not knowing who I could trust, what was real, and what wasn't. Everything I thought I knew was a lie."

Tears pricked my eyes. This was why he seemed

more comfortable with animals, keeping people at a distance. He didn't trust anyone not to hurt him. I unlaced my fingers from his, pulling his arm around me so I could cuddle into his side. I closed my eyes, wrapping my arms around him. I wasn't sure what I should say. All I knew is that I wanted to relieve his pain. I wanted to be there for him.

"I'm so glad you're exactly who you say you are."

I stiffened in his arms. Did he know?

He worried that at any moment he'd lose what he had—his home, his job, his friends. I pulled away so I could see his face.

How could I tell him I wasn't who he thought I was? I touched his cheek. "You are not to blame for what your father did."

He laughed without any humor. "That's not how it felt back then. There was speculation and rumors. How could I not know? I lived with him."

"You were innocent. You have a right to be happy, to let people in, to trust they're not going to hurt you." *You were a child.* The words echoed my past. Was I too hard on myself?

Relief passed over his features, his shoulders lowered. "I want that with you."

"I do too." I swallowed down the truth, wanting to show him how I felt. It was imperative that he never forget my touch or the press of my lips on his.

I straddled his lap, cupping his face in my hands. Not able to say the words, I tried to convey them with my eyes. *I believe in you.* If I said them out loud the next three words would be, *I love you.* He wasn't ready. I said the only words that would penetrate. "I want you."

He gripped my hips, eyes flashing with need, want.

I wanted to give him this.

I rocked slowly over his hardening length, kissing his neck and the corner of his mouth. A brief brush of my lips on his, softer this time, more of a promise than a declaration. "I want you, Gray."

I wasn't walking away from him. I wasn't scared. I'd stand by his side like I hoped he'd stand by mine.

He stood, a guttural groan erupting from his lips as if he couldn't believe I was his. His arms banded around me, holding me tight, my legs wrapped around his waist. The pressure of his arms around me made me feel safe. Our mouths met, our tongues tangling as he purposely made his way to my room, lowering me to the bed, whispered promises falling in between kisses.

We ripped our clothes off one by one, never losing each other's lips for long. It was like we couldn't get enough of each other. We had to keep touching, kissing each other to maintain the connection we'd made on the couch when he'd confided in me, when he'd told me his deepest darkest secret.

I was important to this man. He needed me. I had to be the woman he deserved, honest and caring. I'd do anything to be worthy of him. Unfortunately, if I told him my truth he might not be so understanding. He might see me as a weak person, allowing myself to be pushed around by producers for ratings.

When there was finally nothing between us, he whispered against my lips, "Do we need protection?"

I pulled away slightly to see his expression. He trusted me. He wasn't just saying that, he meant it. "I'm on the pill. I'm clean."

"Me too. Are you okay going bare?"

"More than okay." I wanted to erase the secrets, take down the walls, unblock the barriers until there was nothing between us. Nothing that could break us apart. Not even rumors, history, gossip, or speculation. We knew what we had in each other. It was rare and difficult to find. I wouldn't let it go without a fight.

He slid inside with a roll of his hips. "Fuck. You feel so good."

I'd never been so in the moment, only aware of the slickness of his skin, the force of his thrusts, the tenderness of his lips, his touch.

I arched up to meet him thrust for thrust, opening myself to him in the only way I could. An orgasm flowed through me, the suddenness taking me by surprise. It was like a never-ending wave of sensation and emotion. The tears that pricked my eyes on the couch were back, threatening to spill over. I squeezed my eyes shut, willing him not to see.

He kissed each eyelid, the corners of my mouth, my neck. "I've never felt this way before."

His voice was full of wonder.

"Me either." Tears filled my vision.

"You're unforgettable." The words erupted from his mouth. He thrust one more time, deeper than before, shuddering his release, marking me as his.

He kissed me long, hard, and deep in an effort to stamp the words on my lips.

Words swirled in my head, not making full sentences or complete thoughts, words like love, need, want, forever, trust. Words I didn't deserve, words I didn't trust.

He kissed me once more before going to the bathroom, bringing back a warm washcloth.

My heart clenched hard as he carefully cleaned me before settling contentedly on my chest. He threw the washcloth on the floor before gently drawing me to him. H treated me like something, someone, to be treasured. I didn't deserve this. I didn't deserve him. Not when I hadn't been honest with him the way he had been with me.

"That was amazing."

By themselves, the words were cliché. Coupled with the emotion that heavily tinged his voice, the reverent swipe of his hand down my cheek, they were more potent than any drug.

"You're amazing." He punctuated each word with a kiss down my body, his hands cupping my ass as he settled between my legs.

He kissed each thigh, lifting his head to meet my gaze. "Let me love you."

The words hung in the air, before wrapping around us like a promise. "Yes."

He lowered his head, licking and sucking, the occasional scrape of his teeth unwinding the doubt and worries until nothing was left but us, his lips, and my need. By the time he used his finger to ease inside, I was desperate with raw need, fucking his finger and mouth, my thighs quivering. My fingers twisted in the sheets; my skin was slick with sweat.

"Gray, I need you."

My head turned from one side to the other. I ached with the desire to give my body over to the overwhelming sensation of another orgasm. It hovered on the horizon, just out of reach, threatening to be bigger than anything I'd ever experienced. When it finally crashed down like the waves on the shore, I jerked with the force of it, shuddering and moaning, my fingers seeking him. He kissed his way up my body.

He was worshiping me. There was no other way to describe it. As soon as I'd recovered from one orgasm, he'd build me up again.

There were no words to describe the feelings coursing through my body as he cradled my head in his hands, his cock nestled in my folds. I wanted this—him—all night long. I never wanted him to stop.

He rocked inside, every part of our body touching, connected.

He whispered sweet words against my lips, promises of forever. It was too good to be true, empty promises that would eventually evaporate like water in the desert.

The orgasm built inside, softer than before, settling over me slowly. He groaned his release into my neck.

We lay like that for a while, his arms wrapped around me, his finger tracing circles on my shoulder. I drifted off in a haze of contentment.

CHAPTER 17

Gray

Telling Elle about my past made me feel closer to her. Each confession, every revelation wove a pattern in our souls tying us to each other. Being with Elle was something I hadn't dared to hope for—acceptance and understanding—maybe even love.

The night I confessed my past to her, all night long, I'd reach for her, making love until we were spent. Exhausted, my muscles sore, I'd gone to work the next day with a smile on my face, excited for the future.

I wanted happiness with Elle. I took stock of my life as I met with patients, performed exams, and troubleshot problems. I wanted to offer her something that mattered. At the top of that list was a home, one I wouldn't want to lose. I wanted to take that leap—that risk—with her, knowing she'd catch me on the other side if something fell through.

I'd scoured real estate listings on my break to figure out what I liked. I was unsure whether that was a home in town, a farmhouse with a barn and acreage, or a house on the lake. What felt right? It was way too soon for these thoughts, but I wondered what Elle would like too.

I'd always wanted pets of my own, a dog, a cat, maybe even chickens, and a horse. I could envision raising children on a farm, teaching them about animals, gathering eggs every morning, riding a horse, and enjoying nature.

My goal moving here was to do whatever it took to get the clinic. Now, I wanted to do whatever I could to keep Elle, to make my life worth living again.

Taking that risk was worth it if it meant I could have what I'd experienced last night forever. I'd do anything to keep that feeling.

I'd called a realtor then the bank to start the approval process for a mortgage. I wanted something permanent in Telluride, where people supported and loved me. Where they wouldn't turn their back at the first sign of trouble. I'd been so afraid to reveal my past. When I had, Henry and Elle stood by me. I was no longer a scared kid who'd felt alone and betrayed. I was surrounded by people I could trust.

Contractors came in to give estimates on the

kennels. I heard back from a couple of vets about their mobile vet clinics. They were more than happy to pass on their information. I wrote up a proposal of what each would cost. The kennels wouldn't be too expensive. Plus, we could add boarding to our services, bringing in more than enough money to cover the cost. The vet clinic might take more time. It was significantly more expensive, and I wanted to use it to offer free services. I'd need to figure out a way to make it work. I sent my proposals to Ed, hoping he was still on board.

All week I was getting calls from rescues, asking if we had the additional space for them. I wanted to be able to say yes, and hopefully soon, I'd have an answer for them. I wanted to see my dreams, my plans, come to fruition. For the first time since my life imploded, I was in control. I wasn't hiding. I felt powerful as if anything was possible.

I thought I'd been in control before. I'd been hiding in plain sight, not letting anyone in. Not improving, not succeeding, just existing.

I spent evenings with Elle at her apartment, which was significantly more cheerful than mine, and the days finding ways to improve the clinic. I finally took what Ed had said all these years to heart. I tried being more sympathetic, more personable with the clients. It was difficult at first, but each day it got easier. I attributed the change to Elle. Her positive attitude and happiness naturally spilled over to every aspect of my life. I smiled easier. I was less grouchy, less likely to snap.

By the end of the week, Ed gave the go-ahead for the kennels. I immediately called the contractor with the best estimate, getting on his schedule.

On Saturday, I went to see houses while Elle worked, trying to figure out what appealed to me the most. I kept coming back to the idea of a farm. Open spaces, a home with a porch, a swing, a view of fields, a barn for animals, room to expand.

The next Thursday was Halloween. In the past, I usually stayed in with the lights off, pretending I wasn't home and avoiding the few kids that lived there.

This year, Elle planned to hand out candy at her shop. The thought of doing something on a holiday, greeting kids, was outside of my comfort zone. She suggested I participate as a way to prove to the towns-people I was interested in becoming one of them, part of the fabric of the town. I'd resisted Henry's suggestions to join him for town events in the past, never feeling a part of it the way he did having grown up here.

I opened the door to her shop in the charcoal suit we'd agreed upon. The shop was decorated with skele-tons, ghosts, and streamers. It looked amazing.

Piper sat in one of the stylist's chairs, leaning toward the mirror with a make-up wand of some sort while Henry sat next to her.

I was just about to greet them when heels sounded on the wooden steps. "Gray. You're here."

I turned my head to see Elle coming down from her apartment, stilettos marking her descent, emphasizing the curve of her hips. Her hair hung past her shoulders, sleek and straight, with none of her natural curl. She wore a tan blazer, a white button-down shirt with a press lanyard, and a narrow skirt hugging her curves.

My mouth was dry. She looked sexy. "Yeah. There weren't any emergency calls this afternoon."

She smiled wider as she approached me.

The beauty of her smile made me slightly dizzy. My heart thudded in my chest. The rest of the room, Henry, and Piper faded away until it was only Elle and me.

Stepping close, touching the lapels of my jacket, she tilted her head. "You look so handsome."

"You look—" there weren't words for how beautiful, hot, and gorgeous she looked. "Unbelievably sexy."

Her eyes held a naughty gleam. "Wait until later, I saved some candy for you."

"Oh, yeah?" My voice turned gravelly at the thought of bending her over a desk, playing out a naughty secretary scene with her in this outfit. I hoped she was referring to herself as candy, not Halloween. My dick swelled, confined by my stiff pants. I wished we were alone, that there wasn't candy to hand out or responsibilities.

Then her forehead wrinkled. "Where's your Superman shirt?"

This was why I hated Halloween. It wasn't the children running around asking for candy, it was having to wear a costume. It usually made me feel stupid, like I was a child playing a game. I wanted to impress Elle, make her happy. "It's under my shirt."

Her lips twisted into an adorable pout I wanted to kiss off her. "How will anyone know you're Superman?" She stepped back, gesturing at her hot as fuck outfit. "Without your costume, I look like a boring attorney, not Lois Lane."

"They made me wear a costume too. Yours isn't as bad as mine." Henry called over, reminding me we weren't alone, cooling my desire for a second.

Then Elle stepped closer, slowly unbuttoning my shirt. My cock twitched in my pants as my breath hitched. I wanted to grip her hips and pull her against my erection so she could feel how she affected me. Instead, I tried to take a few deep breaths, focusing on something unsexy like the dog I operated on this morning.

"What's your costume?" I tried to focus on Henry, glad my voice hadn't cracked.

Henry stood, pulling his sister to stand next to him, both in red and black outfits with fake guns on their hips. "We're Deadpool and Lady Deadpool."

Elle smiled. "I think you guys look great. I wish I

could have convinced this guy to wear a more adventurous costume."

Lowering my voice, I whispered in her ear. "You'll feel plenty adventurous when I get you alone tonight."

Elle shivered. "I can't wait."

Her hands settled on my chest, the warmth seeping through the Superman t-shirt before she pushed the button-down shirt open. "There. Perfect."

Logically, I knew she was referring to my costume, but I wanted to believe she'd meant I was perfect. I wasn't the tarnished kid whose dad was arrested in a federal raid. I was a man, one worthy of her attention, maybe even her love. "Thank you."

She smiled up at me, something simmering in her expression, awareness, desire, longing.

She probably wasn't aware I was thanking her for more than unbuttoning my shirt. I was thanking her for coming into my life, being there for me, supporting me, being someone I could count on, and more importantly, pushing me to be a better person.

Piper brushed past us, grabbing a cauldron overflowing with candy. "We'd better get out there. The kids will be coming by soon."

"I already set up a table and chairs." Henry followed Piper outside.

I lowered my head, dropping a chaste kiss on Elle's lips. "I can't wait to be alone."

Without waiting for a response, I grabbed the second cauldron of candy, pushing open the door to a gust of wind. Clouds drifted across the sky ominously, partially covering the almost full moon.

As soon as we were settled, the first family with what looked like three superheroes stopped by the table, saying, "Trick or Treat."

"Oh my gosh, what adorable costumes," Piper gushed. "Is your dog a taco?"

Behind them on a leash, was a bulldog in a taco costume.

The child nodded.

"How cute." Piper walked around the table to take a picture of their dog, petting him.

The mom asked me, "Aren't you the new vet?"

"I've been here four years now, but I guess I'm new compared to Ed." I smiled at her.

Her kids grabbed candy, arguing over which one was the best.

"Well, I think it's great to see you out." Then she turned her attention to her kids. "Did you say thank you?"

Elle nudged my shoulder with hers. "I told you coming out tonight was a good idea."

I felt like a teenager hanging out at a table at prom, but I had to admit she was right. Maybe if I made more of an effort, I wouldn't be the "new" vet anymore.

More families stopped by until the street, which had been blocked off, was crowded with people. I kept going into the shop to grab more bags of candy to refill the cauldrons.

By 8:00 p.m., the crowd had thinned. Elle and Piper started to clean up.

I was exhausted. I'd started the day early with surgeries. I was ready to have Elle all to myself.

After Henry helped me carry the table to the back storage room, Piper asked, "You want to head to the bar for a while?"

I was about to refuse when Elle squeezed my arm. "I'm really tired."

I got the impression she wanted to spend time with me too.

We said our goodbyes to Piper and Henry. I grabbed Crew to take him outside while Elle mentioned grabbing some snacks. "Don't change."

She raised a brow but didn't argue.

After a quick walk, where all I could think about was Elle in her Lois Lane outfit, I took the steps two at a time, pushing open the door. My pulse was already racing, my mind stripping Elle out of that skirt, slowly lowering it to the floor, revealing the black lace thong she liked to wear so much. The thought of that tiny scrap of lace between her ass cheeks preoccupied my mind, urging me on.

Elle stood by the counter dumping chips into a bowl. It was a purely domestic scene until she popped a chip in her mouth, licking her finger. Turning to find me standing in the doorway watching her, she slowly drew her finger out of her mouth with a soft popping sound.

Fuck. Thoughts of her dropping to her knees and sucking my cock overtook all reason. I unclipped Crew, hanging the leash by the door.

Then I stalked toward her, gripping her hips like I wanted to do when I first saw her earlier in the evening, pulling her back against my crotch. The scent of her citrus shampoo filled my nostrils, reminding me of her naked skin.

Elle turned her head slightly, looking up at me under her lashes. "Are you happy to see me, Clark?"

"I am. Very happy." I breathed into her neck, biting her sensitive skin lightly.

She gasped, arching her back, rubbing her ass against me. "You took long enough. I've been waiting for you."

My mind raced with possibilities. Elle bent over while I pounded into her, her sitting on the counter, legs spread while I feasted on her, her on her knees. "I want to fuck you right here."

"So do it." Her voice was breathy, her words an invitation I couldn't refuse.

My cock hardened. My hands drifted up her sides, cupping her breasts, weighing them in my hands. Her nipples were so hard I felt them through her clothes. The moment was surreal, making me dizzy with desire. How was I here with her when a few weeks ago I was perfectly content being alone?

I unzipped her skirt, tugging it down over her hips, groaning at the sight of the scrap of lace barely covering her center. I removed my clothes, toeing off my shoes, desperate to be inside her. She made quick work of her shirt. When she placed her hands on the counter, bending over, spreading her legs for me, all my blood shot straight to my cock.

I gripped myself with one hand, the other testing her thong. It was soaked. "You're so wet."

She looked over her bare shoulder, her eyes full of lust. "All for you."

Her words touched something deep inside me, something that had been buried under fear and shame. Elle was mine. It might not last, it might explode in my face, or it could be the greatest thing I ever experienced.

The feeling was heady. I slipped a finger under the lace, sliding through her folds, then slipping one finger inside her hot, wet heat. Growing thicker as she rode my fingers, I gripped my cock tighter, giving it a tug. When I added a second finger, she said, "I need you. Inside."

Her words were desperate, needy. When she caught sight of me working my cock, her eyes darkened. "Gray. Please."

"I'll give you anything you want." I nudged her feet farther apart before dipping my knees to slip inside. Once I was balls deep, her walls tightened around me; I pulled out to the tip, thrusting back inside her with more force than I'd ever used. Something about the costume, the position, and the feelings swirling around me, made me desperate for her.

Her tits bounced with each thrust, urging me to move harder, faster. I spread the globes of her ass so I could see where I entered her. Her slick heat surrounded me, sweat covered my skin, my muscles bunched tightly with restraint. I wanted this to last. Her moans urged me on, my thrusts long and hard.

I reached around, pressing on her clit, her pussy clenched, spasming around me. Her moans echoed off the walls. The sensations were too much. The tingle started at the base of my spine, flowing through my body, leaving me light-headed. I covered her back, kissing her lightly before pulling out. "Let me get a washcloth."

I washed up in her bathroom, wetting a washcloth to clean her. She turned to face me, her expression satisfied, yet something was churning under the surface. Her eyes looked uncertain as if she couldn't believe what we'd shared, that I was here.

"Are you okay?"

"Yeah, that was—"

"Hot?" I gave into my baser urges referring to it as a fantasy. The sexy librarian outfit was an excuse for all the untold emotions simmering under the surface of our skin.

Her determined eyes held mine. "It was more."

I wanted to shrug it off, but she was right. It was

more. I connected with her on a visceral level. I kissed her softly. "I felt it too."

She sighed, swaying into my body, her nipples grazing my chest. I sucked in a sharp breath. I'd never get enough of her.

"Are you hungry?" she asked, breaking the spell.

"I'm starved." I grabbed some chips from the bowl.

She smiled tentatively. "Thanks for coming tonight, for being a good sport."

"It wasn't that bad." There was something more vulnerable about standing in her kitchen naked and eating chips than the sex we'd shared.

"I think people were surprised to see you. It's good for them to see you participating in community events. It shows you want to be here, that you're happy. A man who wears a Superman costume, handing out candy to little kids is more approachable than one who hides in his apartment on Halloween."

That made me pause. Is that how people saw me? I sounded like a coward. That's how I'd been living my life, in fear of being found out, afraid to take risks.

"You're the best thing that's ever happened to me." The truth of those words rang between us, filling the space, making me shiver from the intensity.

She encouraged me to be the person I was underneath, the one I'd been hiding all this time. She helped me be the person I was meant to be.

CHAPTER 18

Elle

Finishing up with my client, I cleaned my tools and swept up the hair clippings. I'd been floating since last night. Each moment with him made me fall deeper and harder.

Alice emailed me a new contract for the proposed barbershop spin-off show. Emily upped the ante, offering more money than before. My past had been elevated to a ticking time bomb status. I had no plan for how or when to talk to Gray. Fear of rejection, of ruining the best thing that had ever happened to me kept me frozen. I wanted to enjoy what I had with him, not ruin it with the truth. I emailed Alice back telling her there was no amount of money I'd take to be on TV again.

In the afternoon, Emily called.

Adrenaline kicked in as I remembered how persuasive Emily could be. Back then, I was under contract. I had to do what she said. I was no longer that young girl who couldn't stand up for herself.

I went to my office for privacy, debating whether to ignore her call. I knew she would keep calling. She wouldn't let up. She might even come here. Then what would I do? The thought of her invading what had become my safe place left me feeling weak.

I wanted her to understand nothing she could offer would entice me to come back.

"Hello." I gripped the phone tightly.

"Giselle! Hi, how are you?" Her voice was infused with enthusiasm and warmth.

I cringed at the use of my given name. Her tone was something I'd gravitated toward as a lonely child. Now I saw it for what it was, an attempt to manipulate me.

"Emily. What can I do for you?" I purposely kept my tone professional. I didn't want her to act like we were friends because we weren't.

"Alice said she sent over the contract." Her tone was incredulous. She probably wasn't used to chasing people down after sending them contracts.

Anger boiled that she'd use my sister to get me back. Emily knew how protective I was of her. "She did."

"This is an amazing opportunity. It could really solidify your career as an actress and a hairstylist." Emily was in full producer mode, spinning how amazing the opportunity was for me when in reality, she was just trying to keep her job.

Frustration with the situation bubbled over. "I don't want to solidify my career as an actress. You and I both know no one considers reality stars actresses."

Emily laughed lightly. "There are plenty of stories of reality stars who've gone on to be successful. A few have had amazing acting careers."

She was right. It was possible, but the ones who went on to be actors didn't keep doing reality shows. They quickly cut ties with the original show, only taking serious acting offers. "It's irrelevant because I don't want to be an actress."

I'd always been afraid to tell Emily the truth. I didn't want that world. When I was in it, it was all any of us were supposed to want. Now, I wasn't sure if that was ever true or if you just got caught up in it with no way to escape.

"What about your barbershop idea? You can't buy exposure like we want to give you." Her tone was incredulous.

"I don't want that kind of exposure anymore. My shop is doing great." Panic filled me that she would show up here with cameras in tow. It wouldn't be positive exposure. It would look like I craved attention, that I wanted Telluride to be on a cheap reality show. It wouldn't endear me to the locals. I couldn't even imagine how Gray would take it.

Emily paused for a few seconds. "Alice said you're in Telluride? That's hardly LA."

"I don't want to waste your time. I'm not moving back to LA; there's no chance I'm signing another reality show contract. I'm done."

"It's so hard to get there, too." Her voice trailed off. I hoped she wasn't thinking of a plan to travel here, or a way to convince me to change my mind.

Telluride was difficult to get to. That fact solidified the cozy, protective feeling I got coming here. She was about to invade my space, destroying everything I'd built. I couldn't let her do that.

"After everything we've been through?"

Anger surged through me, hot and thick like lava boiling out of a volcano, melting everything in its path, changing the terrain permanently. "*We* haven't been through anything. I was practically raised by the producers on that show. It wasn't a good experience. It ruined my reputation."

She scoffed. "We made you famous."

"*In*famous. People think I'm that person on the show, a bitch with no morals," I said without missing a beat, letting the truth fall out of me, making me feel stronger.

"Who cares what people think if you're making tons of money and people want to be you?"

I could almost see Emily rolling her eyes, waving a

hand at me as she had in person when we'd had difficult conversations.

"No one wants to be me. They are fascinated by the hurtful things I did. You may have been able to manipulate me when I was younger, but not anymore. I'm not your puppet. You can't pull my strings, dangling money and fame in front of me. It won't work." I wanted to tell her to stay away from Alice too, but she was an adult. She had to make her own decisions, living with them like I had.

"You're making a huge mistake." Emily's voice was hard. She rarely moved from persuasion to anger. It usually wasn't necessary.

"That's what you think. I think it's the best decision I've ever made. I'm finally happy with who I am." My tone lightened. I was finally doing what I wanted. I'd never go back.

"I'll give you a few days to reconsider." Her words rang in my ears.

"I'm not going to change my mind. Bye, Emily." I hung up. Worry that she wasn't done with me, that she'd show up here, settled like a knot in my stomach, squeezing tighter and tighter. Was it too much to hope I'd never hear from her again? That I could start over here?

With Emily contacting me, I needed to talk to Gray sooner rather than later.

That part of my life felt so long ago like it happened to another person. I couldn't imagine meshing that part of myself with who I was now. I knew as soon as I told him about it, that part of my life would become part of me again. I wouldn't be Elle; I'd go back to being Giselle.

I'd seen the comments when the show was canceled. There was speculation that we'd never find a job acting. We'd live off our parents' money, become addicts, get arrested, have a mental breakdown. People wanted us to fail. When I was Giselle, I felt like I was doomed to screw up, to live up to their low expectations.

Initially, there was speculation about what I was doing, why I hadn't signed on to do another show. For the most part, it had died down. It was easier to fade into the background with the show off the air. That's where I wanted to stay. I didn't want to acknowledge that part of my life. I wanted to pretend like it never happened.

The more time I spent with Gray, the more I worried he wouldn't accept that I'd played a role or the fact that part of my life was over. I wanted him to support me the same way I did him, but our situations were different. He was innocent, swept up in the drama of his dad's mistakes. I'd made a decision to be on a show, playing a villain, doing it for years. I needed to tell Gray and face the consequences because each day, I was falling in deeper with him. The problem was, I had no plan for how to do that.

* * *

FRIDAY EVENING WAS my daddy-daughter event. I decorated the shop for the event, adding streamers and balloons, covering some of the *boys only* and *caveman* signs with colorful fabric. I felt jittery with nerves, more amped up than opening day.

"Relax, it's going to be great," Piper said as I checked again to make sure I hadn't forgotten anything.

Snacks from Baked in Telluride were arranged on a table in the back. The bags we'd prepared for the girls were lined up on a table by the door. Each bag had Smoke & Mirrors printed on it, the handles tied together with a pink ribbon. Inside the bags were instructions for the styles we were teaching, various hair ties, bobby pins, barrettes, ribbons, a hairbrush, and a hand mirror. I'd gone a little overboard, wanting the night to be a success, hoping the dads would come again or tell their friends.

I smoothed my hands over my black pants. "I hope so."

When the families started arriving, the dads looked nervous while the girls were excited. I relaxed when I saw the girls' enthusiasm, asking each child how she liked her hair styled. I planned to show the dads a few braids and twists. I wanted each girl to go home with something custom, whether it was a special barrette or ribbon in her hair.

I got each family settled in a chair, going over a

style with the group, then making my way around the room to assist. Even though Piper was here with me, it wasn't enough. We needed more staff in the future. The guys needed a lot of assistance. Once they got the first style done, we started on the next one. By the end, each child's hair had a braid, a twist, or a bun.

The success of the evening gave me more energy.

We gave them time to eat some of the food and ask questions. The tension from the stress of the evening was just leaving my shoulders when one of the little girls ran up to me, her dark hair wrapped in tightly woven braids. "Miss Ellie?"

I crouched down on her level, my lips tipping up in a smile. "It's Elle."

"Miss Elle, thank you so much for helping my dad."

It was a simple thing, yet I was overcome with emotion. "You're welcome, sweetie."

"I can have braids like all the other girls at school do."

I squeezed her hand.

Her dad stood behind her, holding a younger girl who'd wanted her hair twisted into curls. "I'm a single dad, so it's difficult. I'm so grateful you offered this. It's been a fun evening for the girls. Hopefully, I can replicate it."

"If you have trouble, come on in. We can help you." The idea of this dad wanting to be able to style his daughters' hair was so endearing.

"Thank you so much." He gave me another grateful smile before taking the older girl's hand to walk out.

I talked to each dad as they left. Each one was grateful and hopeful they could competently take care of their daughter's hair. One said he was happy to be able to do a simple bun for ballet classes. One said he hoped to impress his wife. It was more than I could have hoped for when I initially planned the event.

When Piper closed the door after the last family left, I pressed a hand to my chest. "That was—so much more than I was expecting."

Piper nodded, smiling. "It was fun. Meeting single dads wasn't a hardship."

"Hey, no hitting on the clientele."

"There's something about a man taking care of his children. So hot." Piper bustled about cleaning up the trash.

I had to agree. "I think I underestimated how much dads want to help their daughters."

"It was fun. We should do it again. We can probably expect some new dads to come, maybe some follow-ups to perfect their technique or learn new things. Even the girls loved being pampered."

"Maybe we could offer birthday parties." I was brimming with ideas lately.

"Look at you, already planning our next event."

It felt good, too. It wasn't free vaccines like Gray was providing. Even so, I finally felt like I was doing something good with my life.

We cleaned up, taking down the decorations so the shop was back to being a boys-only man cave for the next day. All the pink, glitter, and hair ties were removed. It was an amazing event, but my bread and butter were men. They didn't want to be covered in glitter when they sat down.

"I'm going to get going. I'll be working late tomorrow." Piper gathered her things.

I smiled. "Thank you so much for helping tonight."

"It's my job."

"It's more than a job. I hope you consider me a friend." I hugged her, a little surprised by my own overt display of affection.

"Of course, I do." Her tone was slightly admonishing.

She had no idea friends in my past were untrustworthy.

The bell tinkled above the door.

"Is it over?" Gray held a bouquet, looking around as if he expected a child to pop out.

"All done. You should be proud of Elle. She was amazing tonight." Piper touched his arm before sidling past him to leave.

Gray's gaze stayed on me.

"Are those for me?" I walked up to him, warmth blooming in my chest.

He held the flowers out to me.

I took them, burying my face in the blooms. "They smell amazing."

"You're amazing." His eyes were filled with pride.

He wrapped an arm around my shoulders, pulling me close. No one had ever given me flowers before.

"It went well?"

"It went better than expected. The girls loved it, and the men were happy to learn something so they could help their daughters."

He kissed me then let me go while I locked up, turning off the lights so we could head upstairs.

"I told you, you were worried for nothing."

I unlocked the door to the apartment, stepping inside. "I've never tried to do something like this. I had no idea what to expect. I have a few other things I want to talk about with the person in charge of town events."

"Like what?" he asked, grabbing waters out of the fridge for us.

I grabbed a decorative vase from under the sink, filling it with water for the flowers. "I know the town does trick-or-treating at the shops, but I was thinking about a stroll around town for customers to sample hot cocoa and cookies while browsing the wares from each store. The shop owners could hand out food and drink for free or samples of their products. Maybe around the holidays?"

I'd been thinking about handing out goodie bags with fliers for upcoming tutorials like the one I had tonight as well as coupons for free and discounted haircuts.

"I think that would be something people would come to," Gray said thoughtfully.

"I hope so." I arranged the blooms in the vase, wondering if I should talk to him now about my past or enjoy tonight's success.

He wrapped an arm around my shoulder, pulling me into him. "I'm so proud of you."

"Thank you." I enjoyed his praise but holding my past from him kept me from enjoying it completely.

He lifted my chin with his finger, kissing me sweetly.

I had to tell him.

Gray pulled back slightly, his finger still pressed lightly under my chin. "What do you say we celebrate in the bedroom?"

I wouldn't ruin this moment by bringing up the past. "I'd love to."

His eyes heated. He picked me up and carried me across the threshold like I was his bride. When we reached my room, he placed my feet lightly on the ground, his arm wrapped around my waist, holding me pressed against him. He stared into my eyes for a few seconds, something I was afraid to acknowledge brimming in them; then he kissed me like it was the first time, as if he were asking permission for more.

I wanted to give him everything he ever wanted. My fingers tangled in the hair on his neck as we kissed, enjoying the moment. There was no need to rush. We had all night.

We lingered over removing each other's clothes, kissing the spots we unveiled, savoring each other's touch. It was like we were saying we appreciated each other, loved one another, even if no words were exchanged.

I slowly sank to my knees, looking up at him.

His hand rested in my hair, a question in his eyes.

He was telling me I didn't have to, even though I wanted to. I wanted to give him everything. I wanted to show him what he meant to me.

I gripped the base of his cock, pumping him once, twice, while I watched his eyelids flutter, his head tilting back in ecstasy when I sucked him into my mouth. A heady feeling of power I'd never gotten while doing this before, flowed through me. A blow job was expected with the other guys I'd been with. This was a gift I was giving him.

I increased the pressure, my rhythm, the suction of my mouth until he finally groaned in frustration, hauling me up to sit on the edge of the bed. I wanted to make him feel good. At the same time, I wanted him inside me.

"Lay back."

I spread my legs, my knees falling open, the cool air on my pussy.

He knelt between my hips, blowing on my clit, my legs trembling with desire. "You're so fucking beautiful."

The truth of his words was evident in his tone. "Thank you."

"I'm going to drive you crazy. The same way you did to me." His voice was a low growl, determined.

"I look forward to it." I grabbed onto the comforter, bracing myself.

He squeezed my ass, bringing me to his mouth. He knew what I liked. He quickly built me up, driving me to the brink, pulling away before I went over.

When he lifted his head, I scrambled up the bed, eager for him.

"Knees," he said.

I slowly turned to my hands and knees, feeling a little vulnerable not being able to see his face, my ass in the air. That night in the kitchen didn't seem quite as intimate when we were playing the role of Clark Kent and Lois Lane.

He pressed lightly on my upper back as if he wanted me to drop down to my forearms. I resisted the pressure until he draped himself over my back, making me not feel so alone or distant from him. He kissed my shoulder, whispering in my ear. "Do you trust me?"

"Yes." Tenderness washed over me.

"If you drop down to your forearms, it will feel even better." His tone was rough as if he were holding himself back. His need for me had me slowly lowering myself.

"Okay." I felt more open to him than I'd ever been.

He sat up on his knees. His fingers parted my folds,

stroking me before slipping inside, quickly bringing me back to that edge he'd left me on earlier. When I was riding his fingers with wanton abandon, he removed his fingers, replacing them with his cock. I whimpered at the sensation of him filling me up, his fingers gripping my hips. He was deeper than any other position, his balls slapping against my ass with each thrust. Each thrust touched a spot inside of me, an intense burning building to something huge. I didn't want to stop. I could feel something building inside, threatening to explode, to burst my preconceived notions of what things could be like with Gray.

He let go of my hips, reaching around to cup my breasts, tweaking my nipples, the sensation shooting directly to my core. One hand drifted down my stomach, circling my clit, pressing hard.

I went over the edge, free-falling, hoping he'd catch me. My pussy clenched around him; tremors shook me. He lightly bit my shoulder as he continued to thrust before finally emptying himself inside of me.

"Don't move. I'll clean you." He slapped my ass lightly before moving off the bed.

I lowered myself to the comforter, not planning on moving anytime soon. He made me feel so good, loved, cared for. Guilt seeped in that I was hiding something from him.

He placed one knee on the bed, washing me with the warm cloth, throwing it in the direction of my hamper. He rolled me so I was flat on my back. He'd propped himself on his elbow, looking down at me, his hand resting possessively on my hip.

His expression was full of awe. "I love you, Elle. I never thought it was possible to love someone, to trust someone again, but I do."

A lightness spread through my body, making me feel dizzy. No man had ever said those words to me. Coming from Gray, a man who didn't trust easily, it meant even more. "I love you too."

It felt good to finally say the words. I'd been thinking them for a while. I'd wanted to wait until I was sure of his feelings. I'd wanted to wait until I told him everything about me, but would he even feel the same way about me after I did?

"You make me happy." His fingers traced circles on my hip.

"I am too." That was the indescribable feeling swirling in my gut, filling the hollow of my chest cavity. Working on the show had been toxic, the people surrounding me tearing me down instead of lifting me up.

This thing with Gray was the opposite. It was better than I'd imagined. I never wanted it to end.

CHAPTER 19

Gray

I was flying high on this thing with Elle, yet there was a feeling hovering on the edges of my peripheral, a sense of impending doom. Elle was the best thing that ever happened to me, and good things never lasted.

Stepping into Elle's shower while she walked Crew before work, I tried to focus on the things I could control. Those things seemed few and far between. I might not get the clinic. I might not get the house I wanted. Elle might not be perfect for me. Anytime I went down the spiral of my past, I tried to rein it in. Nothing bad had happened since I was eighteen. The little voice in my head whispered, *"That's because you haven't taken any risks. You haven't had anything worth losing."*

A chill ran down my spine despite the warmth of the water and the smell of Elle's citrus body wash. I had to believe better things came from putting yourself out there and taking risks, than hiding in my cold, sterile apartment until a contract for the clinic rested in my hands. I couldn't keep waiting for life to start when it was in front of me, waiting for my next move.

Stepping out of the shower, I quickly toweled off. A few clients were due in clinic this morning before I could see some properties. I'd narrowed my wish list down to farms, and I was excited to see what the realtor found for me.

I wished Elle could join me, but she had appointments this morning.

Dressing quickly, I texted Henry, asking if he'd come with me to give his opinion. He'd grown up on a farm. He might notice things I didn't. He was quick to respond with a *hell yes*.

I was cautiously optimistic that one of the properties I saw today could be my future home. Maybe even the home I shared with Elle. I loved that she lived above her shop. Her commute was convenient, but it didn't stop me from hoping she'd call my new home hers one day.

The things that mattered to me were increasing, making me feel like nothing or everything could go wrong.

I jogged lightly down the steps, excited to see Elle before I headed out. Alone in the shop, the smell of freshly brewed coffee permeated the air. She sat on the stool by her computer at the front counter, Crew sleeping at her feet.

I slipped my arms around her middle, resting my chin on her shoulder. "Hey, you."

She smiled, turning her head to kiss my lips briefly. "Are you going to look at properties today?"

Straightening to my full height, my hands on her waist, I said, "I wish you could come."

"Me too." She turned on the stool, spreading her knees to accommodate me, her arms wrapped loosely around my waist.

"I invited Henry to come. We might get a drink after."

She looked up at me. "I can't wait to see what you choose."

I should tell her what I was thinking, how important her opinion was. My heart rate picked up. "I want you to see it before I make a decision."

She tilted her head, considering me. "Yeah?"

"I want you to like it too." I couldn't say I wished she'd share the home with me one day. It was too soon, despite our declarations of love last night.

"That's—"

The bell above the door sounded. A blonde woman stepped in, younger than Elle by a few years, with different color hair, but the resemblance was uncanny. They could be sisters.

"Alice, what are you doing here?" Elle tilted her head slightly.

I loosened my hold on her, giving her space.

Alice's nose wrinkled. "What? I can't visit my big sister?"

I stepped back so Elle could slide off the stool. She moved slowly around the counter, pulling Alice into a hug. "Of course, I'm happy to see you. I wasn't expecting you, that's all."

Crew moved to stand next to Elle, his tail wagging while he waited for Alice to notice him.

Elle stepped back from Alice, her shoulders tense, her back stiff.

It made me think there was more going on here than just a sisterly visit. Why hadn't Alice called before coming?

"I came to see what was so great about this town that you won't leave."

The tension in the room was palpable. I didn't remember Elle saying her relationship with her sister was contentious.

I stepped closer, placing a hand on Elle's lower back to make a statement. "Hi. I'm Gray."

Alice's eyes flickered to me. Her eyes widened. "Is this the reason you don't want to come back? You're—"

I didn't know what Alice intended to say because Elle cut her off.

"I'm glad you're here, but I'm working today. I won't have time to show you around. I can let you into my apartment." Elle gestured upstairs.

I didn't like the idea of Alice taking my time with Elle, but I couldn't interfere because she was her sister.

Alice waved her off. "I can show myself around. I'll check out that cute trailer that sold coffee I saw on the way in. What was it called?"

"The Coffee Cowboy," I offered. Something about this woman set me on edge. Maybe it was the calculated look in her eyes as her gaze flicked from Elle to me or the flashy way she dressed. A revealing tank, jeans so tight they were practically painted on, sky-high heels, and oversized sunglasses were perched on her head. This woman looked like a California girl.

Alice pointed at me. "That's the one."

I wasn't sure whether I should stay or go. Glancing at my phone, I saw my first appointment would be in the clinic soon. "I have to run. It was nice meeting you, Alice. I hope I can spend some time with you while you're here."

I touched Elle's elbow, guiding her to the door. I wanted to ask what she was doing here, but not with Alice watching our exchange. Pausing to face her, I said, "I have to go. I'll see you later?"

I didn't want to sound so needy, so vulnerable.

Elle bit her lip. "I'm not sure what Alice has planned or why she's here. I'll text you later, okay?"

She finally glanced up at me, uncertainty swirling in her eyes.

I wanted to give her whatever she needed.

"Sure." I kissed her lightly on the lips before I walked out the door.

The impending doom I'd been worried about just showed up in the form of Alice.

I couldn't shake the bad feeling all morning. By the time I met Henry at the first property, I wanted to cancel the showings, and head to the shop to make sure Elle was okay. I wanted to reassure myself that nothing had changed between us.

My phone dinged with a notification when I turned down the lane. Parking, I pulled out my phone, my heart rate picking up when I saw the headline: *Dean Stanton up for Parole After Serving Twelve Years in Prison for Money Laundering.* When I'd set the alert on my phone, I thought I'd want to know. Now, I wasn't so sure. My skin prickled; the hair on my neck stood up. I closed the notification, not wanting to read the full article. Why now? I was finally starting to live life again. He was going to come crashing into my life, dragging up the past, ruining my future.

It might be headline news again. There might be speculation as to what happened to his family. Ed might find out. I might lose the clinic, Elle, everything. I tried to push it out of my mind, into a box I could open later when I was alone and able to decipher the possible ramifications.

I rounded the hood of my car, my stomach in knots as I greeted Henry with a curt nod.

He leaned against the driver's side door of his truck with his brow raised. "What's up with you?"

I sighed, looking at the property we were here to see, not really seeing it. I wasn't ready to talk about my father, even if Henry knew the story. "Elle's sister is in town."

"Yeah?"

I looked from the house to Henry. "I have a bad feeling about it."

"Why?" His voice was incredulous.

"She doesn't talk about her family much. I'm sure it's nothing." Except it didn't feel like nothing. Between Alice's arrival and my father's pending parole hearing, it felt like a volcano getting ready to erupt. I had a feeling it would destroy everything in its path, leaving nothing behind to rebuild.

My realtor, Allen Grim, pulled up in a black Audi. He climbed out. "You ready to look at some houses?"

Henry nodded. "We are."

I fell in step next to him, trying to focus on the reason we were here, to find a home. A place to live and grow, maybe raise a family. I tried to ignore the worries, the doubts, the thought that Elle might decide she didn't like it here. I wasn't enough to make her want to stay.

The first house was in poor shape, with only two bedrooms and one bath. It needed an addition and renovations. It was a bigger job than I wanted to take on. The second property had a pond. It was pretty. I wasn't sure about the safety of having a pond on the property if I wanted kids someday. Now that I'd been honest with Elle, it felt like anything was possible.

After the third showing, Allen said, "You don't seem interested in anything we saw today."

I tried to refocus on the homes we saw, thinking objectively about them.

Henry rubbed his chin. "This one would be good for you. Enough property for some animals, but not too much you'd need someone to help you with the land."

"Yeah, the house is in good shape." Whoever had inherited the property had done some nice upgrades for resale. This was the house I would consider if I weren't so concerned about what Alice's arrival meant.

"Think about it. Let me know if you'd like to see anything a second time. I'll email you any listings I find that meet your criteria." Allen nodded at me, then said to Henry, "It was nice meeting you."

"You too." When Allen got in his SUV to leave, Henry continued, "Is it Elle?"

"I'm not sure what her sister coming into town unannounced means."

"It might not mean anything, but it's a small town. We'll find out soon enough."

My stomach churned with uncertainty and dread at the thought it was happening all over again. This time would be worse than the last. I wouldn't be able to move across the country to reinvent myself. I'd chosen to stay here. Telluride was my home. I wasn't sure if Elle felt the same.

"You need to consider this one." Henry tilted his head to the property we'd just seen.

This house was perfect. The quintessential farmhouse with a wraparound porch, new siding and roof, even a tire swing hung from the large tree in the front yard. A newer stable had been built next to the original barn. There was plenty of room for animals. Inside, the kitchen and bathrooms had been renovated. The five bedrooms had been changed to make it three with one large master suite. It was move-in ready, with a higher price tag to match. I could see Elle and I sitting on the porch, planning our future.

"It's an option."

"A good one. Don't wait too long."

He turned to his car, dropping his hand on my shoulder. "You need to stop worrying about Elle. If it's meant to be, she'll stay. Her sister won't be able to convince her to leave. If she goes, she's not the woman for you."

My stomach dropped at the thought of trusting her not to change her mind. "Alice asked if I was the reason Elle was staying here. It made me think she wasn't happy about it."

"You can't ignore your intuition if something doesn't feel right. Although, it might not be what you're thinking. Maybe Elle and her sister just don't get along."

I sighed, letting the breath out slowly. "You're right. It could be nothing."

"Want to grab dinner?"

"Sure." The alternative was going home to brood about what Alice's arrival meant for me, if dad's parole hearing would make national news, or if my life was about to implode.

We climbed into our respective vehicles, heading into town. I'd moved away from home twelve years ago, always expecting my past to come back to haunt me. The irony was it didn't happen until I finally believed I could move past it.

CHAPTER 20

Elle

*A*ll day, there was a buzzing in my ears. I smiled. I tried to focus on conversations with my clients. It took everything in me not to find Alice and tell her not to reveal my past to anyone. She'd left right after Gray because my first client for the day walked in.

Why was she here? Why had she come unannounced? Especially after she'd said she had no interest in visiting.

She wanted something. There was no other explanation. The only thing I had that she wanted was notoriety, and the ability to get the producers to film another show.

What would she do to get what she wanted? Would she tell everyone in town who I was, destroying my reputation, possibly my business? Would she make it so I had no choice but to return home? I couldn't imagine leaving Telluride. It had become a safe haven for me. I hated that Alice was bringing my old life here.

I was walking on a tight rope, waiting for an explosion to go off. At any second, my whole world could implode. Everything I'd worked so hard for would disappear.

I wanted to go back to this morning, lying in bed with Gray, enjoying the safety of his arms around me. I'd never felt more content. It was all because of him and this town. I belonged here. It wasn't a passing feeling or sentiment. I felt it down to my bones.

I'd do anything to get Alice to keep her mouth shut. She had learned one thing from the show: you capitalize on other people's weaknesses to get what you want. I needed to pretend her visit didn't affect me. That I wasn't ashamed of my past.

My back ached with the weight of stress. Alice stayed out all day, not returning for lunch, to chat, or to hide out in my apartment.

I should have asked if she was here with anyone, and how long she intended to stay. I was so shocked at her arrival I couldn't process anything but that I hadn't spoken to Gray about my past. He had no idea. My fingers shook with the need to talk to him before she did.

I texted him before closing.

Elle: Can you meet up tonight?

Gray: I'm at the bar with Henry. Stop by after work.

Was Alice at the bar? Would she say anything to Gray? Fear slid cold as ice down my spine. I was off-kilter, like when I was filming—my future being determined by producers, ratings, and the other castmates. My old life clashed with my new one. I mistakenly thought I could separate the old Elle from the new, but it wasn't possible.

I shut the door after my last client, changing the sign from open to closed. Stress made my body feel energized yet at the same time exhausted. I cleaned up in record time, taking Crew for a quick walk. I felt bad for leaving him after being at work all day. I had to get to Gray before Alice did. I needed to control an uncontrollable situation, stop the train before it ran over unsuspecting pedestrians playing on the track.

I fed Crew, patting him on the head before leaving. Locking up, I walked to the bar, dread increasing with each step. Opening the heavy wooden door, I squinted, adjusting from the bright sun to the dimness of the bar, searching for Gray. Adrenaline coursed through my body leaving me shaky. I felt desperate to find him. My heart dropped when I saw him at a high-top table with Henry and Alice.

I made my way to him, searching for any sign she'd told him about my past. When our eyes met, he smiled, happy to see me. I took a deep breath trying to steady myself. I still had time.

He stood when I approached, pulling me in for a hug. I savored the feeling of his arms around me, wondering if it was the last time.

I leaned back to get a better look at him. "How were the showings?"

"Good. We found one that might be an option." He exchanged a look with Henry I couldn't decipher.

He didn't seem as happy as I thought he'd be.

"That's good." I sat next to him, smiling at Henry who sat across from Gray. I hesitantly asked Alice, "What have you been up to?"

"I toured the town. It didn't take long." She rolled her eyes. She didn't like Telluride. Her reaction, although predictable, annoyed me. The question, *why was she here*, skirted along my skin like a bug.

Alice shrugged, a conniving smile crossing her face. "I ran into your boyfriend and his friend. I thought I'd be friendly."

The pit in my stomach grew bigger. Alice being in town could only mean one thing, my past was about to crash into my present in the worst way possible. I couldn't ask her why she was here in front of the guys. That opened me up for her to say everything I feared. I went for the easier question. "How long are you staying?"

Alice dipped her head at me. "That's up to you. I came back to convince you to come home."

I shook my head, trying to clear the panic that made it difficult to form coherent thoughts. "Los Angeles was never my home." Huntington Beach was our hometown; Telluride is my future.

I was afraid to look at Gray, worried he could pick up on the tension between us. I sensed Henry giving Gray a worried look.

Alice was quiet, considering me.

I wanted her to let it go, to say she was here to see me.

Henry's finger traced the edge of his glass as he looked from me to Gray, one brow raised.

"If you came here to convince me otherwise, you're wasting your time." My teeth ground painfully together.

Alice studied me before flicking her gaze to Gray. "Is *he* the reason you want to stay?"

"He's one of them. Even before we met, I planned to stay. I opened a business that's finally gaining ground. I'm happy here. I like the community and the people." I couldn't go back to Los Angeles, not when I felt like a carefully wrapped package on a conveyor belt, going around in circles while someone else pushed the control buttons.

Alice shook her head in disgust. "Does he know

everything you gave up to be here?"

Childishly, I wanted to slap my hand over her mouth to stop the words from leaving her mouth. Instead, I used my eyes to plead with her, to will her to stop talking.

She had all the power.

I resisted the urge to place a hand on Gray's forearm, asking him if we could go somewhere quiet to talk.

It was too late. The anticipated crash of my past and present raised every hair on my arms and neck, sending cool chills down my spine.

"What did you give up coming here?" Gray tipped his beer to his mouth, his body deceptively calm.

Everything hinged on my answer.

"Nothing. I gave up nothing. I came here looking for a fresh start. It's exactly what I got." I gave Alice one last warning look before turning to Gray, hoping he'd listen.

"You don't want to be with your family?" Henry asked.

"I miss them, but this is my home." To Alice, I said, "You're welcome to visit anytime. Please stop begging me to go back. I'm happy here."

I sensed Gray's shoulders lowering, his fingers relaxing from a fist.

Alice slapped a hand on the table, making everyone jump, her voice rose with each word. "How can you walk away from the show, the contract, the money?"

My face burned hot; my fingers twisted together in my lap. The buzzing in my ears increased to a feverish pitch. "Alice, this is not the time nor place."

"What's she talking about? What show?" Gray shifted slightly to face me. His words were cold, hard.

I wanted to say nothing, but she'd already said too much. I'd have to tell him the truth I'd been avoiding.

I closed my eyes briefly, shoring up my courage to reveal my greatest shame, knowing this would change everything, the way he looked at me, his feelings for me. I opened my eyes, keeping them trained on Alice, daring her to disagree with me. "When I was sixteen, producers with cameramen showed up at our school. They got permission from our parents and the school to interview us for a reality show. I was young and stupid. I didn't realize what happened on that show would be memorialized forever."

I was stating facts because Alice and Henry were present when what I wanted to do was explain the impact of that show on my life, the lonely nights, the stomach pains after the producer pushed me to do something I wasn't comfortable with, and the shame after I gave in.

"What show?" Henry shifted in his chair to get closer.

Alice smiled smugly. "Huntington Beach, then later, it was Hollywood Hills."

"Never heard of it." Henry's eyes darted from me to Alice.

I shrugged as if it didn't matter when it was the single, most impactful event in my young life. "They were scripted, sold as reality. Mainly teenagers and twenty-something women watched them. It was trash."

My words were calm, confident. My heart beat loudly, competing with the buzzing in my ears; sweat trickled down my back.

Gray held up a finger. "Wait. You're saying you were on a reality show where cameras followed you around?"

I couldn't tell from his expression what he was thinking. I wanted to touch him but my past was between us. "I thought it would be fun. They told us we'd be actresses."

"It was a reality show," Gray said carefully as if he was trying to work out what I was saying in his head.

"Right. But they told us what to say, who to date, what silly pranks to pull. A producer was by my side telling me everything I needed to do to get ratings. I didn't realize until it was too late that viewers thought it was real when it wasn't."

Honesty was the only choice at this moment. Baring my soul, hoping he'd give me a chance to explain. "I was ashamed of what I'd done. It wasn't me. The second show followed us as we tried to go to school, get jobs, and essentially, become adults. That's when I realized the impact of the first show. Clients would approach me at the salon I worked at, calling me names."

A cheater, a homewrecker, a slut, an attention whore.

I hoped Gray saw it. The unusual situation I was in, how lost I must have felt.

"Do you think we could go somewhere to talk about this?" I felt like I was sitting on quicksand, the situation quickly spiraling out of control, my feet sinking deeper into the muck, so deep, I'd never get out.

I placed a hand on his forearm, willing him to look at me, to tell me everything was going to be okay. Instead, his eyes were on the table, the muscles under my fingers tensed.

"Oh, come on. It was an amazing opportunity. Your name in the gossip magazines, paparazzi following your every move, VIP passes to all the hot clubs, designer clothes to wear." Alice's voice grated on my nerves.

"That wasn't a good thing, Alice. It was horrible."

Henry was on his phone, probably scrolling for any information he could find. I wanted to beg him not to read the articles, to give me a chance to explain.

I was torn between defending myself and giving into the sinking feeling in my stomach. An awful realization stole over me. I didn't deserve Gray or this life. I never did. My life changed when my parents approved of me signing the contract. I couldn't go back in time to make a different decision. I had to live with my choices.

"I don't want to do another show. It's not me. That

life is toxic. I want my barbershop to be a success; I want to make a home in Telluride." *I wanted a life with Gray.*

"I like not having cameras follow me around. I'm free to make my own decisions, my own choices. No one here knows." That was going to change. People would look at me differently, talk behind my back, wonder if the articles were true. I'd lose clients. People might confront me on the streets about my behavior on the show. The thought made me feel sick.

"They're going to find out." Henry shot Gray a pointed look.

"You're making a huge mistake." The disgust in Alice's voice was evident. "Have you even looked at the contract? They're offering you a ton of money."

"Do you want the money and the fame? I've tried to protect you from that lifestyle. Maybe that was my mistake. You only saw the good, not the bad." I felt defeated. I'd failed her as much as my parents had me.

Alice's face was incredulous. "You were famous. You had money, designer clothes, guys throwing themselves at you."

My face heated. "Those things are empty. The guys always want something, the girls aren't your friends. They want the fame and money for themselves."

Alice liked those things. She wanted them. Nothing I said dissuaded her.

"You're famous," Gray said, eyes cold, unseeing.

Henry turned his phone so Gray could read the

headlines: *Huntington Beach's Favorite Reality Star Villain Moves to LA.* The first line of the article read, *Cameras will follow the stars...*

Gray grabbed Henry's phone scrolling through the article. I wanted to beg him not to read it, to listen to me. It was no use. It was too much to expect the man who said he loved me last night would believe me over whatever was printed in that article. Why had I expected anything else?

Gray ran his fingers through his hair.

"Please, can we talk about it?" I pleaded.

"What is there to say?" He gestured at the phone. "I never knew you at all. You're apparently a trashy reality star, a mean girl who cheats with her friend's boyfriends."

I shook my head frantically. "No. No. You have it all wrong. None of that was real. It was scripted. We were told what to say, what to do."

"Were you handed a script each morning?" Henry asked pointedly.

My stomach dropped.

"Not exactly. We were told what was supposed to happen, what would make viewers tune in. They didn't want us to be nice. We were supposed to get into trouble, gossip, talk behind each other's backs, pretend to date each other's boyfriends. None of it was real. I never dated that guy." I pointed at the picture of me kissing Chad.

"You're kissing him on camera." Then Henry blew out a hard breath. "It says your name is Giselle."

I wish Gray would say something, anything to let me know what he was thinking. "I shortened it to Elle when I came here. Not to be deceitful. To start over where people didn't know me. Have I ever given you a reason not to trust me?"

Gray's face softened.

Of anyone, he should understand. He was judged for his father's actions.

His eyes sharpened on me. "Do you have cameras following us? Did you? Was anything real?"

He was so used to protecting his past, he couldn't expose himself to mine. I'd never overcome the film, the articles, the pictures, the comments. I was that person. I was Giselle.

"What? No. Of course not." I squeezed my fingers together, desperate for him to listen.

"How can I believe anything you say when you kept this from me?" He threw the phone on the table, standing so fast his chair tipped back before righting itself.

"I hope you know I'm not that person." My voice was thin, quiet, defeated.

"I met you a few weeks ago. Hardly enough time to know you. I can't believe I trusted you when everything was a lie, even your name."

He turned to go, taking all my hopes and dreams for the future, with him.

I hesitated only a second before following. He burst out the door, pausing on the sidewalk to suck in a deep breath.

"Gray. Can we talk about this? I'm the same girl who was with you last night. I love you. You love me." I reached out for him, letting my hand drop when he laughed without any humor, shaking his head.

"I'm asking you to give me the benefit of the doubt. I didn't want to tell you about that person because she wasn't me. I was influenced as a teenager to act a certain way. I got caught up in that world. I'm not proud of it. But as I got older, I rebelled. I wanted out." The sick feeling in my stomach intensified. "At that point, I'd already signed a contract for the spin-off show. The money was good. I thought I could at least use the money to open my own business. When the second show wasn't as successful, I got out. I moved here to live the life I wanted. I want you, Gray."

"Don't." He held his hands up to ward me off.

"I want this town. I want my shop."

He kept shaking his head slowly.

He didn't believe me.

"I can't be around you. You have no idea what you've done."

His words pounded like drum sticks in my head. "What are you talking about?"

He looked around us to make sure no one would overhear before his eyes settled on me. "My dad's up for parole."

"When did you find out?" I licked my dry lips, my brain frantically trying to pull the pieces together.

He looked away, his eyes unfocused. "This morning. After I left you. It's only a matter of time before the town, and Ed, puts it all together."

"No one knows about the show. Alice told you and Henry. It doesn't mean the whole town knows." My voice sounded as weak as I felt.

"You're crazy if you believe that. Your sister isn't out to do you any favors. She'll take you down to get what she wants, pulling me down with you."

"She was promised a spot on the show if I signed on." Had Alice been so far sucked into that world that she was desperate to do anything to get on TV?

"Exactly. She'll do whatever it takes to get you. She'll bring producers and cameras here. They'll dig into what you're doing here. They'll dig into me. Someone will make the connection."

I placed my hands on my hips, frustrated he couldn't see beyond his past or what he'd always feared. "Will they? I know this is what you've feared your whole life, but don't you think you're overre-acting a bit? You've been here for years. The people know you. They won't blame you for what your father did. I don't. Henry doesn't."

"I want to take over a well-loved business. The community trusts Ed. Once they find out my past, they won't trust me with their animals or their money. That taint doesn't ever leave unless—Fuck!" He ran his fingers through his hair, leaving it standing on end. "I'm going to have to leave again."

The pain and utter heartbreak on his face was my undoing.

I took a step back instead of closer. The show wasn't toxic. I was. "I'm so sorry, Gray. I never intended for this to happen."

I'd been so worried about what people would think when they found out about me, I hadn't considered what it meant for Gray. The last thing I wanted to do was make things worse for him. I wanted him to be happy. I wanted Ed to give him the clinic.

"I have to go." He walked away, not looking back.

This time, I didn't follow. He was right. I ruined everything.

I walked home, my heart pounding in my ears, my skin clammy. I didn't bother returning to the bar to see the disgust on Henry's face or the triumph on Alice's. I needed to be by myself. I needed to figure out how to move on when it felt like my world had caved in.

Gray didn't want anything to do with me. The more he read about me, the less he'd remember Elle.

CHAPTER 21

Gray

I walked in the direction of my car, not seeing where I was going, not hearing anyone's greetings as I passed them.

How had everything fallen apart so spectacularly? This morning, I'd been so happy. Last night, we'd said we loved each other. I'd contemplated moving in together.

Now, I wanted to sever her from my life, pretend she never existed. I wanted to rewind, going back to that moment in my office, the one where I'd let the shadows in her eyes suck me in, and tell myself to run.

I was tempted to read more about her, even though that one article had said it all. She'd cheated with her friend's boyfriend on TV. Who did that? Her name wasn't even Elle. Nothing she'd said to me was real. They were carefully orchestrated lies to make me think I'd met a different person, one who was caring and kind.

I wasn't sure what her end game was. She ended up being no different than my father. She pretended to be someone she wasn't. She'd carefully built a life on stilts, one that would blow over at the first gust of wind. Then take me down with her. I was drifting on the sand, like tumbleweed twisting first one way then another, with no direction, no anchor. I was on my own.

I ignored the buzzing of my phone, probably Henry trying to reach me, to make sure I was okay. Opening the door to my truck, I wondered where I could go. My apartment wasn't a refuge. The only place that felt like home was Rigby's Ranch, with its animals, old-fashioned barn, home-cooked meals, and hospitality. The thought was a punch to the gut. Elle's past threatened to destroy that.

I drove there, slowly numbing myself against what I'd felt with Elle last night and this morning. I turned off my dreams about the future, a home, and the clinic.

I pulled off to the side of the driveway, hoping no one would see me so I could be alone for a few minutes. Paul wouldn't mind. I'd come here often over the years to think. I headed straight to the barn, the familiar smell of horses and hay comforting me. I greeted each horse softly as I passed by each stall, finally stopping when I got to my favorite horse, Blaze. I stroked his nose as the tickle of tears invaded my eyes.

He nuzzled my neck, silently asking for a treat. I grabbed an apple from the burlap sack that hung on the wall, handing it to him.

The tension in my neck eased slightly as he munched on the apple. The horses shuffled in their stalls, grunting and snorting. Why couldn't everything be this easy? Blaze pushed on my neck, eager for more. I grabbed a second apple for him.

"What are you doing here?" Paul asked curiously, walking inside.

I offered an apple to Blaze, not ready to talk.

He raised his brow. "Hiding out?"

"You could say that."

Mr. Rigby went about his business, putting feed out for the horses to eat. I continued to stroke Blaze's neck. Paul didn't prod me to speak or ask what was wrong. I appreciated the silent support emanating from him. I knew he'd listen if I wanted to talk or leave me alone if I didn't.

When he'd finished, moving toward the door, I said, "Wait."

He turned. "Yeah?"

I needed to talk to someone. This was bigger than anything I'd encountered before. I didn't want to keep running. I wanted to stay. "I found some things out today. Things that could change the way people look at me."

"What could possibly change the way we look at you?" He settled on a hay bale against the wall, crossing his arms across his flannel-covered chest.

"I found out Elle used to be on a reality TV show. She wasn't a nice person." That was putting it mildly. Cheaters were the same as liars.

He was quiet for a few seconds. "Is she a nice person now?"

"She is. Or at least I thought she was." How did you ever truly know a person? I thought I knew who she was, but she had this whole life she kept from me. It was the same as the situation with my father. He had a secret life that blew up in a big way. Hers would too.

His eyes narrowed on me. "What's the problem?"

I bristled that he didn't understand the gravity of what she'd done. "She never mentioned being on this show, and she lied about her name, who she was."

He tilted his head. "Is she fundamentally different than the person she showed you?"

I sighed, the weight of what Alice revealed on my shoulders. "I don't know. I don't know who she is anymore."

His gaze knowing, he asked, "Don't you? Is there a reason she was a certain way on this show?"

"She said she was a teenager when she did it. Producers told her what to say and do. That none of it was real." I didn't like to make excuses for people.

"You don't believe her." His tone was matter of fact.

I hadn't in the bar. Thinking back, I saw the pain in her eyes, the utter torment about what happened, her shame, the embarrassment. "I don't know what to think."

He shook his head, leaning forward, his elbows on his knees. "Don't you?"

"I don't know what you mean." I shifted on my feet, stuffing my hands in my pockets.

Blaze grunted, probably because I wasn't paying attention to him.

"What's your gut telling you?"

It was telling me to run, cut all ties, start over. Something held me back. "I still love her. I can't believe everything I knew about her was a lie."

There was a sinking feeling in my stomach that I'd made a mistake in shutting her out. I wanted to know why she'd done what she had. Why she felt like she couldn't come to me.

"Maybe it wasn't. You said she was young when she was on the show, manipulated by producers. Maybe she wasn't *that* person. Where were her parents during this?"

"She never said."

"If she didn't have anyone looking out for her best interests, except a reality show producer, do you think she made the best decisions? If she was handed money for acting a certain way, would she turn it down? If she was surrounded by people telling her how amazing she was, to keep doing what she was doing, what do you think she would do? What would you do in that situation?"

"I have no idea." I rocked back on my heels.

I had the support of my parents. Even though my dad turned out to be a criminal, they were there for me, for the most part. He even made sure the feds couldn't take the money he'd set aside for me. He had taken care of me in his own way.

Paul's eyes were thoughtful. "I met her that one time. I didn't sense she was dishonest, or not who she said she was. Maybe you should talk to her some more. We all make mistakes. I wouldn't want to be held responsible for the things I did at sixteen."

He stood, walking out of the barn. He had a point. I was immature when I was that age. I didn't want to be held responsible for what my father did. But wasn't what she'd done different? She was being held responsible for what she did, not someone else.

I sat on the hay bale he'd vacated, pulling out my phone to search for her name, Giselle Carmichael. Pages of gossip site articles came up, outlining every salacious, outrageous thing that happened on that show. Mostly high school drama. Who was dating who, who said what, pranks, outrageous invitations to prom... I couldn't believe people cared enough to watch it. The comments were nasty, calling Giselle an attention whore, a slut, a boyfriend stealer, a bitch. I had to stop reading because it made me sick. Had she read these? Is that why she said it was toxic?

She said she moved here to escape the nastiness. I wanted to know more. Not only how she'd survived growing up in the spotlight but why her sister wanted her to go back to it. I couldn't imagine cameras following me in high school, capturing every stupid thing I said, every awkward moment.

I dropped my head into my hands. Had I completely fucked up by not hearing her out? Would she be willing to talk when I'd calmed down, or was it too late? Was she already considering going back to LA?

"I thought I'd find you here." Henry stood at the entrance to the barn, watching me uneasily.

"I just talked to your dad."

"Did he give you good advice?"

I ran my fingers through my hair. "I might have overreacted. I should have heard her out."

"I don't know. Isn't she the exact kind of person you need to keep your distance from? Aren't you worried about someone connecting you with her, your dad, and her past?

"I suppose it's possible. My father's up for parole. He might be in the news, or it could blow over quickly." It had been twelve years. Would people care anymore? Maybe they'd see that my dad was responsible for his own actions. It had nothing to do with me. I had this prickly sensation that I should give Elle that same consideration.

Henry was quiet, considering me.

"What happened when I left?"

"Elle never came back. Alice seemed gleeful. She said once everyone in town finds out who Giselle really is, she'll have no choice but to go back and sign the contract for the show."

"That's fucked up."

Henry shook his head in disgust. "I'd never hurt Piper like that."

"The power of money and fame is hard for some people to ignore." Like my dad, a teenage Elle, and Alice.

Henry sighed heavily. "Maybe you should talk to her."

I'd reacted just like those assholes in the comments. I believed those articles, not the person she showed me. She couldn't be that good of an actress to fake what we'd had the last few weeks, could she?

CHAPTER 22

Elle

I was crushed. Tears ran unchecked down my cheeks as I curled into the fetal position on my bed.

This morning I laid in bed with Gray, his arms around me as he whispered how much he loved me. How could that all change in a few hours? He'd gone from happy and in love to angry and disgusted with me.

I couldn't blame him. I'd lied to him. I'd omitted a big part of my life. It was immature to think I could move on from it. That I could pretend it didn't happen. That I wasn't that person deep down. A better person would have said no, would have broken the contract, walked away.

I'd have to come to terms with the idea I'd always be Giselle; the past was a part of me whether I liked it or not. I'd put on a brave face, doing my best to deal with whatever people had to say about it.

It was only a matter of time before it got around town. People would turn on me. I could only hope that men wouldn't care as much as women and that they'd still frequent my business. Or in time, maybe people would forget. As long as I kept my head down, continued to live my life with integrity, maybe they'd forgive me.

There was no chance that Gray would. He didn't trust easily. I knew my past could damage his future, but I still waited to tell him. The reality was he wouldn't have dated me at all if he'd known. Wasn't it better to have experienced that love than never to have loved at all?

I'd wrap myself up in the feeling I had when I was with him. I'd have to hold on to that for the lonely nights ahead. One thing I knew for certain, I wouldn't go back to LA. Smoke & Mirrors had to succeed. There wasn't another option for me. My savings was shored up in these walls.

My phone buzzed. My heart soared, hoping it was Gray telling me he wanted to talk. Then it sunk when it was Alice.

Alice: I'm downstairs. Let me up?

I didn't want to talk to her, but maybe she'd leave if I did. I dragged myself out of bed, running a hand through my hair, hoping it wasn't too knotted. I knew without looking, my face was red and swollen from crying. I didn't care if Alice saw the damage she'd done. Even though I thought she might do something like this, the reality still hurt.

My limbs were heavy as I made my way downstairs, unlocking the door to the barbershop, pushing it open for her.

She smiled tentatively. "Oh good. I wasn't sure you'd want to talk to me."

"I don't." I gestured for her to come in so I could lock up behind her.

She faced me, awkward silence between us.

I crossed my arms over my chest at her triumphant expression. I wasn't a pawn in this game of hers. "What do you want?"

Her forehead wrinkled. "You don't want to talk upstairs?"

"I don't want you in my space." I didn't trust her. My apartment was my refuge. The place I went when I wanted to forget about my past and revel in my present. Alice tore it down in one day.

"I'm sorry. I didn't mean to tell your friends. I thought they knew."

"You thought they knew about my past?" I searched her face for any sign of insincerity. Her eyes darted to the left as she clenched her jaw. She was lying. The anger built, making it difficult to stay calm.

"Yeah. I can't believe you didn't tell him. Aren't you supposed to be dating?" She was deflecting.

"Don't turn this around on me. You knew exactly what you were doing. You want to destroy what I have here so I'll have no choice but to go home with you. You want to be on a trashy show so badly, you'd sell out your own sister? You'd ruin everything I've built?" I gestured at the shop, the thing I was most proud of.

Her lips drew into a straight line as the silence stretched.

"That's not going to happen. Do whatever you have to do, then leave. You're no longer welcome here."

Her face fell. "I never intended—"

"Yes. You did. You came here and did exactly what you intended to do. You told me a few weeks ago you had no intention of coming here. Then all of a sudden, you're here for a visit, telling everyone, knowing I hated that life. You want to destroy me. That's not how sisters treat each other. You're supposed to be there for me, support me. You're not supposed to manipulate me so you can get what you want." As heartbroken as I was by her actions, it felt good to lay everything out.

Alice pinched her lips together. "I don't understand why you won't come back. Why won't you do the show? Why are you being so selfish? You had your shot, let me have mine."

I closed my eyes against the onslaught of memories,

Alice standing next to Emily as she manipulated me. I thought I was protecting her when she was right next to me the whole time, learning from the best. "You need to leave."

"Why can't you help me for once? Why can't you let me have the dream?"

I slowly opened my eyes, my heartbeat slowing, a calm overtaking me. "I'm happy to help you go to college, or get your feet under you. I'm not helping you get on a TV show. It ruined my life."

"You're so dramatic. You made a lot of money, you partied, had a good time. It was amazing." It was like she was grasping for the memory she had of me.

"It wasn't." My voice was flat. I felt numb. "I don't know why you're here. You're not going to change my mind."

"I don't know either." She turned to go.

"If your plan is to send a producer here with cameras to convince me, don't. I won't participate. I'll never talk to you again, and I won't forgive you for bringing those people back into my life. I own my life now. I decide who gets to be front and center to see me succeed or fail, not some producer, not a cameraman, and certainly not you."

Alice's eyes flashed with anger. "You're going to regret this."

"I already do." I uncrossed my arms, opening the door for her.

"You're so selfish."

"If you want to be a good sister, you won't tell anyone else about the show. You won't ruin my reputation in this town." If I wanted them to know, I'd tell them. It was time I put myself first. It was a good feeling. I thought I'd come here to find myself when I was here all along. I was afraid to come out, pushed down by other's expectations, but I was here. I knew what I wanted, what I needed to do to get it. If Gray wasn't it, I'd survive. I'd come out stronger on the other side. I wouldn't let anyone tear me down again."I won't tell anyone else." Alice pulled the door out of my hand, slamming it so hard the closed sign bounced off the window. I locked it, blocking out her, the world, Gray, and anyone else who wanted to hurt me.

I headed toward the stairs to my apartment when a sharp knock on the door jarred me. Thinking it was Alice wanting to continue our fight, I pulled the door open, finding Piper. "What are you doing here?"

"Henry told me what happened. I brought reinforcements." She held up a bag of ice cream and wine.

"Come on in." I led her upstairs to my apartment.

"Aren't you mad?" I asked as she pulled out the food.

Her eyes shot up, her mouth dropping open. "Why would I be mad at you?"

"I lied about who I was."

She placed a finger on her chin, then shrugged. "Did you? You go by a shortened version of your name. I wouldn't want to admit I was on a trashy reality show either. I can't believe I didn't see the resemblance before now. I never watched it, but I remember reading some of the gossip columns."

She reached out to tug on one brown lock. "Dying your hair isn't exactly hiding your identity."

"This is my natural color."

She smirked. "Exactly. You aren't hiding, you're revealing yourself. This is who you are. Not that Giselle on TV."

"That girl made the worst decisions." My lips twitched as I allowed myself to consider Piper's take.

"Every sixteen-year-old makes bad decisions. It's a rite of passage. You were unlucky enough to do it on TV. Was any of it real?"

"No. The show came out later saying it was scripted. By then, the viewers didn't want to admit they'd wasted years watching a fake show."

"I'd be pretty pissed too." Piper barked out a laugh, covering it with her hand. Then we were both laughing over the absurdity of the situation, the show, and the shitstorm my life had become.

Covering my aching stomach, I said, "I can't believe you're here."

Warmth flooded through me, heating the areas cooled by Alice's revelation and Gray's departure.

"We're friends. We don't turn on each other just because you have a secret in your past you're embarrassed about."

Relief flowed through me at her words. The sentiment reminded me of a friend I'd had before I was cast on the show, Kelsey. She was more serious and studious than me. We'd been friends since elementary school, but the producers didn't want us to hang out with anyone not on the show. I'd always regretted losing her friendship. Piper reminded me a little of her. Maybe I should reach out to Kelsey to make things right. "Gray won't be so forgiving."

"Give him time," she said quietly.

"He said he loved me." The words rolled off my tongue, beautiful in their simplicity. My chest throbbed with the loss.

"Do you love him?" Her eyes softened.

I nodded, miserable at the prospect of not being able to say it to him again.

"It'll work out. He'll come to his senses." Her tone was uncertain, feeding into my doubt.

"You've met Gray, right? He's the most rigid person I've ever met. I'm not sure he will." The pit in my stomach got bigger.

"He's never been with anyone else like he's been with you. You're different."

"I hope so." My shoulders ached from the tension of worrying all day about Alice revealing my ugly truths to the man I love and my new friends.

Piper pulled a couple of bowls out of the cabinet. "Are you worried your bitch of a sister will tell everyone?"

I pressed a hand to my twisting stomach. All the

worst-case scenarios I'd imagined flashed through my head, one worse than the other. "About the show?"

"Yes." She turned away, pulling open drawers until she found the silverware.

I closed my eyes briefly. If she did, it would be over. The truth would come out.

"Aha." Piper held up the ice cream scooper.

"She said she won't, but do you think people will turn on me if she does?"

She scooped ice cream into the bowls. "There might be a few that will. If you stay, and you tell people you're not like that anymore, that you don't want to leave, and this is your home, I think they'll come around."

"That's all true. I want to stay here." My stomach settled at my pronouncement. I grabbed the wine opener, needing something to cover the worry, the doubt, and the dread. I untwisted the cork, pouring two glasses.

Piper pushed the bowl of ice cream toward me. "Wine and ice cream heals everything."

Gray was another story.

I took a bite of the ice cream, not in the mood to bury my feelings with junk food or wine. I didn't want to numb myself or forget. I wanted to immerse myself in the way I felt with Gray, holding on to that feeling until it faded with time. I wanted to remember what it felt like to be loved, cared for, and trusted.

"He'll come around. You'll see."

"You're so confident." I wanted to believe her even though nothing had ever turned out in my favor.

"I know Gray as much as anyone can. I've known him longer at least. He doesn't open up. He doesn't have girlfriends. He certainly doesn't bring them to my parents' house. He felt something for you. I don't think he'll walk away. At least not forever."

She sat at the island, digging into her ice cream.

I wanted to talk to him. He didn't know the whole story. He didn't know what it felt like to live under a microscope, feeling like you had no choices in your life.

"I want him to know I'm different. I'm not that person anymore."

Piper dropped her spoon in her bowl, placing her hand over mine. "Anyone can see you're not that person."

"I don't feel like that person anymore. But reading the articles, seeing the pictures and comments, brings it all back—the pressure to act a certain way, the shame that came with it when I did, the feeling like I was on a hamster wheel I couldn't get off."

"Everyone deserves a second chance. If Gray can't see that then he's not the guy for you."

That might have been true, but her words drilled a hole in my heart.

"Have you texted him since?"

"No. I wanted him to have a chance to calm down. I was hoping he'd come to me." It might be too much to hope for.

"I'd reach out then, let him know you want to talk."

"Yeah, that's a good idea." I didn't want to walk away, to close this chapter in my life. I wanted to fight for him. I was wrong not to tell him, even if I had reasons—reasons I could only hope he'd eventually understand. I pulled out my phone, the empty screen taunting me.

Elle: I'd like a chance to talk to you. I know I don't deserve it. I wasn't upfront with you. I omitted a huge part of my life, but I'd love a chance to explain, to apologize. I love you.

I put the phone down as if it had the power to bite me. My heart beat loudly in my ears.

"I've never been this invested in someone. No one ever mattered to me like this. As if my whole existence depended on him listening to me, loving me. I'll be okay without him, but—"

"You'll be so much happier with him."

I slumped, taking a large bite of ice cream. "Exactly."

We ate in silence for a few minutes.

Straightening, I said, "There has to be something I can do, to prove how much he means to me, that I'm not that person anymore."

"I think you already have. The person you showed him wasn't that girl in LA. He needs to realize that on his own."

My heart slowed, the perpetual buzzing in my ears dulled. "I hate waiting around, not knowing what he's thinking or feeling."

"You're good, Elle Carmichael. Whatever happens, you're a good person." Piper hugged me.

I let those words seep into my bones and my soul. I was a good person. If Gray couldn't see that then he wasn't the man for me.

CHAPTER 23

Gray

*A*t home, I read Elle's message, knowing I needed to reconcile the person she was with me with the person she was before.

I sifted through every scenario in my head. What would the town think if they found out about Elle's past? How would it affect me? What would happen if the town found out about my dad?

If I wanted people to judge me on the person I was now, shouldn't I do the same for Elle? She'd never given me any indication she was a cheater or untrustworthy. She was interested in helping animals, insisting on raising money for Athena's injuries, interested in helping the rescues, supportive of my decision to have a mobile vet clinic.

She didn't seem like the same person who said and did nasty things on TV. Maybe it was a role she played like she said.

I wanted Elle to be upfront about her past even though I hadn't been with mine. I hadn't been upfront with anyone in my life: Elle, Henry, or Ed.

I should talk to Ed, explain why it was so important for me to make a home here. I called him, leaving a voicemail when he didn't answer, asking if he could meet me in the office early Monday morning. I needed to talk to Ed before I talked to Elle.

Gray: I want to talk too. Can we meet on Monday evening after work? There's something I need to take care of first.

Elle: Of course. Thank you.

Her relief came through over the text.

I wanted nothing more than to hear her voice, to hold her hand as she explained everything. This time, I'd listen. I just hoped what she had to say didn't make me feel differently about her.

* * *

MONDAY MORNING, I went to the office early to speak to Ed. I'd tossed and turned all night, wondering if I was making a mistake in telling Ed the truth. The vision of a future with Elle, free of my past, motivated me to go through with it. Henry and Elle were understanding. Hopefully, Ed would be the same.

Guilt weighed heavily on me that I hadn't been willing to listen when Elle told me her story. I hoped Ed would give me the benefit of the doubt I hadn't with Elle.

I paused in Ed's doorway, my limbs stiff.

Ed looked up from his computer. "You wanted to see me?"

I closed the door, sitting across from him. "There's something I have to tell you."

He turned to face me. "It sounds serious."

I clasped my fingers tightly together. "It is. It could affect the clinic, what you think of me."

Ed waited patiently for me to continue.

I swallowed around the ache in my throat. "My father is in federal prison, serving time on charges of money laundering. I haven't had contact with him since I was eighteen. I was living with him when his house was raided by the feds."

Ed's eyes widened. "You've never talked about it."

"No. I only recently told Henry and then Elle." I couldn't tell what Ed was thinking. Was he shocked? Disappointed?

"I don't want my past to affect you or the clinic. My dad's up for parole. He might be in the news again. People might put it together, figure out I'm his son. It could be bad for you. I understand if you don't feel comfortable selling the business to me." My heart pounded in my chest as I waited for his response.

He crossed his arms over his chest. "Why are you telling me now?"

"Partly because my dad's name could be in the news again, but also, something about Elle's past came up this weekend. It blindsided me, made me think she wasn't the person I thought she was. I don't want my past to become an issue. I don't want you to think you made a mistake in selling the business to me.

"More importantly, I wanted you to know that Telluride is my home. I want to buy a house. I have plans for the clinic. I hope my past doesn't come back to bite me in the ass, but I have no way of knowing." I sighed, adding the hardest thing I'd ever had to say, "Even if you don't want to sell the clinic to me, I'm staying."

Ed steepled his hands, considering me. "I'm glad you told me. I'm sure some of my older clients might have an issue with it."

I nodded, my stomach dropping. "I completely understand if you want to sell to someone else."

Ed's gaze was steady on me. "Gray, you've impressed me over the years, but I worried you worked too hard. You never really settled here, not until you met Elle. She's good for you. I hope she makes you see there's life outside this clinic."

"She does." She did.

"I don't know what happened in her past to have

you questioning her. I don't need to know, just like I don't need to know your past to know what kind of person you are today. You aren't your father, or what he did. You're hardworking, conscientious, and caring. I wouldn't feel comfortable handing my business to anyone other than you."

I was prepared to tell him I understood. I was okay with his decision to let me go. I was prepared to walk out of here, looking for another job. My mind scrambled to catch up to what he was saying.

The thing that stood out to me was that he wasn't surprised. He didn't take any time to think about it. "How long have you known?"

"Since you started. I looked into you. I wanted to hire someone with the potential to take over the business. You were young yet determined. I wanted to make sure there wasn't a reason you wouldn't be a good candidate."

"If you knew, why did you hire me?"

Ed shook his head. "You went to college then vet school, moved here, and you were friends with the Rigbys. There was no blemish on *your* record. There was no reason for me to think you were bad for the clinic. I wanted to give you a chance to prove yourself and you have."

"I don't understand." He knew. He always knew, and it didn't matter. An uncomfortable feeling washed over me. If Ed could judge me on the person I was now, I should do the same for Elle.

"You're a good person. You're not a reflection of your father. I'm sure Elle and Henry told you that." He spoke each word carefully as if he wanted it to sink in.

"They did."

"Believe them. Believe me."

I'd felt tainted by my father's actions since I was eighteen. Logically, I knew I wasn't a criminal but the shame, guilt, and shock stayed with me. I feared it was only a matter of time before it caught up to me. Then people wouldn't find me worthy. I was so busy looking backward, I hadn't looked to the future. I hadn't even thought I deserved one. That's why I spent so much time working. It's all I thought I was good for. I didn't deserve the same committed relationships as other people did. I held on to Henry, knowing deep down I didn't deserve his friendship.

Elle needed me. She needed my support. I wasn't there.

I stood. "I have someone I need to talk to."

I had appointments. I couldn't leave, but I needed to talk to her now.

I wanted to leave Ed's office to get to her. I couldn't believe I'd waited all day yesterday to speak to her. I'd sat at the Rigbys' dinner table pretending everything was okay when it was the opposite. The whole day of appointments stretched before me, a barrier to talking to her, to making things right.

I tilted my head slightly. "Thanks for listening to me."

"I'm here for you, Gray, whether you want me to be or not."

"Thanks." I was grateful to Ed for being one of my supporters, one I'd overlooked. He'd watched out for me in his own way. He held off on selling me the business because he wanted what was best for me. He knew I wasn't living my best life.

I started to walk out of his office, hoping this evening wasn't too late to talk to Elle.

"Don't you have something to ask me?"

I paused, my hand on the doorframe, looking back at him. "No."

"You don't want to ask me if I can take your appointments so you can talk to Elle?"

Had Alice told everyone about the show? "How do you know about Elle?"

He gave me a pointed look. "You said something from her past came up. It has you questioning yours, so it must be something important. Did you screw things up with her when she needed your support?"

I hadn't thought about what my withdrawal of support would mean for her. She was worried her secret would get out. That there would be gossip and it would affect her business. What must she be feeling right now? I'd abandoned her when she needed me. The feeling of someone needing me, depending on me, took hold. "I have to see her now."

"That's what I've been trying to tell you." He stood,

placing a hand on my shoulder. "I'll take care of things here. You go get your girl."

"I will. Thanks, Ed."

He nodded. "Now get out of here."

I hoped I wasn't too late. That Alice hadn't convinced her she had nothing left here to fight for. I took long strides to my truck, not pausing when Anne asked where I was going. All I could focus on was that Elle might have already decided to go back to LA, the show, and her old life. That was the last thing I wanted.

I hoped that when she said she wanted to stay, she was telling the truth.

CHAPTER 24

Elle

I went through the motions at work on Monday, knowing I would see Gray soon. I wasn't sure if I should look forward to clearing the air or dread it. His reaction at the bar didn't give me much hope.

The weekend had been tortuous. I went through the motions, going to Crew's training class, my mind replaying the scene at the bar, Gray walking away from me. Piper came over for Sunday night dinner, saying Gray was at her family's home. I felt bad she'd missed it so she could support me, but not enough to send her away.

I wanted to ask her if she knew what Gray needed

to take care of, but I couldn't. It felt too middle school. Too much like the old Giselle. I'd wait for us to talk on Monday evening. Hoping it wasn't to say he wanted nothing to do with me.

Monday morning at the shop was slow, so I told Piper to take an early lunch. I was taking down the Halloween decorations, putting them into storage boxes when the bell over the door rang.

"Are you leaving?"

I looked up, surprised to see Gray, confused about his question. He still wore his white coat, his air tangled as if he'd been running his fingers through the strands the whole way over. My stomach sank as I stepped down from the stool. "No. I don't want to, but if it's what you want…"

He looked around the shop as if he were looking for potential witnesses for what he was about to do, rip my heart out.

I wrapped my arms around my stomach. The thought of not living here, the one place that felt safe, that was mine, stole my breath. I looked around at the barbershop. The idea of closing left a gaping hole in my chest.

"No."

I shook my head. "I don't understand."

I didn't understand the all-encompassing pain spreading from my chest to my extremities or what he was doing here when we were supposed to talk later. Whatever the reason, it couldn't be good. He probably didn't want to wait any longer to sever ties with me. I wasn't ready for this conversation. I never would be.

Gray shook his head slowly. "I'm screwing this up. I wanted to talk to you about what happened at the bar. I talked to Ed this morning. I told him about my past."

"That's great, Gray." My words were carefully measured, unsure where he was going with this conversation. "I don't see how—"

He interrupted, not acknowledging my words. "I knew after I talked to him, I had to talk to you. I had this overwhelming desire to fix things. To make things right. To listen to you. I wasn't ready to talk to you on Saturday, but I am now."

I closed my eyes against his words, needing confirmation that we would be okay more than my next breath. "I explained everything to you at the bar. You weren't ready to listen."

"I am now."

I was disoriented. Him showing up here. The disjointed conversation. Why was he more willing to listen now than he was on Saturday? "I'm not even sure where to start."

The reality was I was afraid to lay myself out there again. I'd begged him at the bar to stop and listen to me. He hadn't. I wasn't sure I could get over the feeling of watching him walk away, ignoring my pleas. If this was a repeat of Saturday night, my heart would shred into tiny strips I'd never be able to put back together. Somehow, I'd survive like I always had.

"I think we need to clear something up first. What do you want? Do you want to move to LA, do another show? If that's what you really want, I won't stop you."

"No, Gray. That's not what I want." I took a few steps toward him, my hand outstretched. When I reached Gray, he grabbed my hand, pulling me close. I reveled in his nearness, something I thought I'd never feel again.

I felt hopeful and wary. I lowered my lashes, hiding the swirling emotions.

"What do you want, Elle?" He tipped my chin up with his finger.

Tears filled my eyes. "I want you. I want a life, here in Telluride, with you. This place," I touched his chest, "you are my safe place. My escape from my past. I made a new life here."

"What about Alice? How does she fit in?"

"I can't believe she came here to tell everyone about my past. I wanted to hide it forever, never acknowledge who I was, or what I'd done. I asked her not to tell anyone else, and she said she wouldn't. But she was right to out me to you. I wasn't being honest with you. I need to ask for forgiveness, be transparent going forward, and hope you can forgive me."

His expression was pained. "I'm sorry I reacted without listening to you first. I have so many questions."

My smile felt brittle. If I spread my lips any wider,

they'd crack wide open. "Do you want to go somewhere quiet to talk?"

"I'm sorry I didn't listen to you the other night. I'm ready to now if you're willing."

Piper opened the door. "Gray. What are you doing here?"

Her tone was cold, uninviting.

I appreciated her loyalty even if I didn't deserve it.

"Is Alice here?"

My lips pressed into a grim line. "No. She left."

"She went back to LA?" he asked.

"That's where she belongs," Piper said, taking off her coat, placing the to-go bag of food on the counter.

"Do you mind handling the shop for a bit so we can talk?"

Piper's eyes softened as she looked from me to Gray. "Sure. Holler if you need me."

Her veiled threat was clear. She didn't believe Gray was here to make up. She was worried he would reject me again.

Gray followed me up the steps to my apartment. When I opened the door, letting Crew out of his crate, he danced around, happy to see us, oblivious to the emotions swirling, dread, hope, fear, and love. We turned to face each other in the kitchen, an awkward silence between us.

"What do you want to know?" I licked my lips, my eyes darting around the room, not settling on any one thing.

"Everything. Tell me everything." Gray's tone was intense.

I sighed. "Let's sit."

We sat on the couch, my knee drawn up between us. "I told you how the producers came to our school and interviewed us, asking all these questions about my friends. They wanted to know if I was jealous of Lillian and Chad's relationship. By then, they were dating. I wasn't jealous of them. I was jealous of what they had. My home was empty, my parents absent, my nanny doing her job. She wasn't a surrogate mother. I wanted to latch on to something, a boy. I was desperate back then for a connection and love. Maybe the producers saw something in me they thought they could use."

My gaze was on the couch between us. I wanted to touch him while I talked even though I didn't have that right. Not yet. I needed to get this out. He needed to hear it, to carefully consider each word even as my heart longed to be in his arms.

"What about your parents? What did they think?"

I laughed without any humor. "My mom thought it was a great opportunity. The producers sold it as an acting job. She left it up to me. I was sixteen. Of course, I wanted to be on TV. The whole school was buzzing about it. We were the lucky ones. When the contracts were offered, I wasn't sure about my role other than I was chosen because I was friends with Lillian. She was beautiful and blonde, nice to everyone. She was popular. People gravitated toward her."

"Why do I feel like you're building up to something I'm not going to like?"

I continued, not acknowledging his words. "I wasn't as outgoing as she was. As soon as I signed, the producers wanted me to dye my hair blonde like Lillian's. It became clear, pretty quickly, they were pitting us against each other. I was supposed to act like I wanted her boyfriend, that I'd do anything to get him."

"The show wasn't supposed to be real. Sometimes it felt that way. Our friendship couldn't survive."

"That kiss between you and Chad…"

"The producers set everything up. I hated betraying my friend. I justified it because it wasn't supposed to be real."

"Lillian didn't feel the same way?"

"No, she didn't. I don't blame her. Any time we questioned what the producers wanted us to do, they'd remind us of the money and ratings, showing us the comments and emails about what the fans wanted. The fans loved the drama, the push and pull, and how Chad was so passive about it."

I shook my head. "When I went to my parents, they reminded me I'd made a commitment, they'd signed a contract."

"You were sixteen." Gray's voice was disbelieving.

I shook my head, not wanting him to absolve me of responsibility. "When they pitched the spin-off, I was an adult. I could have said no."

"Why didn't you?"

"The money, the lifestyle was all I knew. I didn't know how to be me without it. My castmates wanted me to keep it going. Without Lillian and me, there wouldn't be a show. I felt obligated. I figured if people wanted to watch me go to cosmetology school, I'd get paid to do it. By then, the love triangle story was dropped because Chad stayed home. He didn't go to school. Looking back, he was smart. He got out. When I graduated, I got my first salon job. That's when I realized the show's reach. People came into the salon calling me names."

His jaw tightened. "I've seen the comments."

My gaze flew to his, shame filling me. "Then you know."

"I can only imagine how it felt being on the receiving end. Something similar happened after my father was arrested. It wasn't as overt as calling me names to my face. It was more whispers when I walked into a store. Rumors that I was somehow involved."

I closed my eyes against the memories. "It was awful. I hated it. I constantly had this sick feeling in my stomach. I wanted to take the money to open a salon, then I thought a barbershop would be a better idea. Men wouldn't have watched the show. Wouldn't know who I was or what I'd done. If they did, they probably wouldn't care."

I took a deep breath before continuing, "What I told you the day we met was the truth. This place stuck with me after I visited. I loved it here. I wanted to go somewhere familiar, where no one would know what I did or who I was. I dyed my hair back to its natural color and shortened my name."

"Why didn't you tell me?"

I sensed this was the most important question I could answer for him. "I wanted to be someone different. I didn't want to be Giselle, the villain. I wanted to be who I was supposed to be even if I had no idea who that was. My personality was hijacked at sixteen. I was forced to act a certain way. I came here to find myself. Then I realized I am Elle, the barbershop owner, the person who cares about other people, who thinks about their feelings before I act."

He clenched his jaw. "Did you think about me when you omitted your past?"

I hated hurting him. "I did. I planned on telling you the night you told me about your past. You felt so betrayed by your father. He turned out to be someone you didn't know. I realized I was doing the same thing. You'd never forgive me when you found out."

Tears filled my eyes, spilling down my cheeks. I didn't bother wiping them away. Nothing mattered unless he accepted my reasoning.

"After I told you about my past, what was holding you back from telling me?"

My heart was beating loudly in my chest, a slow steady rhythm telling me my words changed everything, yet nothing. "I wanted to tell you, but not when you were so raw. I wanted to tell you later, but I was ashamed by my past, sure you'd want nothing to do with me when you found out. I wanted to revel in us for a little longer, sink into the goodness that's you and me together. I knew I didn't deserve you. That I was living on borrowed time. Unfortunately, there never seemed to be a good time. Then Alice showed up."

"You thought I wouldn't want to be with you if you told me the truth?"

"I don't blame you for walking away at the bar. Some mistakes you can't rectify."

He was quiet for a few seconds possibly considering what he wanted to say. "I can't imagine what you went through. I can't judge you for decisions you made at sixteen when the adults surrounding you didn't have your best interest at heart. The producers manipulated you. Your parents were absent. They should have seen how the producers treated you, what it cost you. They should have protected you."

I opened my mouth to protest, but he held his hand to stop me. "I hadn't told you about my past when we'd met. I was guilty of the same thing. I can't hold you to a higher standard than I do myself. I understand why you'd want to be judged by who you are now, instead of then."

"What does this mean for us?"

He cupped my cheek, tilting my face up. "I love you. Nothing you've told me changes how I feel."

I let out a drawn-out sigh, unsure it was that easy. "I love you too. Is it that easy?"

My heart hung on to his words, hoping he meant what he said. He loved me. He wasn't walking away. He'd stay.

"I haven't been in a relationship since high school, but I know how I feel. I want to be with you. I want to start a life with you here. If that's what you want?" He wiped away my tears as they continue to fall.

I reached out a hand to touch his face, shocked he was here, saying what he was. "It's exactly what I want."

He kissed me softly. I expected to feel like I didn't deserve him. Instead, this felt right. He deepened the kiss, his hands cupping my head, angling me so he could delve deeper.

Gray made me a better person. Maybe I did the same for him. Together, we were better.

I pulled back, looking up at him, tears heavy on my eyelashes. "I love you, Gray."

"I love you." His voice was rough with emotion.

He pulled off my clothes then his as if he wanted nothing between us, not our pasts, our indiscretions, mistakes, or our regret. Hovering above me, his cock gliding through my folds, I knew I'd never get enough of him.

With a smooth roll of his hips, he slid inside, the moment more perfect than anything I'd ever experienced. Our ugly truths laid bare between us, love shining from our pores.

He thrust, long and slow, savoring each push, each pull, each slide bringing us impossibly closer until our skin was slick with sweat; my moans poured from my lips unchecked, uninhibited.

We came together, his forehead resting on mine, our breaths mingling.

We'd never forget our pasts. They made us who we were together. Strong, determined, caring, and loving. Nothing could come between us—not Alice, his dad, or our families.

Gray settled next to me on the couch, sliding an arm under my head, cradling me to him. "You have me now, Elle. I'll always love you, look out for you, care for you. You won't be alone again."

I stroked his face. "I'll be the same for you."

EPILOGUE

Elle

"*H*appy Holidays," I said, handing out hot cocoa to one of the townspeople enjoying the hot cocoa crawl.

I'd pitched the hot cocoa and cookie crawl idea to the town coordinator. She'd loved that it would draw attention to the shops before the holidays. I made up a gift bag to hand out that included coupons and flyers about upcoming events going on at Smoke & Mirrors.

"I'll take over for a bit. Why don't you take a break?" Piper sat next to me at the counter.

"Thanks." I smiled at her gratefully.

Gray and Henry sat on the leather chairs in the

waiting area, hot cocoa in their hands, a tray of cookies on the coffee table.

I placed my hands on my hips. "Did you leave any cookies for the guests?"

"There's plenty." Gray popped another cookie into his mouth.

"I'll go help Piper at the front." Henry stood, joining Piper.

Gray tugged me onto his lap. "I'm so proud of you."

I looped my arms around his neck. "I hope more locals will give the shop a chance."

"These events draw people in; the shop looks amazing; you're bound to get more clients." I'd been staying afloat with the tourists but wanted the locals to embrace me too. I knew it would take time.

Piper and I had gone all out with the holiday decorations: elaborate window displays, twinkling lights around the mirrors, and a tree. Gray was great at grounding me, reminding me what was important. "Thanks for being here."

He smiled softly. "I wouldn't miss it."

There was an ease to us that wasn't there before. We'd bared our souls to each other; there were no more secrets from our past threatening our future. When his father was denied parole, Gray was relieved he didn't need to worry about his father dropping back into his life just yet. It was him and me, our dreams, and our friends. We'd made a family here in Telluride.

"Do you think we can sneak out of here a little early?"

I glanced at the clock. There were only ten minutes left. I wasn't usually open this late on Friday evenings. "I don't see why not."

Gray's expression was a mix of excitement and nerves. "I have a surprise for you."

My heart rate picked up, wondering if he was giving me my Christmas present early. "I can't wait to see it." Our lips met, soft and light.

Pulling back slightly so our foreheads met, I said, "Let me make sure Piper is okay with closing up."

* * *

My hand was in Gray's as he drove away from town. Love for him and anticipation for what he wanted to show me, invaded every part of my body.

Gray glanced over at me. "Are you excited?"

"I love surprises."

Gray shot me a smile before turning his attention to the road. Homes were already decorated for Christmas.

It was the first year I could remember I felt free to enjoy the season the way I wanted to. I didn't have any parties or events I had to attend. I wanted to immerse myself in everything Christmas: the decorations, the baking, the feeling of closeness with my new friends, and the joy of owning a new business.

Gray turned down a gravel lane lined with trees, the

base of each wrapped in twinkling white lights. I gasped. "It's so beautiful."

Gray squeezed my hand. The warmth of his hands and his steady strength and support never failed to anchor me in our relationship.

After passing the last tree, the house came into view. Greenery was wrapped in lights around the porch railing, a fully decorated tree stood on the porch, a candle lit each window. "Who lives here? What are we doing here?"

My first thought was he was taking me to a party, but the windows were dark.

"I wanted you to see the lights."

I unbuckled my belt, eager to see more. "Is it okay if we're here? We're not trespassing, are we?"

"No. I okayed it with the owner."

My eyes caught on a tire swing that hung from a large tree to our right. Did a family live here?

"I want to show you something." I waited while he walked around the truck to help me out.

When he held out his hand, I stepped down. I closed my eyes, inhaling his familiar, comforting scent.

When he turned, I saw the barn for the first time. "Even the barn is decorated."

A large wreath was centered above the doors, and the roof was lined with lights.

Gray tugged me toward the porch of the house, up the steps, pausing at the door.

Was he taking me inside? Did he know who lived

here? I covered my pounding heart with my free hand. "Gray—"

He dropped to one knee in front of me, my hand held in his. He looked up at me, his eyes shining with love, hope, and happiness.

I pressed my hand harder over my heart. *He was going to propose.*

"Elle Carmichael, the day we met, you drew me in without even trying. I noticed your natural beauty; how down to earth you seemed. Each time we met, your concern for other people and animals impressed me. You saw something inside of me. Your love pushed me to be a better person. You made me see that life was more than work, and my future was more than my past."

My heart clenched inside my chest. The moment was surreal—the crisp air, the lights reflecting in his eyes. I wanted to take a picture of this moment, him looking up at me, telling me everything in his heart so I could remember it forever.

"I love you, Elle, more than anything—more than fear, more than doubt. Marry me. Make a life with me here in this house. We'll fill this home with love and the barn with animals. We'll be there for our kids, making sure they know they're loved."

His vision was so clear. I could see us living here, dogs, kids, friends, and family. I fell to my knees in front of him, cradling his face in my hands. "Of course, I'll marry you."

I kissed him, returning every sentiment he'd said into the kiss until my cheeks were wet, and my hands were shaking. Pulling back from him slightly, I caressed his face. "You own this house?"

He smiled, the expression of a man who had everything he wanted. "I do."

I raised a brow. "I thought you didn't find any houses you liked?"

"I saw this house the day Alice visited. I knew it was perfect then. I wanted to buy it even though I wasn't sure if I'd screwed everything up with you that day. When we got back together, I wanted it to be a surprise." He tucked a piece of my hair behind my ear. "I wanted to ask you to move in with me, but it wasn't enough. I wanted you by my side in every way that mattered. I wanted to build a life with you. I wanted everything I thought I'd never have."

"I want that too." I was in awe of him and the beauty of this moment.

The Gray that had run from anything permanent was now running toward me, holding on tight with both hands. I never wanted him to let me go. I thought it was our pasts that made us infamous when it was our love that was unforgettable.

BONUS EPILOGUE

Gray

Nine months later

That evening, I finished writing notes on the chart for my last exam of the day, closing out my computer.

Ed popped his head into the office. "Can you come out front for a minute? I have something to show you."

The sale of the vet clinic was finalized over the summer, but Ed still worked part-time when he wasn't traveling.

Intrigued, I stood, grabbing my things to leave for the day, closing then locking my office door. "What is it?"

Ed smiled. "It's something you have to see for yourself."

I was surprised when we passed through the lobby,

nodding at Anne as we walked out. I sensed her get up to follow us out.

"What's going on?" My voice trailed off when I saw a large van in the parking lot, still running, with another vet's name on the side. "What's this?" Elle stepped out of the truck, her arms held wide. "This is your new mobile vet clinic van."

She smiled cautiously as if she was afraid of my reaction.

"I don't understand." My gaze shot from Elle to Ed then back again.

"Elle told me about her plan," Ed said.

"What plan?"

"She wanted to see what your budget was for a van before she called around to see what was available."

"This vet clinic just bought a new van, so we were able to get this one for a fraction of the price. I mentioned how you planned to offer free vaccinations and exams. I think that helped." Elle's eyes were soft.

"This is amazing. I can't believe you were able to find something." My mind was racing with thoughts of love; this woman continued to surprise me with her huge heart. She was never that mean girl Giselle. Elle was there the whole time, waiting to come out.

Elle held up her hand. "It was luck. They bought a new van this past week, so they were looking to unload it."

"I can't believe you did this for me."

Ed stepped back, heading inside the clinic.

She took a step closer to me. "Don't you see, Gray? I'd do anything to make you happy. That doesn't stop because we say I love you. I'll show you every day for the rest of our lives."

I think she sensed that I'd always worry about the what-ifs. I appreciated her showing me how great we could be if I let go of that fear. "I don't think I could be happier than I am now."

She tilted her head, a smile playing on her lips. "Are you sure about that?"

"What do you mean?"

"I know you just moved into the house, and things are busy right now, but…" She shrugged, her eyes held a hint of fear.

"But what?" I couldn't imagine what she was leading up to.

"And I know we haven't talked about it. I know it's a surprise. A shock really…" Her voice trailed off.

I gripped her shoulders. "Elle, tell me what's going on. I'm imagining all sorts of things, like you moving back to LA."

"I'm pregnant." She bit her lip as if she were worried about my reaction.

My fingers loosened their group on her shoulders. "Are you serious?"

She smiled, tears in her eyes as she nodded. "Yes."

A lightness took hold of my body; my eyes stung with unshed tears as I stepped closer to her. "I can't believe it. I never thought…"

"You never thought it was possible? You never allowed yourself to hope for a future, me, a baby, a life together?"

My hands cupped the back of her head, tilting her head up. "Yes, to all of it."

"Are you happy?" Her voice was soft.

"So happy." I lowered my mouth to hers, pouring all my emotions into her. The thought of my life with Elle stretched out before me like the fields on my new farm. The mountains in the distance representing the exciting things we had to look forward to.

The End.

COMING SOON

Mountain Haven Series

Coming October, 2021

Adventurous Love, the second book in the Mountain
Haven Series

I'm a city girl at heart but when a dear friend invited
me to stand up in her wedding, I decided to embrace all
Colorado had to offer. I was not expecting Henry
Rigby—the ruggedly handsome best man—a lumbar
jack fantasy come to life. Flirting with him was more
dangerous than any wilderness adventure I'd imagined.

For more information about Lea Coll's Mountain
Haven Series, click here:
https://www.ladybosspress.com/infamous-love

ACKNOWLEDGMENTS

To Kristen Proby, whose advice has been invaluable. I wouldn't have created this amazing new world in Telluride without your inspiration.

To the readers and bloggers who've read and reviewed my books—I appreciate it more than you'll ever know. There's nothing better than connecting with readers. To know that something I wrote resonated with you. I read to be in another world for a few hours and I hope that you enjoy spending time in the world I created.

ABOUT THE AUTHOR

Lea Coll worked as a trial attorney for over ten years.
Now she stays home with her three children, plotting
stories while fetching snacks and running them back
and forth to activities. She enjoys the freedom of
writing romance after years of legal writing.
She currently resides in Maryland with her family.

To learn more about her books, please visit Lea's
website. (https://www.leacoll.com/books)

BOOKS BY LEA COLL

Mountain Haven Series

Infamous Love

Adventurous Love

All I Want Series

Choose Me

Be With Me

Burn for Me

Trust in Me

Stay With Me

Take a Chance With Me

Annapolis Harbor Series

Hooked on You (previously titled Easy Moves)

Only With You

Lost Without You

Perfect for You

Crazy for You

Falling for You

Quick Snap Novellas

Lucky Catch

Trick Play

Download two free novellas, *Swept Away* and *Worth the Risk*,
when you sign up for her newsletter.
(https://landing.mailerlite.com/webforms/landing/v5z3m1)

Made in the USA
Coppell, TX
08 July 2021